MEGALODON IN PARADISE
HUNTER SHEA

D1253552

SEVERED PRESS
HOBART TASMANIA

MEGALODON IN PARADISE

For Courtney Block, orca queen.

"Adversity makes men, and prosperity makes monsters."
--- Victor Hugo

1954

The whole thing had gone FUBAR faster than two eagles fucking in mid-flight.

Chet Hardy knew it would the moment they'd deployed him here, but he'd kept his opinions to himself. Doing otherwise would have landed him in deep shit.

Would it have been deeper than this? Not a chance. Imprisonment in the brig back home in Norfolk for desertion would have been preferable to this.

Oh well. It was too late for that now.

A crashing wave nearly tipped the life raft over. Chet's ass left the bench for a terrifying moment, his short life flashing before his eyes, lungs stinging from the salty spray. He landed back inside the raft with a heavy thud, his teeth clacking so hard, he felt one or more of his molars pop like light bulbs. Daggers of pain speared his face from his jaw to the top of his skull. He winced, tears fleeing from the corners of his eyes.

There was no time to wallow in misery. The next wave came barreling toward him. He screamed, his voice drowned by the fury of the ocean.

This time, he missed the brunt of the wave, but there was another hot on its heels. He had to get the motor going and push past it or he was going to drown.

"Come on, come on!"

Yanking on the pull chain with the little strength he had left, Chet alternated between cursing and begging for mercy from a god he hadn't prayed to since grade school. Blood poured from his mouth, the taste of old pennies cutting through the brine.

Bracing for another impact, a shard of tooth stabbed into his newly exposed gum. For a moment, his world went black. He didn't even feel the wave as it tossed the boat into the air.

Somehow, both he and the boat landed in one sodden piece.

Angry fingers of lightning danced on the horizon, as if searching for him, drawing closer . . . closer.

If there was thunder, he couldn't hear it over the angry belching of the ocean. His ribcage rattled deep enough to upset the rhythm of his heart.

Chet went back to coaxing the outboard motor to life. But no matter how hard he pulled, it stayed silent and dead.

Just like everyone else.

A wave splashed down ten feet behind him, pushing the boat toward what remained of the destroyed shore. He kicked the engine, flopping onto his back, staring up at the black and gray swirling clouds.

Even if you get this bitch running, then what? he said to himself. *If the storm doesn't kill you, that, that* thing *will. How many people get to choose the way they die?*

More tears came.

He should have demanded they listen to him. And if they hadn't, he should have kept insisting until they chalked him off as mentally incompetent and shipped him off this damn hellhole. He wouldn't be the first guy to lose his shit and get sent packing.

Now he was the last man standing, or floating, and there was no hope of getting back home to Portland, Maine.

A powerful gust of wind slammed the boat, skittering it over the churning water, flying against the current.

Jesus H. Christ! That had to be almost eighty miles an hour. It air dried his face and threatened to flay the flesh from his skull.

Now he was further from the demolished beach, back to the drop point for those man-killer waves.

He wasn't even sure how he ended up in the life raft. He remembered watching everything unravel—the warning klaxons, people running to man their positions, the shouting followed by screaming, the roar of gunfire, the cracking of the ship's hull, more screaming, water gurgling as it consumed the ship, people begging for help, others wailing in their death throes, someone barking orders that no one could understand, and worst of all, the sickening crunch of bones as they were masticated to powder.

Something had exploded behind him and there was fire. The orange glow gave light to the horror around him.

It charged and retreated, taking bloody souvenirs each time. Chet had a bead on it once, but his hands shook so much, he dropped his gun in the water. Not that it would have made a difference. Shooting the abomination was like taking a pellet gun to the side of the Empire State Building.

Chet Hardy looked back and his heart froze.

The onrushing wave dwarfed all of the ones previous. This motherfucker could wipe out a baseball stadium as easily as a gorilla could swat a fly on its back.

He was good and fucked.

But at least he would die quickly. He wouldn't have to suffer through the agonizing, terrifying process of drowning. No, this sledgehammer was going to break him in half the moment it touched him. If he was lucky, he wouldn't feel a thing.

If life were fair, he'd have a cigarette handy. Even traitors were allowed one last puff before getting put down by the firing squad. His hand patted the pocket by his chest where he kept his Zippo lighter. It was still there. His mother had given it to him as a going away present four years ago.

Little did either of them know how far he'd be going.

"I can't come back from this one, Ma," he said, his eyes widening as the wave reared up, cresting higher and higher.

He didn't have a girl back home to mourn him, but he worried about his mother. They'd lost his brother at the battle in Clervaux and it had nearly killed her in the process. How much could a mother take?

He pictured her sitting in their living room, he and his brother on either side of her, laughing about the time Randall put on that magic show in the yard, charging people a penny for admission, every trick going wrong. Randall plowed right on, undaunted by his mounting failures. Chet, his assistant, broke down and cried after getting water poured in his pants when the funnel trick failed.

The roar of the wave was deep enough to dislocate his bones, snapping Chet from his reverie.

Please, oh please, don't let it hurt.

A continuous barrage of lightning strikes illuminated the dark wall of water.

Chet looked into the eyes of his death and shit himself.

The wave wasn't alone.

It was swimming within the deadly tide, mouth wide open, headed straight for him.

Chet feebly raised his arms, as if they had the power to stop the cold certainty of his demise.

"No, dear God, no!"

Like old Jonah, Chet and the life raft were swallowed whole, descending into the blackest, foulest chasm this side of Hell.

CHAPTER ONE

PRESENT DAY

Ollie Arias was a small man and only seemed to shrink with age. Born two weeks late, he came into this world a wailing, dripping, pink tangle of stunted limbs. Despite his "extra roasting time," as his mother like to say, his appearance and lung development were that of a premature baby. The doctor doubted his own estimation of Sarah Kay Arias's pregnancy term later that day in the dark and comforting confines of his wood-paneled office. Little Ollie spent his first three weeks free from the womb in NICU, much to the worry of his parents.

Being short of stature wasn't much of an issue until middle school, when all of the other kids seemed to sprout overnight, leaving him deep in the dust. That's when the taunting began. He could endure *shrimp* and *short stuff* and even *midget*, but for some reason, when they called him *alligator arms*, he'd fly into a rage. His mother spent many a day alongside him in Principal DaCosta's office, his knuckles sore or bleeding. He may have been small, but he was a furious fighter, even with his limited punching reach.

By college, he was a veteran barroom scrapper. Topping out at five feet, he was often the subject of cruel, beer-balls induced jokes. He was always happy to show them the error of their ways. It got to the point where even his tightknit crew of college friends didn't want to be around him. Who wanted to go out for a night with someone that was going to get them in a fight, arrested, or at the very least, thrown out of the very place they wanted to be? Ollie didn't blame them, but he sure as hell missed them. His senior year, which should have been fun and full of the promise of better things to come, was instead lonely and melancholic.

So Ollie stopped going out, closed his rabbit ears and sank deep within himself where it was safer, though not much fun. Like a chameleon, he could disappear in any setting, rendering himself invisible at will.

Invisibility was easier. It kept him from getting too hurt, from taking big chances and making big mistakes.

His father used to joke that he'd inherited the old man's luck, which he equated to a three leaf clover or a twisted horseshoe. Ollie was quite adept at zigging right when he should have zagged left. Ollie used to say he was King Midas's evil twin brother, his touch turning gold to lead.

Because of his propensity to anger and his inability to find success, he was wary of making any waves, big or small.

So he chose inertia.

It was his ability to fly under the radar that kept him in his job with Envirotech, a large, multi-national company with over fifty thousand employees. Ollie worked in their Minnesota branch, just five miles from where he was born, and ten from his alma mater. Waves of layoffs and reorgs always passed him by, as few others than his supervisor were even aware of his existence. He'd once changed his nameplate on his outward facing cubicle wall to read COG. No one seemed to notice, so he'd left it that way. It had been there for over three years.

A homebody, Ollie had two passions: movies and playing the lottery.

When it came to movies, he loved everything. The classics, B-movie horror, art house, big-budget special effects orgies, romcoms, foreign films, documentaries—it didn't matter. He subscribed to every streaming service out there, ensuring that he wouldn't miss a thing. After work each night, he'd go home, make dinner (he was a good cook who kept a neat house) and watch two or three movies before drifting off to sleep in his plush lounge chair, the most extravagant purchase he'd ever made. It was more comfortable than his bed.

As for the lottery, he played them all: the daily numbers, Lotto, Mega Millions, scratch offs, Powerball, and even Keno if he had time to kill. He was the guy who made you groan with frustration if he was ahead of you on the lottery line, spending up to $50 a day, rattling off numbers at a feverish pace.

Overall, he'd break even on good years, come up a little short on most. The thrill he got every time he checked his numbers—spine stiffening, gut clenching, heart racing—was the high point of his day.

His other, smaller passion was going to the annual knife show in St. Paul. He loved knife fight scenes in movies like *Crocodile Dundee*, *Captain America: The Winter Soldier*, and just about any karate movie ever made. He'd bought a couple of cool-looking blades but stuck them deep into drawers. He didn't trust himself to carry one around. If the wall he'd built around his temper ever cracked . . . well, that was another world of trouble he didn't need. It was fun just to look at the knives and relive some of his favorite action-packed scenes within the safety of his own head.

The night he watched *Where's Poppa*, a very black comedy from the 70s starring George Segal who played a man trying to scare his aging mother to death so he no longer had to care for her, Ollie's heart raced and raced and raced until he almost called an ambulance. During the movie, he'd plucked his phone to check the latest Powerball drawing. The pot was the third largest in history, a staggering eight hundred and ninety million dollars.

When he saw that all six of his numbers matched the night's drawing, he dropped the phone and ticket. The phone landed in his tumbler full of Dr. Pepper. It quickly shorted out. Barely able to pause the movie, his fingers suddenly the size of sausages, his bones fusing together, nerves struck with palsy, he walked on unsteady pegs to his bedroom where he kept his laptop.

After booting it up and going to the lottery website, he realized he'd forgotten the ticket. His feet barely touched the floor as he ran to retrieve it. Panting, his vision going fuzzy, he checked again.

"Holy crapping Christ!"

Ollie passed out.

When he came to, he checked the numbers again, just to make sure it wasn't all just a dream or hallucination.

It wasn't.

He spent the rest of the sleepless night reading up on what should be done when one wins an enormous lottery. The Internet was chock full of horror stories of past winners now wallowing in debt, but there were some very helpful sites as well. The web giveth as easily as it tooketh away, as Ollie liked to say.

The next morning, he called a lawyer that he'd vetted through Angie's List and was in the office by midday. Opting to get the single payout, it was estimated he'd be the recipient of over four hundred million dollars.

"I'd like it if we can make it official in a few days," Ollie said.

His fancy new lawyer, Tad Fulhaber, a man as tall as he was wide with disturbingly red, chapped lips and a lazy eye, said, "That would be best. We have quite a few things to get in order first."

There was one thing Ollie very much wanted to get in order.

It was just like any Tuesday at work. The office was quiet, people sipping coffee and checking email. Ollie was quiet, but he wasn't deleting junk mail and prioritizing work requests. No one seemed to have noticed that he hadn't come in the day before without explaining why he'd taken the day off.

That wasn't surprising.

Just before eleven, he jumped from his chair, shut down his computer and rolled his neck, bones cracking. Walking past his desk, he ripped the COG nameplate from his wall and stuffed it in his pocket. He opened his supervisor's door without knocking.

"Bill, you got a minute?" he said.

Bill Chapman looked confused, studying his face as if he were seeing him for the first time. He pulled his lips back in a tight line and said, "I'm a little busy at the moment Ali...guy."

Ollie knew full well that Bill referred to him as Alligator Arms when he thought Ollie wasn't around. He'd heard him say it more times than he could count. Everyone loved Bill, but Ollie knew he was a complete dick. If only they could have blended in with the wallpaper like he could, his secret superpower, and hear the things Bill said about *them* behind their backs.

Ollie closed the door. "Yeah, well, I don't give a shit."

When he reached into his pocket, Bill stiffened, his eyes going wide.

At first, Ollie was confused.

Then he realized what had gotten Bill's asshole so puckered.

He tossed his nameplate on Bill's desk. It bounced off the top rack of his Inbox and skittered across the desk, knocking a pen and some paper to the floor.

"What, did you think I was going to shoot you?"

Bill stared at the nameplate, then narrowed his eyes at him.

"Are you out of your mind?" Chapman said, spittle collecting at the corners of his mouth.

"Maybe."

When Ollie jerked his arms up, fingers curled into claws, Bill flinched. That made Ollie laugh.

Bill did his best to recover. "I'm two seconds away from firing you."

"That's one second too slow, because I quit, asshole."

Bill smiled. "That works for me, though it means no unemployment for you."

"I'm not going to be needing that."

"Didn't anyone teach you not to burn bridges? Whatever job you must have might not pan out. Then you'll be begging me for a reference and it isn't going to happen."

Now Ollie smiled.

"The only person who'll be begging is you, Bill."

Bill dropped the nameplate in the garbage and looked down at a pile of paper, dismissing Ollie. "I'll have security up in a few to make sure you only take what's yours."

"You might want to ask them for a few empty boxes. You have a lot of crap in this office."

Bill looked at him as if he were a leprechaun speaking Portuguese. "Look, you quit and you said your peace. Good for you. As you can see, I really don't care. You're not irreplaceable, you know. I'll have a temp agency fill your spot by tomorrow."

Ollie rapped twice on his desk. "Good luck with that. Well, you have a wonderful life."

Bill clicked his mouse a few times, eyes now trained on his computer screen.

Ollie paused before he opened the office door. "You might want to check your email. I think I accidentally selected all employees when I sent my goodbye present to you."

That got Bill's attention. He straightened in his chair, pulling closer to the screen.

"What the hell is this?"

Ollie so wanted to stand behind him right now and see the slew of replies to the email. But it was much better to watch the color drain from Bill's face.

"*That* is a bunch of short audio files I collected of you over the years. You have a big fucking mouth. I don't think there's a single person you haven't torn down when their backs were turned. For once, being short and inconsequential came in handy."

Bill clicked through email after email. He then opened one of the files, the one where he was talking to someone on the phone how much he'd like to bang Evelyn, the head of HR. In his words, "I'd love to break my cock off in that big ass."

Ollie's heart swelled when he saw the man's jaw muscles tense to the point of popping.

"You little gator-armed fuck," Bill seethed.

"Oh, I already have a bunch of those recordings with you calling me that. I kept them to myself. But I'm sure everyone else is being enlightened."

Bill jumped from his chair so fast, it wheeled away and smashed into the wall. "Get the hell out of my office!"

His face was so red, Ollie thought he looked like a baboon's ass.

"That's actually the very next thing on my to do list," Ollie said. "Enjoy your office . . . while you still have it."

The moment he closed the door, he heard something thrown across the room. It sounded like one of Bill's heavy Manager of the Year awards.

"What's going on in there?" Tatiana asked. She was a beautiful Jamaican girl who brought a tray of treats around the office each morning and afternoon. She'd always passed by his cubicle, never once asking him if he wanted anything.

"Hey, are you free this evening?"

She arched an eyebrow so high, he worried it might rocket off her head.

"Come again?"

"I'd love to take you to dinner. Maybe we can see the new Jennifer Lawrence movie afterward."

She looked down at him as if he were an insect.

"I don't think so," she said, her head turning towards Bill's office when something heavy thumped against a wall.

"You sure now? This is your last chance."

"Oh, I'm sure."

He took a muffin from her tray, tossing it from one hand to the other. "Okay. But you'll be kicking yourself by the weekend."

"I highly doubt that."

"I'm sure you think you do."

Sauntering down the row of cubicles, he couldn't help but notice the escalating chatter as people opened their email and listened to the audio files. Standing by the elevator, he inspected his knuckles.

"Well, look at that. You just kicked some serious ass and didn't even get a bruise."

CHAPTER TWO

"I can't believe they all made it."

"Come again?"

Ollie pulled his head back from the doorway and proceeded to elbow his martini all over the gleaming mahogany bar. He grabbed a fistful of cocktail napkins and blotted the vermouth.

"No need. I've got it," the bartender said.

"Sorry. I forgot you were there," Ollie said, checking his pants. Only a few drops stained his tan slacks. Of course, they had to be right on his crotch.

Now he'd have to wait until it dried. There was no way he was going in there looking like the punch line of the phrase, *No matter how much you shake and dance, the last two drops go in your pants*.

The entire upscale nightspot, Minneapolis's finest, was all his tonight. He could hang out in the second floor bar as long as he wanted. He'd read about Club 17 in the local paper and had always wanted to go. However, going stag to a banging nightclub was a surefire way to never make it in the front door.

Well, he'd arrived tonight Han Solo. Funny how many doors money tended to open.

He'd sent the invitations to his college friends two weeks ago, complete with round trip airfare, car service and hotel accommodations. They'd all RSVP'd, but deep down, he never thought all of them would show.

In fact, he was pretty sure none of them would make the trip. It's not like an all expenses paid jaunt to Minnesota in February was the opportunity of a lifetime.

But they were all here, right below him, drinking cocktails and talking as if eight years hadn't passed since they'd parted ways after graduation. Sure, at first their conversations were stilted, awkward, with a lot of "damn, I forgot how insanely cold it gets here" and "you look exactly the same as you did back in college" when in fact all of them had changed dramatically. Ollie knew. He'd spent the last month flipping through the yearbook, the one that contained nary a picture of him.

The bartender, a middle-aged guy as slim as a cigarette, gave him a fresh martini.

"Oh, thanks," Ollie said, taking a sip of the chilled liquor. It was his second in the past hour, which would make it one more martini than he'd ever drunk in his life. He wasn't too keen on the high-octane taste or the way it singed his tongue and throat, but he needed something to take the edge off.

Plus, if you wanted to attain any level of sophistication, you had to learn to enjoy a good martini.

Jeez, why am I looking to James Bond movies for life lessons? he thought. *Because 007 is a freaking badass, that's why.*

By the time martini number two was finished, his brain was buzzing and his feet and hands felt as if they'd been filled with helium. Inspecting his pants, he rapped on the bar and said, "Wish me luck."

"Good luck, sir," the bartender said, his smile so good it almost seemed genuine.

He called me sir. Wow, that sounded weird.

Then again, he'd experienced a lot of weird things over the past several months. People who never gave him a second glance now deferred to him. He knew their angle. He wasn't stupid.

Taking a deep breath, he opened the doors to the second floor landing and paused a moment, watching his old friends. He'd made a silent entrance, so no one noticed he was there.

Lenny Burke had his elbows on a bar-top table, checking his phone while laughing at something Tara McShane said. They'd called Lenny "Stump" back in the good old dorm days, on account of an enamored one-night stand announcing to everyone at a party that he was hung like a tree stump. They'd laughed their asses off, not quite sure if it was meant to be a good thing or an insult. The guys were in no mind to see for themselves. Lenny would tell them, "Come on, you know what they say about us black guys? I hate to tell you, but it's all true." Lenny had gone a little soft in the middle and his trademark dreads were a thing of the past. He wore glasses now, looking the part of the absentminded professor, though Ollie knew he was a market research consultant who worked from home.

Tara McShane, or "T-Mac," had lost her freshman fifteen and then some. She looked like the after picture in one of those fad exercise commercials. Her face was more angular now, but her green eyes still sparkled, catching the strings of fairy lights hanging over their heads. She'd cut her hair so short it was just shy of a buzzcut, and she wore a little black dress so tight, he could see the top band of her thong. She'd most definitely blossomed since he'd last seen her holding her diploma on the big stage.

Steven "Cooter" Combs knocked back a beer and was quick to order another. A country boy from Alabama, he'd always been the life of the party. He was strong as an ox and had a liver that was nigh indestructible. He still looked like a farm-raised mountain of a man, but he was now completely bald and had a scar that ran in a perfect line along the left side of his head. He'd dressed up for the night, sporting a yellow power tie and suit. Ollie chuckled, remembering Cooter telling him he'd rather vote for a Democrat than become one of the faceless corporate masses. He'd said ties were nothing more than fancy nooses. Ollie would have to ask him if he'd voted for Obama.

By Steven's side was a pretty blonde with perfectly tanned skin. She wore a red dress with a plunging neckline. In fact, it plunged far enough for Ollie to tell that she did her tanning in the nude. Or topless, at least. Her hair was so sun bleached it was practically white. She had to be Scandinavian. Lord knows there were plenty to choose from in Minnesota. He knew her name was Heidi, which was another clue, and that she and Steven had been married for a few years. She was the one Ollie was worried about.

Last but not least was Marco Conti. He'd never been given a nickname because everyone thought knowing someone named Marco was cool and slightly exotic, even though he came from Newark, New Jersey. The guy was a born wheeler dealer. He'd gotten them all fake IDs and had somehow blackmailed a teacher into giving Ollie an A in his philosophy class when it looked like he'd flunk out at the end of freshman year. Ollie had been too afraid to ask for details. Marco had been the tarnished brainiac of the crew, a whiz at economics, who they assumed would be in jail before he hit thirty for insider training. He'd emerge from some country club prison ten years later and move to a picturesque sea town in Spain.

Judging by his scuffed shoes and ill-fitting suit, it appeared things hadn't turned out the way they'd all thought they would. His hair was still thick and black as an oil spill; his Roman nose and strong jawline used to make the sorority girls swoon. Ollie would be with those girls vicariously through the exploits Marco revealed to him while they drank PBR on Wanderly Hill, right next to Smith Hall where Marco had most of his classes.

Ollie enjoyed watching them from here, just as he'd been happy to simply be in their orbit in college. When he wasn't being a thin-skinned ass, he'd filled his days and nights observing this odd collection of strangers who somehow grew to be a family. He'd thought of them as the living embodiment of *St. Elmo's Fire*, though he'd always wished they could find someone like Demi Moore to pledge her allegiance to the group (and become his sex slave). Being cast aside from that family had hurt deeply, but he knew, after a year of therapy where he did a lot of couch punching and teeth gnashing, that he was the only one to blame.

And truth be told, he'd never encountered people he felt so close to before or since.

Which was why he had asked them all to come here tonight.

Asked, but never in his wildest dreams expected to see this happy reunion.

Taking a deep breath, he leaned on the rail and said, "Excuse me, this is a private party. I expressly told the bouncer no riffraff."

Five smiling faces beamed up at him.

His entire body was lighter than a ghost's. It had nothing to do with the martinis.

"Is it possible your hair has gotten even redder, you shifty ginger?" Lenny said. They stood around a table, drinking and laughing, falling back into the old routine of ragging on one another, all in good fun.

His old friends gave him a round of applause as he entered the room. He took a bow and was pulled into their circle by Steven, his big arm looping around Ollie's neck.

"Hey, at least I have hair, unlike some people," Ollie said, his tongue feeling as thick as a mattress. He'd have to slow down if he wanted to coherently explain why he'd dragged them all into the Arctic in the dead of winter.

Steven ran a meaty hand over his shiny dome. "You'll n-never believe this, but it all fell out literally over one summer. My pillowcase and shower drain were so hairy, I thought they were goddamn Tribbles."

He still has that slight stutter on words that start with 'n', Ollie thought, though it was less pronounced than back in the day.

"Oh, that's terrible," Tara said, her manicured hand over her mouth.

He waved her concern away. "I was horrified at first, but I've grown to love it. No fuss, no muss."

"Not to mention he has a wife who grew up with a crush on Mr. Clean," Heidi said, her fingertips grazing the thin, pink scar.

Steven knocked back one of the shots of tequila he'd ordered for the table and said, "Come to think of it, my hair fell out while we were getting ready for our wedding. Methinks my wife may have poisoned my follicles in order to fulfill her twisted fantasy."

Heidi giggled huskily, slapping his arm. "I can't believe it took you this long to figure it out."

"An-any of you turn out to be cops or divorce attorneys?" Steven asked, his cheeks ruddy, a drop of tequila suspended on the tip of his nose.

They laughed, assuring him that he would never find someone as beautiful as Heidi, so it was best to accept his fate.

Lenny turned to Marco and said, "I don't see a ring, but I'm going to assume you're a baby daddy to at least one Jersey rug rat."

For just a moment, so brief Ollie would never have seen it if he wasn't studying everyone so intently, Marco's face took on a menacing sneer. It was quickly replaced by his patented cavalier countenance. "I hate to disappoint you, bro, but my swimmers have stayed in their own pool."

Raising his glass for a toast, Lenny said, "To the man who invented condoms and his war against child support payments."

Marco joined in the toast but his smile was miles away from his chestnut eyes.

"So, T-Mac, what have you been up to?" Ollie asked. He'd had a crush on Tara when they were freshmen. She was dating Lenny at the time, then Steven, then Marco. The word *dating* may have been stretching things. What it all boiled down to was that Ollie was the one guy in their group who never had a chance with her. Truth be told, even if he'd had a shot, he wasn't keen on getting sloppy fourths.

Tara laughed, her gin and tonic sputtering from her pursed lips. "Wow, I haven't been called T-Mac in ages."

"You'll always be T-Mac to me," Ollie said, clinking his glass against her own.

Slow your roll, Ollie said to himself. *Yeah, Tara is hotter than ever, but don't leave yourself open for disappointment.*

"I forgot how much I liked that nickname. Who called me that first? Was it you, Lenny?" she said.

"That was way too many beers ago to remember." He turned to Steven. "Though I do remember bestowing Cooter on your country ass."

"Please don't call me that."

"What, you too good to be old Coots McGoots?"

"Too good, too old, and n-not liking being called a slang word for vagina."

They all went silent.

Steven stared hard at Lenny, gripping the edge of the table until his knuckles turned white. For a moment, Ollie thought he was going to punch Lenny.

"Especially coming from a guy who was called a sawed-off dick." He broke into a grin, popping the bubble of tension.

"Nice one, Coots," Tara said.

Maybe things will turn out different with Tara when she hears what I have to say, Ollie thought.

He remembered it was Tara who had bestowed the nickname Raging Bull on him after a particularly nasty bar fight. At the time, he thought it was a damn cool nickname. And it was, until things fell apart.

Now, here was his chance to put things back together again, despite the odds. Not that he considered the improbability of chance anymore. Winning Powerball had a way of making you dismiss insurmountable odds.

Under the table and out of sight, he dug his thumbnail into his palm hard enough to jolt some sobriety into his brain. It was too easy to think that just because he was a gajillionaire, he could have anything, and anyone, he wanted. Tara had been a party girl back in the day, but she wasn't a freaking bauble on a shelf that would fall into his cart just because he could afford it.

Tara eyeballed the pack of cigarettes on the table next to her drink. She looked to Ollie. "You think I could light up?"

"You can do anything you want. The place is ours tonight and we make the rules."

She sparked her lighter and took a deep drag, her eyes rolling up in her head until he could only see the whites. "Oh, it feels so good to smoke in a public place. Even better than peeing in the woods."

"You were a world class outdoor pisser," Marco said.

"I have an abnormally small bladder." She blew a perfect smoke ring. "Anyway, to answer our host's question, I was a veterinary assistant for the past few years, at least until my boss died in a car accident. That was five months ago. Out in the boonies where I live, there isn't much call for vet assistants. So, I'm down to my last month of unemployment and enjoying daytime TV."

Lenny tenderly placed a hand on her shoulder. "I'm sorry to hear that."

She shrugged. "Shit happens. I'm pretty sure I won't end up a bag lady. My sister lives down in Nashville. I might relocate and take my chances there. At least it'll be an improvement in the nightlife, food, and music departments."

"That it would," Steven said. "Heidi and I spent a week there during our honeymoon. I think I gained five pounds."

"More like ten," Heidi said with a devilish smirk.

Lenny ordered another round of drinks. Everyone set to work finishing what they had.

Marco gnawed on his thumb, just the way he used to eat away at his nail during final exams. Ollie saw that there was practically no nail left, the skin red and raw and mangled.

Ollie felt the weight of the unspoken, the questions they all had, pressing down on him. He desperately wanted another drink, but knew it would put him over the edge. No, better to do it now.

"So, I guess you're wondering why I brought you all here," he said.

"Obviously to brag about how you've made it big time in the world," Marco joked.

"I gotta say, your invite had me curious," Steven said. "And thank you for the extra ticket for Heidi."

"I wanted to meet her. Besides, I couldn't do this properly if she wasn't here."

"Please don't let it be something maudlin or depressing," Lenny said. "I'm working on my new year's resolution to stay positive."

Tara chortled. "The only resolution you make is to not make any resolutions." She nudged Ollie. "Okay, Raging Bull, spill it."

Looking into her eyes, Ollie almost forgot everything he'd rehearsed in front of his mirror for weeks. He hadn't counted on the overwhelming rush of nostalgia and emotions he'd thought were long lost.

"What'd you do, win the lottery?" Marco asked, chuckling when Ollie's mouth refused to obey his commands.

Ollie started to giggle, which turned into uncontrollable laughter. He leaned his elbows on the table, spilling the remains of Heidi's drink.

His friends looked at him as if he'd had ten drinks too many. They were right, of course, but that wasn't why he was laughing.

When he was able to catch his breath, he said, "As a matter of fact . . . I did."

"Wait. What?" Marco said.

Ollie wiped a tear from his cheek. "I won the lottery."

"Holy shit, that's fantastic," Lenny said.

"Not just any lottery. You remember the Powerball drawing for just under a billion dollars?"

Tara grabbed onto his arm. "The one that was won by one anonymous person?"

"Yep."

"You're the guy?" Steven said.

"I'm the guy."

"You're joking, right?" Marco said.

"If I am, this night is going to bankrupt me."

There was a long pause, then an explosion of congratulations. There were hugs all around, even from Marco who had never been much of a man-on-man hugger.

"That is just awesome, bro! Holy cow. How did you manage to hold it in all this time?" Marco said. A waiter delivered their next round and they had several toasts.

After they'd had a sip—or chug—Ollie replied, "I won months ago. It's easy to keep a low profile. Trust me, the less people that know the better."

Lenny draped an arm over him. "I'm so happy for you. You were always a good guy, even when you were being an asshole and breaking a bottle over someone's head. And thank you for bringing us all together to share the good news. This is really special."

"You haven't even heard why I asked you all to come."

"You mean it wasn't just to party with your favorite drinking partners?" Steven said.

Ollie smiled. "Oh, it's partly that. Look, I have a proposal and I want you to just sit back quietly and take it in. Okay?"

He motioned to the chairs around the table. Everyone took their drink, and then took a seat. Ollie stood before them like a kindergarten teacher about to start story time.

"Look, ever since college, my life has been . . . well, let's just say unspectacular. I work, I eat, I watch movies, I shit, I sleep and repeat. For my last birthday, I watched *Sixteen Candles* alone and fell asleep with a pint of Cherry Garcia on my chest. And that was the best day I'd had all that month."

The look of sympathy in their eyes, especially Tara and Heidi's, made him swallow hard.

This is not a pity party, butt wipe. This is supposed to be a celebration.

"Just take that as an example of how exciting things have been. Now I have all this money and I didn't know what the hell to do with it. Even though I was kept anonymous, I was still besieged by goddamn vultures, all wanting a piece of the pie. After a while, I had to sever ties with just about everyone I knew. How all these people found out, I'll never know."

"You have the money now to pay someone to find out," Lenny said, raising his glass.

"True, but I really don't care. I've been living in a cabin I rented up at Lake Vermillion, trying to figure out what I want to do with the rest of my life. Of course, there are charities I want to help out, but I had to decide where I wanted to live and what I was going to do with all this time I now had on my hands. I sure as shit don't want to keep freezing my gonads up here."

"That's why I moved to South Carolina," Tara said. "I don't own a winter coat or snow shovel."

Ollie said, "Yeah, you weren't easy to find. But like Lenny said, I was able to pay someone to do that for me. Anyway, when I really thought about it, I realized the best times of my life were all when I was around you guys. And if I was going to be able to enjoy the rest of my life, it was probably best to spend it with you."

"You may n-n-not crash in our guest room," Steven joked. "I haven't told Heidi yet, but I'm planning on putting a pool table in there."

She gave him a massive eye roll that said there was no way a pool table was ever getting in that room.

"I'll see your guest room and raise you," Ollie said. "No, I have a much better idea. I'd like you all to live with me."

There was a long pause.

"In a cabin at Lake Vermillion?" Lenny said.

Ollie grinned. "It only has one bedroom. So I was thinking, how about an island?"

"An island. What island?" Tara said.

Ollie's heart was beating so fast, he was sure they could hear it thump away every time he opened his mouth.

"It's a private island. In Micronesia."

"Micronesia? Where the hell is that? Is it near Tunisia or something?" Lenny said.

Marco backhanded him. "Your grasp of geography is stunning. Are you sure we graduated from the same college? It's north of Australia, east of the Philippines."

"That is correct, sir," Ollie said. "It's three square miles of pure paradise. I don't just want you all to visit. I want you to live there, with me, permanently."

"Permanently as in we can n-never leave?" Steven said, his tone belying that he was quite serious.

"It's not a prison. You can come and go as you please. In fact, you can do anything you like. I'll make sure you not only get to live in one of the most beautiful places in the world, but that you'll also never need to work a day in your life."

No one spoke for what felt like ages. Drinks were left untouched. It was as if all of the air had escaped the room.

In nightclubs, no one can hear you scream, Ollie said to himself. He felt sweat break out on his temples and upper lip.

Lenny, bless his heart, was the first to break the silence.

"Where the hell do I sign?"

CHAPTER THREE

Ollie was peppered with questions.

"What's the name of the island?"

"Grand Isla Tiburon."

"Sounds pretty."

"It's gorgeous."

"Is there anyone living there now?"

"Nope. It's been deserted for decades."

"So, are we just gonna beach bum it?"

"Far from it. I'm going to have homes built for everyone who comes, along with a lot of cool amenities. Think of it as a gated community with everything you need at your fingertips."

"What about food and basic necessities?"

"And internet and phones?"

"And porn?"

"All taken into account. There's a company that can set up a VSAT communications system so you won't miss a single thing on the web. Satellite phones will also be provided so you can stay in touch with your family and friends. As for general supplies, we'll have monthly deliveries, but can get anything we need at a moment's notice. We won't be in the middle of nowhere like Easter Island. There are hundreds of nearby islands, including the capital, Majuro. You won't lose any of the technology you now have, though you may want to ditch it at some time. I'll make sure there's Wi-Fi so your porn is portable."

"How long until it's ready?"

"I've been assured we can move in by the fall."

"This sounds like an enormous undertaking. I'm talking billionaire territory. I know you won a huge jackpot, but how is it going to cover all of this?"

Ollie knew Marco would say that. He was a numbers guy, after all.

"The cost of doing business is a lot cheaper in Micronesia than the good old US. Plus, I was able to get the island for . . . well, a little more than a song, but you get the drift."

"What's the deal with the island? Does it get wiped out by typhoons every two years?" Lenny asked.

"Maybe it's haunted," Steven added with a smirk.

"No and no," Ollie added. "It was a former military holding. They abandoned it a few years after the war."

"The war? Which war?" Tara asked.

Ollie felt his confidence stagger. "The big one."

"Vietnam?" Lenny said.

"You don't mean the Gulf Wars," Marco said.

Slapping his forehead, Ollie said, "World War II. Jeez."

Heidi's eyes went as wide as ostrich eggs. "World War II? It's been abandoned since the forties?"

"1954 to be exact."

"Probably littered with unexploded ordnance," Lenny said. "If you send people out to build, they could be stepping on a literal minefield."

"Or the ground or water could be toxic. Militaries don't give a crap about the environment," Tara said.

Marco held up a finger. "I'm assuming the Australians were the ones that owned it."

"As a matter of fact, it was an American base of operations," Ollie said. "It's part of the Marshall Islands, which I'm sure you've all heard of. Which is why they were willing to work with a fellow American to take it off their hands."

Tara's mouth dropped open. "Wait. The Marshall Islands? As in the Pacific Proving Grounds?"

"What the hell is that?" Lenny asked.

Marco took a quick nibble at his thumb. "That's where we did a bunch of nuclear testing. You ever hear of the Bikini Atoll? They, like, blew the shit out of the place."

Steven leaned into the table. "Bikini Island is still there, but there was another island, I forget the n-name, that was completely obliterated when they set off the first thermonuclear bomb. Boom. Gone. Like it n-never even existed."

Heidi added, "The military had to evacuate whole populations to other islands hundreds of miles away. Not just until things blew over. Forever."

"We set off all these bombs without warning the civilians. It was a total travesty," Tara said.

Ollie's heart galloped. He knew he'd eventually have to address this. He just didn't think it would happen this soon.

Lenny looked at everyone with hawk's eyes. "How does everyone know so much about this stuff?"

In unison, they answered, "The History Channel."

"At least until they went all ancient aliens, hillbillies, and pawn shop cheats," Marco said.

Ollie had to act fast.

"Everything you said is true. The Marshall Islands are the site of one of the biggest crimes against a race of people since the American Indians. There are, in fact, islands that are uninhabited because of nuclear contamination. Grand Isla Tiburon, I assure you, is not one of those locations. In fact, it was nowhere near the nuclear testing. They had to keep it free and clear of all that craziness."

"Why's that?" Steven asked.

"They had a lab or something there. You have to remember, this was back during the Cold War, and there were spies everywhere. They had to find places as remote as possible to do top secret work."

Marco raised an eyebrow. "Yeah, well, we know that only good things come from under the cloak of secrecy. You get nuclear bombs from Los Alamos, all kinds of diseases from Plum Island, not to mention those Montauk Monsters that washed up on the beach."

Lenny interjected, "I think if anything that evil came out of this place, we'd have heard of it seventy years later. And the Montauk Monster was a rotted raccoon. Nothing evil about a drowned raccoon. Sounds like the coast is clear, right, Ollie?"

"Absolutely. The military put it in writing that there is nothing left behind harmful to humans or the environment. Even the EPA gave it a total clean bill of health. It's empty because, to be fair, the Marshallese are poor people. They don't have the resources to repatriate the island and build it back up. And once the military was done with it, there was no one left to give two shits about the place."

Heidi looked at him with thinly veiled disgust. "So you want to take advantage of other people's misery?"

Ollie had to ball his hands into tight fists, under the table, of course, before he spoke.

"Not at all. In fact, part of my plan is to donate millions of dollars to the neighboring islands to improve their health, schools, and infrastructure. I'm going to employ them to help rebuild the island. And when I die, it's being willed to the Marshallese people. I'm not a monster. We did a wrong down there. Here's my chance to really do something good in the world . . . and with my friends, to boot."

"That's actually kinds of sweet," Tara said, her hand over her heart.

"And amazing that it came from you," Steven joked. He cast a quick look at Heidi, whose gaze wiped the smile from his face. She'd definitely need more convincing, just as Ollie had suspected.

"So, there's nothing on the island?" Lenny asked.

"In fact, all there is is one building, the old main lab. It's supposed to be totally empty. I'll have it torn down."

"Don't do it right away. I'd like to check it out," Lenny said.

"You still into that whole abandoned buildings thing?" Tara asked.

"It's called urban exploring and it's a rush like you've never experienced. I'll take you all in there, show you how it's done."

"Sounds creepy and dangerous. Count me out," Heidi said.

Ollie felt their attention waning. "Look, I'm not saying that you have to stay there forever. I'm just asking you to come share this amazing adventure with me. I plan to make trips to the other islands and work with the kids there, local hospitals, you name it. I promise, it will be the most amazing experience of your life. You can leave any time you want. If you do, I'll still make sure you and your kids never need to work a day in your lives. "

Marco stared at him for an uncomfortably long time. Ollie could hear the little calculator keys tapping away in his head. He finally said, "Look, I'm going to be honest with you. I've got nothing to lose, so you can count me in. My concern is that you're not being taken for a ride, Ollie. You'd need independent surveyors going out there to make sure the island truly is safe."

"Which is why I want to hire you on immediately as my right hand man and financial advisor. I have people now, but I don't trust them like I do you."

"You don't have to do that."

"I know. But I really want you running the show."

In fact, Ollie had never been as close to another person as he had to Marco back in college. They were roommates from totally different worlds, but they made it work. Ollie loved to listen to Marco's exploits and big plans for future world dominance. He'd always been so brave, so smart, so sure of himself.

It was clear a lot of that bravado had leeched away over the years. Ollie hoped this would give Marco his groove back.

Tara tapped out a cigarette. "I have to say, this has been the craziest twelve hours of my life."

"Look, there's no rush. I know this was a lot to lay on you. Take your time and think about it. I only ask that you give me your answer by the end of the month, just so I know how much building has to be done."

Lenny pushed away from the table. "That seems fair. I can tell you now, I'm in with Marco. I fucking hate market research and I haven't had a date in over six months. My parents moved to Alabama to be near my dumb-ass brother. I'm free as a bird. Now if you'll excuse me, I have to take a whiskey crap."

Everyone groaned.

When he left, Tara said, "Well, he hasn't changed."

"If that's true, I'm n-not going in there after him. I roomed with the guy for three years. I kn-know the horror to come," Steven said.

"I almost forgot!" Ollie exclaimed. He pulled his phone out and went to his pictures file. "This is Grand Isla Tiburon. Tell me it isn't gorgeous."

He handed it to Tara. Steven, Heidi, and Marco gathered around while she swiped through shot after shot of white sand beaches, palm trees and crystal blue water. When Lenny returned five minutes later, they were still looking.

You should have shown them the pictures first, Ollie admonished himself. Of course, he was just beginning to sober up, so he could blame it on a liquor-soaked brain.

When he looked at his cell phone, he saw it was eight in the morning. Time to head back home and get some sleep.

They emerged from the club with hands shielding their eyes from the sun. They looked like vampires.

Tara hugged him and kissed his cheek. "Look, I really need to think about it. It all sounds amazing . . . and kind of scary. You understand, right?"

He looked into her emerald eyes and wondered if he'd still want to go through with everything if she didn't come.

"I do. I'll send you, all of you, every scrap of information I have and everything that Marco and I discover so there's total transparency. I want us to be safe more than anything."

"I know you do."

In a few minutes, they were gone, headed back to their hotel. Ollie got in his new Land Rover and drove to the cabin.

She'll go, he said to himself over and over. Above all else, she'd do it just knowing they would help the Marshallese people. She'd always done charity runs and volunteered at the Girls Club and soup kitchens. It was part of the reason why he'd chosen Grand Isla

Tiburon. It would give her a chance to impact people's lives on a grand scale.

She had to go.

Ollie pulled down the shade and was out the moment his head hit the pillow.

Oddly enough, he dreamed of mushroom clouds.

CHAPTER FOUR

NINE MONTHS LATER

Ollie wasn't sure if he could have accomplished everything without Marco. When it came to the worlds of business, real estate and finance, Ollie was as experienced as a Bigfoot optometrist. Whatever areas Marco lacked, he was very skilled at finding the right people with the right expertise.

They'd moved to Grand Isla Tiburon two months ago. It was important to be there to watch over the final construction phases. At first, they'd lived in tents—tricked-out teepees that were the stuff of old time sultans and cost a pretty penny—waiting for the first home to be finished. Ollie had to admit he was reluctant to leave the tent. It had been pretty freaking cool, like camping on steroids. His mother hadn't let him join the Boy Scouts.

However, it was hot as hell and the tent would turn into an Indian sweat lodge most nights. Plus, no matter what he did with the fine netting, the bugs always found their way inside.

The heat didn't diminish the beauty of the island. The shore was lined with soft white sand, with clusters of palm trees everywhere you looked. The crystal blue waters of the Pacific cradled the island like a baby in the womb. He'd thought it would be a flat island, but it had its share of peaks and valleys.

He was still getting used to the bugs, most of which looked like something out of a Bert I. Gordon monster movie. Luckily, they didn't seem intent to drain him of his blood. The cry of gulls was omnipresent during the day.

When it came to the design of the houses, or bungalows as he preferred to call them, Ollie opted for simplicity rather than opulence. The whole idea of coming out here was to live in peace and harmony with nature. The bigger the bungalow, the more work that had to be put into upkeep. Plus, he wasn't comfortable with gold showers that could fit six, sunken pools in the living room, or sprawling estates with rooms that would only collect dust.

There was a lot of bamboo and teak, with mosquito netting over the canopy beds.

The last thing he wanted to do was flaunt his wealth in the faces of the Marshallese who would work on the island. It would become their island in time. No need to set a ridiculous standard they'd struggle to maintain.

All of the homes were was a single-level raised structures because of the propensity for flooding, not just during the rainy season, but when any kind of storm swelled the surrounding Pacific. Global warming wasn't just a term used out here to push a political agenda or get people to be more PC. No, to the Marshallese, it was a frightening fact that forced them to adjust not just their way of life, but outlook for the future. They didn't care whether the changing weather patterns were manmade or just a cyclical function of the planet. All that mattered was that it was real and called for some adaptations to better deal with it. Homes on other islands were wiped out with soul-deadening consistency, and there were only so many times people with little means could rebuild.

Which is why so many Marshallese had simply picked up stakes and moved to America. The US's open door policy was too enticing to resist. Ollie was shocked to learn that there were huge populations of Marshallese in Arkansas of all places! He could think of a thousand other places where rather he'd settle down.

Then again, a lot of the Marshallese he'd been in daily contact with thought he was equally insane for coming down here. The grass was always greener . . .

The five houses were arranged in a ring in the center of the island. Their placement was designed to mirror the natural ring of an atoll, the ovular coral reefs that enclosed lagoons and were in abundance in Micronesia. There was enough distance between each to provide privacy while still being close enough to wave to one another from their front doorsteps. All had two bedrooms with dining rooms that opened up to teak wood decks overlooking the ocean, since the ocean was just about everywhere you looked. Ollie envisioned countless dinner parties as they hopped from house to house, enjoying each other's company over bottles of wine, the moon shimmering on the darkening water.

"The boat should be here in an hour," Marco said, startling Ollie.

"Thanks for the heart attack."

"Anytime."

Ollie said, "I was so excited, I couldn't sleep last night."

"I sweat right through my sheets. That ceiling fan only seemed to make it worse. I had to take a couple of shots of whiskey to sleep so I wouldn't be dragging ass today."

"The air conditioners arrive next week. We'll be sleeping like old cats once we get them in."

"You mean babies," Marco said, drinking from a freshly cracked coconut. A handful of workers were putting the finishing touches on the exterior of Lenny's bungalow.

"Babies sleep like shit." Ollie laughed. "I had a cat, Drusilla, who would sleep through an earthquake. That's the kind of sleep I want."

"I'll just be happy to stem the tide of diaper rash this place has given me." He motioned for Ollie to follow him to his house. "Come on and help me carry the cooler and stuff down to the dock."

There wasn't a cloud in the sky and the sun seemed especially bright. Ollie wiped a sheen of sweat from his forehead. "I'm putting on my suit. I'm staying in the water until the last possible second."

"Hey, good idea. Can we technically call ourselves beach bums?"

"Why the hell not? Who's around to tell us otherwise?"

They changed and each carried a handle on the cooler filled with champagne and flutes. The ice shifted loudly. Ollie worried that the glasses would break, but they made it to the dock in one piece. As soon as he closed the cooler lid, he jumped into the crystal blue water. Opening his eyes, it seemed like he could see forever. Marco splashed next to him, diving under the dock to collect shell fragments.

At best, Ollie was a middling dog paddler. But he could hold his breath a bit and float under the water without panicking.

Visibility under the pristine water was clear as glass. A tightly packed school of fish, a riot of flashing golds and indigo, darted in perfect fluidity in the distance. Ollie kept meaning to study up on the various sea life that would be his neighbors, but getting everything ready was so time consuming. There would be time. Plenty of time.

A large shadow trailed the wake of the departing school. He couldn't make out what it was.

He did know there were a lot of big ass tuna out here. Commercial fishing rights for tuna were one of the mainstays of the Marshall Island economy. Some of them grew to be quite massive. The only tuna he wanted to get up close to came in a can and was best served with mayo, onions and celery.

Of course, it could also be a shark. To say they were in abundance out here was an understatement. In fact, the entire area had been declared a shark sanctuary decades ago. He'd been reassured that they weren't of the man eating *Jaws* variety . . . for the most part. He and Marco had spent many a dusk sitting on the beach with cold beers, watching dozens of triangular shark fins swimming back and forth in the distance.

Ollie spotted the hull of the boat as it cleaved its way toward the island. He popped up and saw Marco climbing up the ladder on the side of the dock.

"Here they come," Marco said, toweling himself off. Ollie could make out the faint outline of Marco's defined abs.

He felt his own flat stomach, having shed the extra pounds of flab that had accumulated during his twenties. Being out here working in the sun, eating better, had chiseled the both of them down to their high school bodies. Marco saw another benefit to their newfound physical fitness—guilt-free drinking. Even hangovers could be easily burned off.

Marco and Ollie helped tie the boat to the dock, exchanging pleasantries with the captain, Joel Elcar. The man had the deepest tan Ollie had ever seen. He assumed it went right down to the man's marrow. When he smiled, his teeth glinted like stars.

"Did they behave themselves?" Ollie asked.

Joel barked a short, hearty laugh, his perpetual grin widening. "They have many questions. Lucky for them, I have many answers."

Elcar's mate, a teen that looked at lot like the sun-kissed captain, set the small gangplank down.

Ollie spotted his friends walking from the stern, glasses filled with what looked like mimosas in their hands. Heidi wore a straw hat with a brim so large, a gust of wind would have carried her off like the Flying Nun. Steven, draped in a hideous Hawaiian shirt, had an arm curled around her waist. Lenny wore long cargo shorts and a black New York Mets jersey. He caught Ollie's eye and gave an enthusiastic thumbs up. "Are you kidding me? This is like something out of a movie."

"Welcome to Fantasy Island!" Ollie said with outstretched arms.

"You're a little tall for Tattoo," Steven said, pointing at Marco.

"All the better to spot de plane," Marco replied, lending a hand to Heidi. She wore absurdly high heels, her ankle almost snapping when a lazy wave made the boat bob up, the gangplank shifting.

"You should probably ditch the shoes," Steven said to her.

"Fashion advice from a *Hawaii Five-O* extra. Nice," she replied with a smile that didn't quite make it all the way to her eyes.

Lenny leapt from the side of the boat onto the dock and hugged Ollie. His jersey was soaked with sweat. "I still can't believe this is real," he said close to Ollie's ear.

"I see you've dressed the part of the islander," Marco said.

"Hey, you should never forget where you came from. Queens and the Mets are part of my DNA."

"You already have drinks, but I think we have something just a little bit better to start things off right," Marco said, opening the cooler. Inside were three bottles of Louis Roederer Cristal Brut. Ollie was no champagne enthusiast, but Marco had assured him the two-hundred-dollar-a-bottle bubbly was miles better than the more popular Dom Perignon.

"Oh, sweet," Lenny said, accepting a glass of the fizzing wine.

Ollie took their mimosas and handed them to the mate where he disappeared into the cabin.

Marco handed him a glass and he almost dropped it.

Why are you so nervous?

He felt as if he were going to rocket right out of his skin. After almost a year of planning, it was finally happening.

"Starting without me?"

Tara emerged from the cabin wearing a white crochet dress that flowed down to her ankles. A side slit revealed a wonderfully tanned and toned leg. She'd grown her hair out since the night in the club and dyed it red, the scarlet ends splayed against the top of her exposed chest.

Ollie had to remind himself to breathe.

"Nope," Marco said. "Just getting our priorities straight."

With a slight shudder, Ollie broke from his paralysis and helped her down the gangplank. He was glad he'd just been swimming. The ocean water masked the sweat that broke out on his palms.

"I was beginning to wonder if you'd changed your mind and caught the next plane back to the states," he said.

"And miss all this?" She gladly accepted the glass of champagne. "Not on your life, Raging Bull."

They all looked to Ollie, their host and benefactor.

Benefactor.

He wondered if he'd ever get used to this new life he'd stumbled into.

A cool breeze came off the ocean. The sun, blue sky and clear water were a backdrop no Hollywood CGI could top.

"Thank you all for coming. You have no idea how much this means to me. There were times I didn't think we'd get our shit together, but luckily, I've had Marco keeping the course. Here's to the rest of our lives and the incredible adventures to come."

They clinked glasses and sipped the wonderful champagne.

Tara leaned into him. He felt an electric jolt shoot up that side of his body.

Steven downed his glass. "God bless us, everyone. N-now, hit me with some more of that hooch."

***

Deep within the stygian blackness of its long slumber, the beast sensed changes in its cold, still world. Vibrations and a flood of new, exotic scents sank below the waves.

The small, active part of its brain registered the sudden deviation from the typical calm that enshrouded it like a frigid, dead womb.

The incessant flood of sensory input awakened something inside it.

Hunger.

But it could not detect what it truly craved.

For the moment, it could only sit and wait.

INTERLUDE, 1950

For Dr. Laughton, it was like working in a damn coffin. On most days, the air conditioning had a hard time keeping the heat at bay, so the coffin was more like an oven.

I'll bet that brings back some memories for that psychotic Dr. Mueller, he thought. *Although this time, he's on the other end.*

He'd been having a difficult time adjusting to this new paradigm of international cooperation in the name of science. He and the other American scientists had not been told the backgrounds of the men imported from Germany and other hiding spots around the world so they would not be biased or prejudicial in their dealings with them.

That only made things worse. As far as Laughton and his contemporaries were concerned, these foreign scientists were all guilty of one atrocity or another.

There was no sense fighting it. It was happening all over the globe. He even heard they were going to set up a lab near his hometown in Long Island, New York with one of these castaways.

To the victors go the spoils, no matter how strange and dangerous they may be.

Though, truth be told, they wouldn't have been able to make such progress without them. These imported minds had been given free rein to delve into the wildest theories and postulates, and with that unfettered permission had come some remarkable results.

Results that they were now working together to refine . . . and control.

He was still trying to figure out how they had managed to genetically engineer the Megalodon. Laughton and his partner Lancaster poured through reams of data, some of it, he was ashamed to admit, that was above his level of understanding. In fact, if he just went by what was put down on paper, he would not believe it was possible.

But the caged beast under the lab was surefire proof that they were right.

Mad fucking geniuses. Though you'd never know it to be around them. They were as cool as igloos, this lot. Quick to smile, always calm under pressure, models of precision and invention.

That disturbed him even more.

There was a knock at his door.

"Come in."

Dr. Brand, his white lab coat smeared with black smudges, came in looking grayer than usual. He really needed some time in the sun, along with a host of vitamin shots. This bunker of a lab was killing him.

"We got a new shipment," Dr. Brand said, pushing his glasses up the bridge of his narrow nose.

That brought a smile to Dr. Laughton's face.

"It's a little early," he said.

"Colonel Pearson expedited pickup and delivery. I've prepped the subjects."

"Thank you, Martin. Why don't you go topside for a while, take a break? You look exhausted." *Not to mention filthy and smell like death itself*, Dr. Laughton thought. He really had to have a sit down with Dr. Brand and convince him to let them do a full workup. He was beginning to fear the worst, especially considering what Dr. Brand did all day.

"I'm knackered. I think I'll just lie down for a spell. If you need me, you know where to find me."

Dr. Laughton watched him go, then placed the files he'd been reading in the safe.

He didn't want to miss feeding time.

CHAPTER FIVE

"I feel like hot garbage," Steven mumbled into his pillow. He'd kicked the sheets off hours ago, but with the humidity, it still felt as if he had a hot, wet blanket draped over his body.

"I have the fan as high as it'll go," Heidi said. She stood over him in her new two-piece bathing suit. When she turned to get a bottle of water from the dresser, he noticed the rear of the suit left very little to the imagination.

It hurt to rub his eyelids. Was that sand? Had he face planted on the beach last night?

"That suit's a little skimpy, don't you think?"

Handing him the warm bottle, she pulled her sunglasses down so he could see her exaggerated eye roll. "As if I'd give your friends their own private show. I can only imagine what Lenny would say. I'm going out in the yard . . . by myself."

Steven struggled to sit up in bed. His tongue tasted like he'd licked a dog's asshole before he went to sleep . . . or passed out, depending on your point of view.

"The yard? It's like a wide open beach."

"You forget about the privacy fence around the cabana?"

"I forget a lot of things at the moment. What time did we crash?"

She gave him two Tylenol and fluffed his pillows. "I think it was around five. I know the sun was about to come up."

Heidi looked as if they hadn't drunk the island dry. They'd been married two years, together five, and he'd yet to see her with a hangover. He suspected some kind of witchery.

"What time is it n-n-now?" He closed his eyes and surrendered to the soft mound of pillows.

"Just after two. You want me to fix you something to eat before I go out?"

"Jesus, n-no."

"You sure you don't want a nice runny egg?"

Steven clamped a hand over his gurgling, cramping stomach. "You're evil, you know that?"

"A girl's gotta have her fun. Go back to sleep. You'll be feeling better by dinner."

"I can only hope."

"We have many more nights like last night and we'll be flying back to Malibu to one of those fancy rehabs."

"Been a long time since I drank like that. I'm getting old. I feel old."

"You're not old. You're just not in college anymore."

With the pillows bunching around his head, it felt as if they had become sentient and were trying to suffocate him. "I think I'd feel less like shit if it wasn't so damn hot."

Heidi threw a towel, sunscreen and a James Patterson paperback in her beach bag.

She said, "What did Marco say about the air conditioners? They're coming in next week?"

"I'll die of heat exhaustion before then."

Patting his bare stomach, she said, "A little sweat will do you good, help you lose a few. You see what it's done for Marco already."

Steven groaned. He'd seen the difference in Ollie, too. Heidi never was into short guys. He'd have to keep a close eye on Marco, though. He trusted his wife, but his past experiences with Marco and the fairer sex were less than savory. Hell, Marco had swiped Tara right out from under Lenny in their sophomore year. Not that Stump and Tara were ever destined to become something serious.

Of course, that was then and this was now. They'd all grown up.

Well, everyone but Lenny.

At least the bed was comfortable. And it was nice to have the windows open, the meager breeze tickling the sweat on his skin. Back home, he'd been paranoid about keeping windows open. Sure, they'd lived in the suburbs, but with so many people around, there was always the potential for a break in or worse. Ever since Mexico, he couldn't shake the feeling that something bad was about to happen. Even after installing a security system around the house and making sure he had pepper spray on him at all times, he never felt completely safe.

It was why he'd jumped at the chance to come out here, despite Heidi's protests. She knew he needed the change too, so she didn't fight him so hard. He was tired of feeling like . . . like less of a man. Jeez, it hurt to even think it. When people saw the size of him, they all assumed he was invincible.

Those Mexican thugs had really messed his mind up good. He'd considered therapy, but then this opportunity came along. Island therapy beat sitting on a couch any day.

Rolling away from Heidi, he said, "Thanks for the pep talk. Go enjoy our tropical paradise. I'm going to see if I can will myself to die."

"You better not. If I'm going to be a widow, I want to live somewhere with lots of options."

She chuckled as she walked out of the bedroom, her flip-flops slapping the bare floor. "Love you, honey," she said before she slipped out the patio door.

Steven grumbled something that may have been translated as "love you back" before an acid burp almost made him christen the bed.

***

Lenny had had the foresight to drink three bottles of water and take three aspirin before hitting the hay. His one-to-one ratio of water to aspirin, the amount differing depending on the quantity he'd imbibed, hadn't failed him yet.

There were a few low clouds in the sky, but they were whiter than the cream in a Twinkie—pure eye candy, not a threat of rain for miles.

He sat on the empty beach in a folding chair, reading over last week's *Sports Illustrated* and enjoying the calming sound of the surf. A row of gently swaying palm trees were at his back. A couple of birds that looked kind of like seagulls dove in and out of the water, probably fishing. Looking out over the horizon, Lenny thought he could see forever, right to the end of the Earth.

"You really stepped in shit this time," he said.

"We all did," a voice replied behind him.

Tara wore a coral bikini and matching cap with her hair pulled through the back. She fanned a blanket out next to his chair and plopped down.

"I thought I'd be the only one alive at this hour," Lenny said. "You need a water?" He opened the lid to the little cooler he'd brought to the beach.

"I'm good. I hydrated like hell so I could get out here. It's too beautiful to miss."

"Somehow, I became an early riser. Even on weekends, I'm up by six. I haven't slept this late in longer than I can remember. Then again, I haven't partied like that since . . . since college."

Tara sprayed sunscreen on her bronze skin. "Did I really do a body shot?"

"Not just one. Three. I don't think Marco minded."

She picked at a tooth. "That explains the pubic hairs."

They looked at one another and sputtered laughing. "Real gross, T-Mac."

"Just telling it like it is, Stump."

For the next few minutes, they sat in silence, staring out at the wondrous view.

"This would be perfect if it weren't for one small flaw," Lenny said.

"You want Ollie to provide a concubine, too? So greedy."

Lenny thought about that for a moment and nodded. "That would be nice. But no, what I'm missing is the Mets-Cubs game. Guess I'll have to watch them on my computer. I'll also have to work out the whole time zone thing."

Tara rolled onto her stomach, taking off her sunglasses and cap. "Ah, a boy and his baseball."

"It's America's pastime and I'm a good old American boy."

"Check that. You're a Marshall Island boy now."

"Or more specifically, a Grand Isla Tiburon boy. I wonder what we can make the pastime here?"

Tara flicked sand at him. "You're doing it right now."

Lenny shielded his eyes so he could watch a pair of marine birds. They were either terrible fishermen or extremely hungry. One of them hit the water hard, kicking up a spray of foam. It leapt back into the sky, something sizeable and flopping in its beak.

"You ever go fishing?" he asked Tara.

"Used to go all the time with my grandpa when I was a kid."

"Maybe tomorrow we can get some poles and see what we get. I hope Ollie has poles."

"We're on an island. I think it's international law that you have to have fishing gear. The only thing I'm gonna catch today is a few more winks. Nudge me in about a half hour so I turn over, will you?"

Lenny checked his watch. He'd ditched the wristwatch his father had given him for his smart phone like everyone else. Coming down here, he thought it was best to get back to basics.

When he looked up, one of the birds swooped down. There was a quick commotion on the surface of the water. The sun's reflection made it impossible to make out any detail.

The bird never resurfaced.

Its fishing partner circled overhead, cawing, until it grew tired and flew away.

Is that a dorsal fin? he thought. *Didn't that guy who brought us here on the boat mention something about sharks? Whatever. It's not like they can get me here.*

Lenny had been a landlubber all his life. The visual out there was a stark reminder of how brutal nature could be, especially in the mostly unknown dark of the sea.

It made him extra appreciative of the fact they were living on a beautiful island where the only thing they had to worry about was when cocktail hour would start.

***

Ollie woke up to a steady pounding in his head. Opening one eye, the room spun, so he closed it tight and prayed for it to settle down.

Knock, knock.

So, it wasn't the thrumming of his heartbeat reverberating around his skull. Someone was at the door.

Mustering up the little strength he had, he cried out, "Come in. The door's open."

"Wow, you look like crap baked over."

Marco slumped into a chair by Ollie's desk, across from the bed. He didn't look much better. His hair was slicked back, still dripping, his skin tone gone an alien gray. One of his eyes was so red it looked like he was in the throes of some holy stigmata.

"You don't look so hot yourself," Ollie said. He tried to raise his head from the pillows and failed miserably.

"That was a rough one."

"I remember everything up until Lenny carrying Steven around on his shoulders and daring us to a chicken fight."

Marco tilted his head back, groaning. "That part had been redacted from my brain, bro. All I know is, when I woke up, I was so sticky, I had to peel the sheets off my chest and stomach. Did one of you try to Krazy Glue something to me?"

When Ollie tried to laugh, the pain drove him back to pained silence.

"I don't think there's any Krazy Glue on the island. You don't remember covering yourself in Fireball?"

Marco got up, went to the kitchen and came back with two cold bottles of water. He tossed the cap and sucked down half his bottle, then handed the other to Ollie. "That's why I tasted cinnamon this morning."

Ollie remembered getting upset when Marco coaxed Tara into doing some body shots. He'd done his best not to let his irritation show. Then again, they were all so bombed, no one would have noticed if he'd thrown himself down on the floor and had a good old-fashioned temper tantrum.

"Anyone else out and about?" Ollie asked, taking a sip of his water.

Ollie's brain wanted to be out and about with his friends on their first full day living as islanders, but his body wasn't up to the task.

"I saw Lenny and Tara on the beach. It looked like they were sleeping. No sign of the mighty Cooter Combs."

It was a very quiet day on the island. Marco had given the workers the next two days off. Most of the heavy construction was already done. There was still considerable work that needed to be completed on the rec center. The gym was finished, but they were waiting on half the equipment. The ten-seat theater had a long ways to go, as did the two-lane bowling alley and pool tables. There was a small room that Ollie had decided would be a library. He'd ordered several hundred books that would get here within the month, which was fine, because the shelves were still being built.

"We did it," Ollie said, his smile delivering tiny daggers of pain to his temples.

"That we did."

"You think they'll all stay?"

Marco finished his water, rubbing the condensation from the bottle on his face. "I don't know. I guess it all depends how things go. It would be a shame to do all this work just to have this as a 'summer island.'"

"Yeah, but it would be one hell of a summer island. Hopefully we can keep building on it."

"Just pray that our investments stay the course. The dividends alone could keep this place going and growing for decades."

"That's why I pay you the big bucks."

Marco stood, patting Ollie's leg under the covers. "That you do. Lenny mentioned a few times about exploring the old lab. I'm sure once he recovers, he's going to want to go right out there."

The military lab was on the northern tip of the island, a series of cement blocks stacked atop one another. There were few remaining flecks of drab olive paint on the pebbled walls. Lenny had requested that they leave it untouched until he got there so they could all go inside together. As curious as Ollie was to see what was inside, he'd agreed and held to it, even though Lenny was thousands of miles away and would never know.

"We could put that on tomorrow's agenda. At this point, I want to see what's inside as much as he does," Ollie said.

"I'll ask Lae to put together a nice dinner so we'll have a pleasant way to cap the day."

Lae Malolo was a middle-aged islander who did housekeeping and cooking for them. She was a master in the kitchen. Her tuna with mango chutney was the stuff of salivating dreams. She came to the island every other day, making sure everything was neat and Ollie, Marco and the workers were well fed.

Now that everyone was here, she'd be coming more often. Ollie had plans to build a house for her small family, both to have her closer to work and to give the Malolos a life they'd never thought possible. He'd seen where they lived now. Four of them in a two-room house that at best would be an expanded toolshed in the states. Once the rec room building was completed, their new house was next on the list.

"What do you think we'll find in the lab?" Ollie asked.

Marco shrugged. "Old files. Rusted office equipment. I'm sure lots of broken glass. I know what you won't find." He turned to leave.

"Oh yeah? What's that?"

"Some horrible failed experiment lashed to a slab like Frankenstein's monster."

Ollie heard the door close.

"You just ruined all the fun."

CHAPTER SIX

The sky was dotted with dark clouds the next day, but still no rain. Ollie had heard that some islands were suffering from a severe drought. Since Grand Isla Tiburon had been abandoned so long, no one knew how much rainfall the island had received over the years. He'd heard last night that there was a huge storm rolling through, but it was going to miss the island by a hefty margin. Getting ready for their little adventure today, Ollie was too distracted to check the news.

He recalled one brief morning shower in all the time he'd been here. Marco had been prepared, working out the fastest, most economical ways to import the water they needed, making sure reserve tanks were built and filled before everyone arrived.

Dying of thirst while surrounded by water was an irony they refused to accept.

Even without rain, the day looked to be a dry washout. Luckily, they had something special in the works.

Ollie laid the supplies Lenny had requested on the beach.

"You did good," Lenny said, giving them the once over.

"I've become very adept with shopping lists," Ollie said.

Tufts of straw colored beach grass surrounded the urban exploring gear. Ollie shooed a formidable-looking spider away. It scuttled deeper into the beach grass.

It was day two and they'd fully recovered from their first night shindig. After a breakfast of eggs, sausage, and rice delivered by Lae to each of their homes, Ollie was surprisingly itching to get inside the mysterious lab.

"Maybe we should just go now," Lenny said, checking his watch.

"You said ten. It's only two minutes after. You have all the patience of a four-year-old."

"Patience? Ever since you told me about a sealed up military lab, I've had to wait nine months for this moment. I could have made and had a baby in all that time. I think my patience is unparalleled."

Ollie couldn't help chuckling. He had to admit, Lenny's enthusiasm was infectious. He looked around to see if anyone was coming.

"Marco said he had to go through some emails. He's got a lot on his plate. But he will be here."

Lenny grabbed a nylon pack, knelt down on the sand and stuffed it with a cord of rope. "We might as well put everything together while we wait."

Because they wouldn't be going far, they didn't need to pack food. But they did have a couple of bottles of water for each pack. It was probably stifling as the Devil's underpants in the lab. Aside from the rope, in each waterproof bag there were flashlights, glow sticks, a headlamp, gloves with no-slip surfaces, pocket knife, a first aid kit, digital camera, respirator and construction helmet. They kept the helmets attached to a line on the side of the packs.

"You sure about the helmets?" Ollie asked. "We're going to look like we're trying out for the Village People."

"You can't be too careful, especially out here where the nearest hospital is a long boat ride away. These old structures look solid but start to fall apart just from the vibration of walking around. I don't want anyone getting de-brained." Lenny got to work on a second pack.

"I don't think that'll be an issue for Heidi," Tara said. Ollie and Lenny jumped.

"Why do you keep doing that?" Lenny said.

"I can't help being stealthy," she said.

Ollie instantly felt lighter than air once he saw that she was dressed for some exploring. She wore jeans, sneakers, and a long-sleeved shirt. She took a last drag on her cigarette and flicked it into the sand.

"Go easy on Heidi. She's not so bad," Ollie said.

Tara sighed. "I'm sure Steven told her about us back in the day. She keeps giving me side eye."

Lenny said, "Can you blame her?"

"I guess not. Maybe dumb blonde jokes aren't the way to go."

"That's the spirit," Ollie said.

"I can't believe we have this whole beautiful island, and here we are, overdressed, sweating, and planning to skulk around some abandoned building."

"You have your whole life to bum around the beach," Lenny said.

Tara smiled. "Wow, that's weird to hear and know it's true. And if we're being honest, I think this is kind of cool. My brother and I used to have this abandoned house in our neighborhood that was our getaway, especially when my parents went nuclear on each other. It was filthy as hell and in retrospect, I know what those balloons all over the floor really were. But it was ours . . . at least during the daytime. At night, we knew the big kids would party in there and we were forbidden."

Lenny handed her a pack. "And that's how little urban explorers are made."

"You enjoy breakfast?" Ollie asked, helping her slip the pack onto her back.

"It was amazing. What kind of sausage was that?"

"Something from the Philippines, I think Lae said."

"And that rice. So sticky and perfect. I did an extra mile on the treadmill this morning because I had to eat it all."

"The gym will be a whole lot more fun once we get the AC installed."

"I didn't mind. I think I'm still sweating out all that booze from the night before."

"Our T-Mac has become diesel," Lenny said.

She sure has, Ollie thought.

"Is it just the three of us?" Tara said.

"Cooter said he'd be here," Lenny said. "Not sure about Hides."

It seemed Stump was doing his best to resurrect their college nicknames and create new ones.

Ollie shielded his eyes from the shafts of sun that pierced the cloud cover. "In fact, here they come."

Tara said, "Huh. Does Heidi know she might break a nail?"

"We hardly know her. She might be into this kind of thing," Ollie said.

"I distinctly remember her saying it was stupid the other night."

Ollie said, "This has to be hard for her. We all have this shared history. She's the outsider stuck in the middle of the Pacific with us."

Tara said, "She's just so . . . so . . ."

"Girlie," Lenny said. "Hides is the epitome of girlie."

"Girlie girls were never your strong suit," Ollie said.

"Which is why I hung around your sorry butts for four years. I also like to think I was there to add a touch of class to your sweat-sock-smelling dorm."

Lenny laughed. "You were all class when you won that burping contest."

"Three years running, if I remember correctly," Ollie added.

"What can I say? I'm the total package—class *and* talent."

"Morning, guys," Steven said, holding Heidi's hand. She had miraculously dressed the part, but Steven was in shorts, sandals and a loose fitting button down shirt.

"Hey there, love birds," Ollie said. "Looks like we picked a perfect day to crawl around indoors. It's only supposed to get cloudier."

"I'd be just as happy zoning out by the water, but I have to admit, Lenny's got me curious," Steven said.

"You sure you don't want to change?" Lenny said.

"That's what I told him," Heidi said. "He doesn't want to listen."

"I'm sweating balls without any clothes on. The last thing I want to do is cover myself up and walk into that oven."

"At the very least, you need sneakers. Go on, we'll wait," Lenny said.

"Are you serious?"

"You'll thank me when we're not having to take you to Majuro for a tetanus shot."

Steven's shoulders sagged and he headed back to his house.

"How are you liking everything?" Ollie asked Heidi.

"I have to admit, this is all pretty awesome. I know I'm going to miss my friends soon enough, but for now, I'm loving it. I haven't taken a day to just sit and read in, like, forever. I read my book from cover to cover yesterday."

"Wait until you see the library when it's done," Ollie said. "I even had Steven send me a list of your favorite authors and books so I could get the stuff you like."

"Did you get my stuff, too?" Lenny asked.

"We can't find *Juggs*, but your adult coloring books are on order." Ollie was pleased to see Tara helping Heidi with her pack.

"Ha, ha."

"And here's the last of the funky bunch," Tara said as Marco came from the other side, scrabbling down the small dune.

"Everything good?" Ollie asked him.

Marco still looked a little green around the gills. The bags under his eyes were still packed, though for a short trip.

"Uh, yeah. Just have a few things to tie up later."

"Take a pack," Lenny said, handing one over.

"Thanks."

Steven came back wearing high-top sneakers and they were off. The walk to the lab was a little over a half mile, made to seem longer as they trudged over the soft sand. This side of the island was the hilliest, spots of grass browned from the sun and lack of rain. Ollie was still amazed by how most of the island still looked like man had never set foot on it. When the military was here, they must have spread out. Either they kept to the area around the lab, or nature had made quick work of covering their tracks.

Walking alongside Ollie, Marco said, "I also gave Lae one of these." He showed him a small walkie-talkie. "Just in case anything happens and we need help."

A shiver ran down Ollie's back. "I thought you said all we'd find is paper and broken glass."

"My job is to plan for every eventuality."

"You're handier than a clown at a rodeo, you know that?"

They had to use their hands and feet to make it up the last dune.

"It's bigger than I thought it would be," Steven said.

"That's what she said," Lenny quickly replied. Tara punched the back of his shoulder.

"Are we going to explore the whole thing today?" Heidi asked with a heavy dose of trepidation in her voice.

"We'll play it by ear," Lenny said, the clear leader of this expedition. "It all depends on what kind of goodies we find inside."

All told, the lab consisted of a dozen connected solid blocks. There were four singular blocks on the perimeter with concrete walkways attached to buildings made of two blocks stacked on one another, with a central building of four blocks dominating the entire structure. It was big, ugly and utilitarian. In other words, pure military.

"Looks like something my niece would build," Tara said.

Lenny led the way down the dune. "The military has great engineers, but they prefer function over form. I don't think they were looking to make the cover of *Town & Laboratory* out here."

Ollie and Marco had been out here before, on their first day on the island. They had both noted at the time that there were no windows. In fact, a long steel door in one of the outer blocks appeared to be the only portal into the place.

"Who the hell would want to work in such a place?" Marco said.

"I think it looks like a prison . . . or a cage," Heidi said.

"For my money, it looks like a sand castle built by a giant kid who had one of those plastic hollow brick things to shape the sand," Ollie said.

"I think we can all agree it's pretty ugly," Tara said.

"Which is why it's going to be torn down next month," Marco said. "So, Lenny, you better get your kicks in while you can."

When they got to the door, Lenny turned to Marco and Ollie. "Any chance they left you a key?"

"Oh, sure," Ollie said. He handed Lenny the collapsible pry bar he'd ordered. "I think this'll work."

"Okay, before I open this door, you all need to put on your masks. I don't know how well this has been sealed up, so I can't tell what gasses might have been stored up inside. I'll let it air out before we go inside, but even then, keep your masks on. I'll bet good money that at least there's asbestos in there."

He jammed the end of the pry bar by the door handle.

"Oh yeah, and make sure you wear your helmets inside, too." Everyone slipped on their masks and unclipped their helmets.

Lenny gave them a thumbs-up. "Here goes nothing."

With a loud grunt, he tugged on the pry bar. The metal door moaned.

Ollie felt Tara's hand grip his arm. Her hand was like a vise.

Pain never felt so good.

The door swung open so fast, Lenny lost his footing and fell on his ass. The pry bar slipped from his hand, looped in the air and landed with a sharp crack on his helmet.

Everyone but Heidi couldn't help but laugh.

Lenny made a quick recovery, jumping to his feet. "And so ends my demonstration of why we need to wear helmets."

"Are you all right?" Heidi asked.

"I'm fine. I have a thick skull under here." He peered inside the dark laboratory. "That's weird. The door wasn't even locked. Maybe the locking mechanism rusted away."

"So it's safe to just go in, right?" Steven said, his body filling the doorframe.

Lenny tugged him back. "Same rules apply. I want some fresh air to flow in there first."

Ollie flicked his flashlight on and tried to pierce the thick gloom. "Look, there are steps going down. The inside is a lot bigger than it looks from the outside."

Tara sidled up next to him, their twin beams sweeping the room. It was hard to make anything out from this distance. She found a broken seashell and tossed it inside. It skittered somewhere in the darkness.

"What'd you do that for? It can't be that deep. We're already at sea level," Marco said.

"That's exactly why I did it. I wanted to hear if there was water down there. If there was, there's no way I'm wading through that diseased soup."

Lenny nodded, only his eyes visible through the mask. "That was really good thinking. You sure you haven't done this before?"

"I just have a high level of self-preservation and a need to avoid infection."

A heavy splash behind them pulled their attention from the open lab.

The ocean's waves hit the beach, but not loud enough to account for the booming sound.

"What the hell was that?" Steven said.

"Dolphin maybe," Ollie said.

"Or a shark," Marco said. "This whole area is part of the shark sanctuary. Sometimes, they'll pop out of the water real quick if there's something tasty looking near the surface."

"Okay, so swimming is no longer an option," Tara said.

"It's all right to swim. Just not too far out," Ollie said. "Marco and I have been in the water practically every day."

He didn't get the feeling that brought Tara much comfort.

They stared at the water for several minutes but saw nothing.

"I think it's safe to go inside now," Lenny said. "Just follow my lead. And you may want to turn your headlamps on, too. The more light, the better. Keep a close eye on the ground. There might be all sorts of stuff lying around, just waiting to trip you up."

Heidi dug her fingers into the waistband of Steven's shorts. "Make one ball and chain joke and you're sleeping on the couch tonight."

Steven raised his hands. "I'm n-not saying anything."

Heidi visibly trembled.

"You okay?" Tara said.

"It's all right. I'm just not a big fan of the dark. I know that sounds childish."

"Not at all," Ollie said. "Here, let's swap flashlights. Mine is a little bigger."

Lenny said, "That's what she—"

Tara punched him again.

"Okay kids, single file," Lenny said, taking the first step.

There were three steps in all. The harsh narrow lights revealed a worn path through the dust.

"You think these are the footsteps of the people when they left here in the fifties?" Steven asked.

Lenny shook his head. "No, this looks more recent. Guess we're not the first people in here."

"But this island was deserted until this year. Who else would it be?"

"No one *lived* here, but I'll bet people still came ashore for day trips," Marco said, wiping sweat from his brow and upper lip. "Maybe there was a storm and someone broke in for shelter."

"Any port in a storm will do," Ollie said. To him, it looked like numerous footprints going up and down the stairs. He trained his light to the corner of the room and found a pile of crumpled paper bags. "Picnic lunch?"

Lenny toed the bags with his sneaker. "They could have been here for decades. Hard to tell. If they were plastic, I'd say it was recent garbage."

It was as hot inside as Ollie had feared. It felt like stepping into a pizza oven. His own hot breath circulated back to him within the filtration mask.

"Found the reception desk," Tara said. She, Steven and Heidi were huddled behind a large, semi-circular desk covered in dust. She opened a leather bound ledger and paged through it, the brittle paper crackling. "It's a list of names, dates and time of entry and exit." She tucked it under her arm.

"Normally, when you do urban exploring, you take nothing with you," Lenny said. "Whatever you touch, you make sure you put it back in the exact same spot you found it. But since the place is going to be demolished, it's a good idea to save some of the history."

"Did you know this place had a name?" Tara said.

"Not a clue," Ollie replied.

She trained her flashlight on the cover of the ledger. In gold inlaid letters, it said : DEEP SEA REBIRTH—OMEGA LAB

"N-n-now that's ominous," Steven said.

"More like creepy," Heidi said.

"Wonder what they were rebirthing," Ollie said.

"Maybe we'll find something they left behind and find out," Lenny said. "That's the real fun of exploring places like this."

Ollie asked to see the book. The pages were almost all filled with impeccably neat handwriting. The year of the entries was 1954. "At least we'll know who was on the island back then. I guess these are ranks. Wonder what WO2 means."

Steven looked over his shoulder. "It stands for Chief Warrant Officer."

Tara said, "How do you know that?"

"Military channel. Oh, and all those books," Heidi said. "If there's a war in it, he'll read it."

"What about this?" Ollie asked, pointing to a line that read *ENS – Charles Duba – 1:23pm / 10:07pm.*

"That means Charles was an ensign."

"What were ensigns in the grand pecking order?" Ollie asked.

"They were low-ranking commission officers. Better than being a grunt," Steven said.

Bang!

"Ah, Christ that hurt!"

All of their headlamps turned to Marco who was hopping on one foot, both hands clasped around his shin.

It looked like he'd smashed his leg on a filing cabinet that had been turned over on its side.

"I told you to look down," Lenny said.

"I looked up for one second to check out the ledger," Marco snapped, hissing in pain.

"Things can turn on a dime in one second in a place like this," Lenny said.

"Maybe we should come back after the wrecking crew smashes some holes in the walls. Then we'll be able to see better," Heidi said.

It was impossible to tell the look Lenny was giving her, but Ollie could guess.

"Where would all the fun be then?" Lenny said.

A sudden gust of wind slammed the door shut, blocking out the little daylight that had managed to venture inside. They all jumped, Steven letting out a high-pitched yelp.

Ollie couldn't help laughing. "It's okay, big guy. No ghosts here. Promise."

Steven made a big production out of clearing his throat. "Just took me by surprise."

Heidi said, "You should hear him when we find stink bugs in the house."

Steven looked down at her fingers literally attached to him at the hip. "This coming from the girl tethered to me."

Ollie scanned the spare room. "Not much else to see here."

Lenny tapped a steel door on the other end of the room with the pry bar. "Care to see what's behind door number two?"

"May I?" Ollie asked. Lenny handed over the pry bar.

Ollie jammed it in the door and pulled. It didn't budge. He tried again, grunting from the strain.

"Here, let me try," Steven said. Heidi shuffled on his heels as he approached the door.

"As grand dictator of Grand Isla Tiburon, I insist I crack this baby open," Ollie said. His short but now muscular arms bulged and shook as he pulled with everything he had.

"I knew it," Tara said. "Now he's a dictator. We were brought here under false pretenses."

The last thing Ollie wanted to do was fail in front of Tara. He'd burst every blood vessel in his body with the effort before giving up.

"Come on, you stubborn fuck."

For some reason, he thought of Michael Douglas and Kathleen Turner in *The War of the Roses*. The divorcing couple was so pigheaded and inflexible, they basically fought to the death. In this case, he was Michael Douglas and this damn door was his own private Kathleen Turner.

Lenny said, "Just pretend it's some ass-wad who made fun of you at the bar."

Ollie gave a last shove and the door flew open as if it had been blasted with dynamite. He tumbled into Lenny, the both of them going down in a heap. The door slammed into the wall, the noise echoing in the empty chamber so loud, it was like shooting nails into their ears.

Something in the room hit the floor with a chest-thundering crash. Tara and Heidi cried out. Marco yelled, "Stay back!"

A plume of dust, like the kicked-up detritus on the edge of a hurricane, billowed out of the room. Shiny motes sparkled under their lights as the roiling cloud washed over them.

Ollie's mask had slipped to the side of his face from the fall. He inhaled a lungful of the dust and immediately started hacking. It burned. He didn't think he could take another breath.

He began to panic.

What if whatever was in the dust was toxic?

I can't breathe! his brain shouted. Spittle dangled from his lips, his ribs aching from coughing.

I can't breathe!

CHAPTER SEVEN

"Somebody help me!" Lenny screamed.

He held tight to Ollie's spasming body, turning him over on his stomach and patting his back. Steven and Tara rushed over.

"Just hold tight. I have to get his mask back on," Lenny said.

Tara grabbed Ollie by the shoulders while Steven looped his arm around his legs. Ollie was gasping and coughing. Tara's headlamp revealed bulging eyes and blue lips.

"What the hell's happening?" she said.

"He took in a ton of that crap," Lenny said. He turned Ollie's mask around so it was in the proper position. "Try to settle down and just breathe, Ollie. You're getting clean air now. Take a breath and hold it in for as long as you can."

Ollie couldn't respond. A tremor ran through his body.

Lenny continued talking him through it. "You're going to be okay. Just breathe, Raging Bull. Breathe. That's it. Now hold it. There. Let it out. Again. See, I told you."

Ollie went still, his back rising and falling steadier now.

Suddenly, he got to his knees and ripped off the mask. Before Lenny could protest and slip it back on, he projectile vomited over his friend's shoulder. Lenny pulled him close, massaging his back as if he were a sick baby.

"You get it all out?"

"I think I just threw up my breakfast . . . from last week," Ollie sputtered.

"Good. Now put your mask back on and try not to barf in it. You wouldn't like that."

"What the heck was that all about, bro?" Marco said.

"He just got a lungful of dust," Lenny said. "He'll be all right. It used to happen to me all the time before I wised up and got a mask."

Ollie gave a weak thumbs-up.

They recoiled at the sound of another crash.

Tara had kicked the exterior door open. She disappeared outside, returning seconds later carrying a big rock. She nestled the rock next to the door.

"We have to keep fresh air coming in," she said. "Ollie, you want to come out and grab some?"

"I'm fine." He smacked his lips. "God, it tastes awful. Like an old closet and . . . and something metallic."

"We can call it a day if you want," Lenny said. "I can always come back tomorrow."

"No way. I'm in."

Lenny looked to his friends. "Anyone else want to go back for cocktails on the beach? I don't want you guys to feel pressured."

Heidi, who had resumed being attached to her husband, looked as if she were going to bail. Then she shrugged and said, "We came this far. It's not like Ollie was attacked by some creature. Just a ton of dust. I'm a scaredy cat, but not that scared."

When no one else objected, Lenny said, "All righty. Let's see what we've got."

It was plainly evident that this inner building was once a hive of activity. Long tables, desks, overturned chairs and file cabinets with empty, open drawers were everywhere. All of the furnishings were made of metal and in varying degrees of rust.

"Looks like someone left in a hurry," Marco said. Their beams of light crisscrossed the room. "Maybe we should take their cue."

"Or an earthquake hit the place," Steven said.

"That's more likely," Ollie said. "There are volcanoes all around Micronesia. A tremor could have knocked everything around."

When Tara hovered over the cushioned back of a chair, Lenny said, "Don't touch it."

Her hand recoiled.

"Why not?"

"Could be loaded with mold. You don't want that on your skin. It's also not a good idea to release it into the air."

"What about the masks?" Steven asked.

"Best not to take any chances," Lenny said. He opened his pack, took out the slim gloves and slipped them on. Everyone got the hint and did the same.

"Okay, so even the cushion can kill you," Tara said, centering her light on a table littered with broken glass and steel pipes that looked like something out of the Mousetrap game. "And you do this for fun?"

Lenny weaved his way around crooked workstations. "Believe it or not, market research isn't big on adventure."

"Then pet strange dogs or call out bingo at a packed bingo hall when you don't have it," Tara said, chuckling.

"That bingo idea is called suicide," Ollie joked, feeling a little better. However, his breath was vile. He hoped no one else could smell it, even through the mask.

The interior building was hotter than the first. They wouldn't last long if some of the heat didn't dissipate.

Marco and Steven went through the file cabinets, having to force some of the drawers open. The screeching metal was worse than nails on a chalkboard.

"Find anything?" Lenny asked.

"Just this," Steven said, holding up an empty bottle of J&B.

A steady *click-clack* caught Lenny's attention. He shined his headlamp on Ollie, who was standing by the wall flicking the light switch.

"Hoping that electricity will magically appear?" Lenny said.

"Sorry. A bit of my OCD kicking in."

"You still do that thing with the light switches?" Steven asked. Turning lights on and off, counting to ten before getting into bed . . . always on the right side . . . and a few other oddities had plagued Ollie when he was younger. It got worse during times of stress, like finals week. They used to try to get him to stop but realized holding him back just made it worse.

"That's funny. I haven't done anything like that in years," he said.

"A place like this is easy to go nuts in," Tara said, gently removing his hand from the switch. "Or pass out. It's pretty hard to breathe in here."

"I agree," Heidi said.

Lenny knew he was losing them. He'd leave the doors open overnight and come back tomorrow. But first, there was one more door that must lead to the central building, the tallest one in the entire lab compound.

It was so hot and damp, their clothes stuck to them like a second skin. Steven had unbuttoned his shirt. His chest and stomach glistened with sweat.

"How about we do a quick look-see in the central building?" Lenny said.

"I like the word quick," Heidi replied. "Think I'll jump in the ocean the second we get out of here."

"Oh yeah. There's n-no way I'm waiting until we get back to the house," Steven said, giving her arm a squeeze.

For just a brief moment, Lenny wondered if Heidi was into skinny-dipping. Sure, she was his friend's wife, but he was still human . . . and a man to boot. It was impossible not to hope.

Lenny jammed the pry bar into the door.

"Everyone have their masks on tight?" he asked before applying an ounce of pressure. They all looked to Ollie.

"Very funny, guys."

Lenny tried to turn the knob but it wouldn't budge.

"Okay, give me room, in case I go flying again."

This time, the door wouldn't budge. Lenny tugged so hard, he farted, which got them all snickering like grade-schoolers.

"Yes, yes, yes, everybody farts. I read it in a book," Lenny said. "Cooter, you want to lend me a hand?"

Steven gave him a hard look. "I don't respond to that anymore."

"Cootsy-wootsy?"

Heidi laughed at that, shoving him towards Lenny. "Go on, open the door so we can get out of here."

Steven grabbed the handle with Lenny. "Ready Stump Dick?"

"Sticks and stones," Lenny said. "On three. One. Two. Three. Pull!"

They threw their combined weight against the pry bar. The door wailed as if it were a living thing, protesting the invasion of its privacy. One of the hinges snapped and the door cracked. It opened with a heavy moan just as the pry bar broke in half.

This time, a dust cloud wasn't there to greet them.

"Do you hear that?" Tara said.

Lenny shined his light inside. It landed on a stone wall seven feet into the room.

"Sounds like the surf," Steven said.

Looking down to make sure there was solid ground beneath them, Lenny said, "Why don't you all come here? We can use all the light we can get."

They stepped through the doorway, the steady undulations of water echoing in the strange chamber.

"Will you look at that," Ollie said, tilting his head up, illuminating the sheer wall.

The temperature in this part of the lab complex was considerably cooler. Lenny sparked the flame of his lighter and watched the flame dance close to his knuckles as a cool breeze fanned it from above. The wind chilled the sweat on the back of his neck.

"What the hell is this?" Marco asked.

They slowly and carefully walked around the wall, which was actually a rounded cylinder or tank, almost like the above ground structure of a well. Lenny pointed out banks and banks of floodlights around the top of the cylinder.

"It's the heart of the lab," Ollie said. "The only question is, what were they doing in here?"

Heidi was the first to spot the ladder on the side of the cylinder. The outer concrete had worn away in patches, revealing gray steel underneath.

The ladder went all the way to the top, connecting with a catwalk that surrounded the circumference of the structure.

"Looks like an observation deck," Steven said.

"Wonder what they were observing that they had to stand so far away from," Tara said.

Ollie grabbed one of the ladder's rungs. "Only one way to find out."

"Hold on, cowboy," Lenny said. "We don't know if that ladder can support your weight."

Ollie tugged on the ladder, putting his feet on another rung. It didn't move so much as an inch. Nor did it make any protestations.

"Seems pretty solid to me," Ollie said. "Besides, it's only twenty or thirty feet to the top. If I fall, you can catch me."

"Don't count on it," Steven said. "You may be a little guy, but you weigh a hell of a lot more than a cat."

Lenny extracted the rope from his bag. "Here, let me tie this around you and I'll find another—"

"Look, I'm just going to go up real quick and take a peek. I'll be fine."

Before Lenny could tell him how incredibly stupid that was, Ollie started climbing.

"Be careful," Tara said, her eyes glued to Ollie.

Lenny put his hand under his mask to flick some sweat from his brow. *He's gone all macho just to impress Tara. I didn't realize he still had a thing for her.*

Of course, they'd all had a thing for Tara back in the day. Lenny was painfully aware that Ollie was the only one of their group who hadn't so much as sniffed a date with Tara. She was a pretty big party girl then. Ollie was shy, her total opposite. To compensate, he'd drink, but then he'd go too far and turn into Captain Belligerent Dickhead. He just never seemed to get on the right wavelength.

For the first time, Lenny wondered if they were all here just for the sake of Ollie trying to do what he failed to do in college. If he failed again, or if she turned him down, would he call the whole thing off and send them back home to lives that included no job and no place to live?

Nah, he wouldn't do that.

But he might break his neck before he ever got his second chance.

"Take it slow, buddy," Lenny called up to him.

"Roger that."

Ollie was three quarters of the way up. So far, everything had held steady. "When you get to the top, loop your rope around your waist and tie the other end to one of the bars up there."

Ollie stopped and looked down.

"Why?"

"In case the whole thing falls apart when you step on it."

Heidi said, "If things start falling down, will we have enough time to get out of here?"

Because the room was shaped like an oval, they couldn't see the door where they'd come in.

"I think so," Lenny said.

Heidi inched toward the exit, tugging Steven by his shorts. "That's encouraging."

"It'll be fine," Ollie said, his voice echoing. "Everything seems real stable."

No one spoke or moved for the next minute while Ollie got to the top, tied himself off and stepped onto the catwalk. He remained still for a moment, making sure all was well.

"See, piece of cake," he said.

"What do you see?" Marco asked.

He'd been exceptionally quiet this whole time, Lenny thought. *Probably adding up the payout on our insurance policies.*

Their lights barely reached Ollie, He was a vague shape that leaned over the lip of the cylinder.

"It's like the tip of a volcano up here," he said. "Except instead of lava, there's water. I can't see anything, though. It's too dark. Kinda reminds me of a bad guy's lair in a James Bond film. Or Dr. Evil's summer lair." They heard him move around. "Wait, there's something up here. Looks like a big chute or something."

The lone, piercing shriek of a klaxon sounded, nearly making Lenny jump out of his boots.

It was followed by a resounding, steady thumping that seemed to come from everywhere within the tomblike building, including above and below it.

The floor shook. It felt as if something were moving beneath their feet. Dull, metallic crashes sounded off one after other.

"What the hell is happening?" Steven said, eyes wide, staring at the floor as if he expected it to burst apart any second now.

Lenny wasn't so sure that wouldn't be the case.

To him, it sounded like the disengaging of locks on the steel bars in a prison, the ear shattering clanging muffled by water and thick slabs of concrete. Something was either slamming shut or disengaging.

After several seconds that felt like several minutes, it stopped.

The sound of everyone's short, frightened gasps filled the void. It didn't last long.

There was a dull buzz, then multiple splashes deep within the cylinder.

"What the fuck was that?" Lenny asked.

Ollie said, "I accidentally hit a button. The trap door on the chute opened and something spilled out. Smells awful. Like a whole cemetery of dead people."

"God knows what was rotting in there all these years," Lenny said. "Take some pictures. After you come down, I'll head up."

"This is so bizarre," Heidi said.

"I guess it makes sense," Tara said. "They called the place Deep Sea Rebirth. You need access to the sea if you're going to be working on it."

Steven placed his hands on the cylinder. "Yeah, but why would you n-need to build something like this? Wouldn't you want to be closer to the water?"

"Or better yet, what were they afraid of?" Lenny said.

When he looked at Heidi, she had the face of a scream queen in mid shriek, except no sound was coming from her mouth.

"Gee, thanks for scaring my wife," Steven said, pulling her close.

"That wasn't my intention. I was just thinking out loud."

Marco put his hands around his mouth and called out, "If you can't see anything, you should come down. We'll have to warn the demolition crew about this. Don't want them falling into the ocean when they knock it down."

Ollie said, "Just a second. I think I hear something."

When he didn't say anything else, Lenny shouted, "Ollie, what is it?"

"I wish I had more light."

The floor rumbled again. It was like standing on the sidewalk in Manhattan when the subway passed underfoot.

"Ollie, get the hell down from there," Lenny said.

"We have to get out of here," Heidi said, dragging Steven like a reluctant dog on a leash.

The sound of the water sloshing in the cylinder escalated. Drops of salty spray rained down on them.

Lenny gripped the ladder. "Ollie, get your ass back down here!"

"I'm coming!"

He looked to the rest of them. "You guys, go. Don't stop until you get outside."

"We can't just leave Ollie up there," Steven said, resisting Heidi's insistent tugging.

"I'll stay. Get Heidi and Tara out of here," Lenny said.

"I'll stay with you," Marco said. When they looked up, it appeared that Ollie was trying to undo the knot he'd made in the rope.

"Me too," Tara said. "Go on, Steven. We'll be fine."

Steven reluctantly followed his wife out the door.

Something struck the side of the cylinder so hard, it sent them sprawling backward.

Ollie cried out.

A wave of icy water barreled down the sides of the cylinder.

Lenny ripped his mask off and screamed Ollie's name.

Water filled his mouth so hard and so fast, he felt like he was about to drown.

***

The beast awoke from its long, dreamless slumber.

Sounds distantly familiar started the neurons firing in its prehistoric brain. Its coal black eyes opened for the first time in decades. The near-death of its imprisonment ended with noise and shuddering and the scent of nourishment.

Meat, redolent with decay and chemicals, sank slowly in the deep, cold water. The beast's stomach fired up like an old truck engine.

It was hungry.

Food—precious, long-ago forgotten food—was so close.

With a swish of its tail fin, longer and wider than a sail, the beast plunged into the cage, nose slamming into coral-encrusted steel. The cage groaned but held steady.

It watched the food sink deeper and deeper until it was out of sight, but never too far to smell.

Ravenous, driven mad by hunger now that its prolonged hibernation had been broken, the beast battered the cage again and again.

For wasn't this what it had been designed and trained to do?

It was an aquatic Pavolovian creation of fury and hunger. Not that it knew or would ever care about Pavlov.

Eat!

That's what it needed to do right now.

With one last burst, the beast crumpled the front of the cage. Iron bars bent like sticks of licorice.

It was free!

Diving toward its food, the beast opened its mouth wide, eagerly awaiting the pungent meat that had brought it to life so long ago.

INTERLUDE... 1951

It was confirmed. Dr. Brand had died of radiation exposure.

This was a shock to no one. The man took chances, was so engrossed in his work that he wouldn't stop. And the powers that be were only too happy to let him continue.

Just another casualty in the pursuit of the future.

Dr. Laughton closed the file folder containing Brand's autopsy results and dropped it on his desk.

"He can still be of value to the project," Dr. Mueller said, making him jump. He didn't know the oily German scientist was even in the room, much less right behind him.

Dr. Laughton whirled round to face him, jaws clenched in fury.

"You may not touch him," he spat.

Dr. Mueller merely smiled.

"It was only a suggestion, considering the good doctor's dedication to what we are trying to accomplish."

"I'm sure that was perfectly normal for you in the war, but here, now, we call it barbarism."

"Is it barbarism when we do the same with my former countrymen?"

Dr. Laughton flashed a wicked grin. "No. That's called justice. And don't play a national pride card with me. I know full well you pledge allegiance to nothing other than *that thing.*"

They all agreed that Mueller was a mad genius. Not the raving lunatic that was depicted in movies. No, his calm, measured demeanor was the perfect smokescreen for the insanity that boiled within him.

There was no doubting his brilliance. Working for the Nazis, the scientist had brought an extinct species of fish, a fish presumed to have been deceased for millions of years, back to life. The discovery of the coelacanth, a fish that could grow to six feet in length, had taken the oceanographic world by storm. Perhaps the world of marine biology had been wrong and the fish, though elusive, had never gone extinct.

Only Dr. Mueller and his associates knew the truth. The coelacanth was just his first success, a remarkable achievement, resurrection of the dead from mere fossilized cells. Even working on the project, Dr. Laughton wasn't entirely sure of how it was done. Everything was on a need to know basis, each scientist assigned to do their part. Only Dr. Mueller knew how to put all the pieces together.

What they had hatched here was no coelacanth.

Dr. Mueller's fingers stroked his goatee. He seemed completely unfazed by Laughton's show of anger and repulsion. The cold bastard.

"That thing will change the world one day. And you should be appreciative that the change will be for the good of you and your country."

"Only because our side won," Dr. Laughton said.

Dr. Mueller shrugged. "Science, great science, knows nothing about race, creed, or color. I actually came to let you know that we're going to do a test run with the creature in one hour. We have several ships at the ready. Care to join us?"

Dr. Laughton turned his back on Mueller, whirled around and punched the smug German scientist.

The blow staggered Mueller, but didn't drop him. Leaning against his desk, the man pulled a handkerchief from his back pocket and dabbed the drop of blood from the corner of his lip.

He said nothing to Laughton. The man simply smiled, then went back to his work as if nothing had happened.

Storming out of the room, Laughton slammed the door, expelling the breath he had been holding, waiting to see if his brief flash of violence would escalate to a full brawl.

He was getting very unprofessional, but it couldn't be helped. This lab was driving him crazy. The project itself frightened him. And he missed home more and more each day.

The doctor was beginning to wonder if any of them would ever be allowed home.

Not after what they had seen.

What they had done.

He looked at the list of names on the clipboard by the door. Twenty in all.

Twenty Nazi war criminals that had been sequestered in secret prisons around the world since 1945. The Allies had captured many more than they let the public know, keeping them hidden from view these past six years.

Allowing those monsters the dignity of a trial was out of the question. Their guilt was unquestionable.

The last thing they wanted to do was give these men a public forum to spew more hate or try to beguile the world that they were, in fact, innocent.

The initial plan was to let them rot, closed off from civilization until they died from neglect, disease, or their own hands.

Oddly enough, it was Dr. Mueller who had proposed emptying some of those prisons for the experiment.

The Nazis were transported to small islands, chained so they couldn't escape. These islands would be close to nuclear tests, the prisoners becoming heavily dosed with radiation. They were then retrieved by specially protected teams and brought back here.

Dr. Mueller had not only brought a Megalodon back from extinction, he had also devised the special formula that gave life to the beast. The ancient shark was a meat eater, but it was so large, it would quickly destroy the nearby ecosystem in its quest for food.

So, it had been altered to respond to a particular type of nourishment—the irradiated bodies of the Nazi war criminals that had been injected with Dr. Mueller's special serum. Again, the ingredients of the serum were known only to Mueller. Laughton had tried several times to gain access to the Nazi's notes, but so far he'd been unsuccessful.

Whatever it was, it did horrible things to the men who were infused and prepared for the Megalodon. Their flesh blackened, became spongy and foul smelling. They looked as if they'd been dipped in hot tar, their cries short lived as it burned out their vocal cords.

The radiation, in combination with the chemical cocktail, was like a shot of adrenaline to the creature.

And like adrenaline, it would wear off, the Megalodon returning to a deep slumber akin to hibernation. Once subdued, it would be transported via submarine back into its specially designed cage under the lab.

It was as ingenious as it was foul. What would they do when they ran out of Nazis? Dr. Laughton knew that Mueller wanted to use the Marshallese that had been accidentally irradiated, but so far, he'd been denied.

But if the creature kept growing and there were more and more successful tests, he knew it was only a matter of time until they gave Dr. Mueller permission to do whatever he had to do to feed the beast. That Megalodon was going to make America an unparalleled super power.

At what cost, Dr. Laughton thought, shuffling into the hallway. *At what cost?*

CHAPTER EIGHT

Ollie was hit by the geyser of water, square in the face. Again, his filter mask was spun sideways. The water stung his eyes, wormed into his mouth and nose. He gagged, the salty tang of the ocean and his own bile burning his throat.

He lost his footing, arms pinwheeling, searching for anything to grab onto.

The slick catwalk had become an ice rink. His feet glided on the slippery metal grating. He spun around, his ribs smacking the rail. His momentum carried him over and he was facing the long drop down.

He tried to scream, but his lungs were too full of water.

The next moment, he was in free fall.

Another explosion of water erupted from the cylinder, slamming him in the back as he slipped and fell over the side of the platform.

There was a sharp tug and he vomited air and seawater.

His descent stopped abruptly as he swung hard into the side of the cylinder. In that brief moment of contact, he swore he could feel something enormous moving around inside it.

Swinging like the blade in *The Pit and the Pendulum*, he spied the rungs of the ladder not far to his right. He reached out with wet hands, his fingertips grazing the metal bar.

Dammit! Keep trying.

There was a heavy thud and more water splashed out. He swung through the curtain of water, which spun him around. He closed his eyes, trying to fight off the dizziness and creeping fear that he was going to die up here, dangling in an abandoned military lab.

That would be just my luck. Win all this money, get things just the way I want them, and fucking die!

He hoped Tara was okay.

As he tried and missed his next attempt to grab the ladder, he rethought that.

I hope they're all okay.

The rope jerked several feet downward as the railing he'd attached it to gave way. He had to get on that ladder!

Whump. Whump. Whump.

It sounded like something was trying to break its way out of the cylinder. A spider web of cracks broke out on the surface, chunks of concrete crumbling down.

Ollie found his voice. "Heads up! This thing is falling apart."

He couldn't hear any replies over the rush of water and terrifying thumps.

Swinging lower, knowing the metal bar was going to give way any second now, Ollie steeled himself for a last, desperate attempt to latch onto the ladder. Water pounded the back of his head, the helmet absorbing most of the blow. It still made him see stars.

"Almost there," he said through gritted teeth.

Three fingers of his left hand touched metal. They curled around it as best they could, his body weight threatening to break his tenuous grasp. Before he lost it altogether, he lunged forward, grabbing another rung with his right hand. It hurt like hell to stop his swinging, his shoulders threatening to pop from their sockets.

But it worked.

He pressed his body flat against the quaking cylinder, holding onto the ladder for dear life. His feet found lower rungs. His body quaked from exhaustion, fear, and the rush of adrenaline. Fumbling for the knife in his pack, he pulled out the blade and cut the rope.

He had to take a few deep breaths before attempting to climb back down.

"I'm coming down," he shouted.

"We're here," Lenny said. His voice sounded as if he were gargling.

Ollie scrabbled down as quickly as he could, praying that no one was hurt. The floor of the lab was covered in half a foot of water. Lenny, Marco and Tara were there to peel him off the ladder.

"You all okay?" Ollie asked.

"Define okay," Tara said. "Alive is good enough for now. You all right to walk?"

"I'm ready to run."

"Even better. Come on."

The four of them sprinted around the cylinder, water sloshing up to their calves, bits of the concrete façade splintering and plinking off their helmets. They made it to the doorway, Lenny slamming it shut behind them. Marco ran smack into a chair, Lenny into the edge of a desk. Ollie and Tara grabbed hold of their arms and kept them moving forward.

They exploded from the lab into the gray light.

Steven and Heidi were waiting for them, practically catching them as they stumbled out, breathless and soaked to the skin.

***

Tara lay on her back, staring at the slate gray sky. "What . . . the fuck . . . was that?"

Lenny was on his hands and knees, coughing out the last remnants of seawater, hocking up great wads of spit. Marco sat with a leg pulled up to his chest. Tara spied a gash in his jeans and a steady stream of blood.

Ollie paced outside the lab door while Steven hugged Heidi, who had calmed considerably.

"Must be whatever storm's cooking out there," Ollie said, pointing to the white caps on the ocean. He thought he spied a few sharks patrolling the surface fifty yards out. "The water is rushing into that . . . that tank, for lack of a better word. Guess it's a little too old for something like that. We're either lucky for getting out unhurt or very unlucky for choosing this moment to traipse on in there."

Marco hissed as he pulled the fabric from the jagged wound in his leg. "Unhurt? Speak for yourself."

Heidi whispered to her husband, "Is unhurt even a word?"

He shushed her.

Tara had watched Ollie's body slam against the cylinder again and again. He'd have some gnarly bruises by tonight.

Lenny was back on his feet, staring at the lab. "I don't know. Everything was fine until Ollie hit that button. Did you see what came out of the chute?"

Ollie shook his head, water dripping off his ears and nose. "It was too dark. It stunk to high heaven, though."

"What happened after we left?" Steven said. Heidi knelt by Marco, examining his wound.

"I'll tell you later, over a good strong drink," Ollie said. "Let's get back and take care of Marco's cut. You okay to walk?"

"Yeah. It looks worse than it is."

They trudged back to the soundtrack of an angry sea. But still, there was no rain, just a stiff, warm breeze.

Tara walked beside Lenny, who seemed deep in thought.

"Bet you never had a little adventure like that," she said. Her thighs quivered as she walked, a cloak of exhaustion draping over her.

"That was definitely unique. I went to this abandoned hospital once in West Virginia. It had closed down in the seventies. The place was huge but falling apart. I actually fell through the floor. Luckily, I landed on my feet and the floor below held steady. I laugh about it now, but I was scared shitless at the time. It was a good thing I had a change of pants in my car."

"Any idea what went on in there?"

Ollie was just ahead of them. Tara could make out the blossoming of a deep, purple bruise on the back of his left arm. She wondered if there was any Epsom salts on the island. A good hot soak and some Motrin would be a big help. Ollie was going to be in a world of hurt later. She'd have to make sure he took care of himself. After all, he'd done all of this to take care of them.

Lenny ran his hand through his wet hair. "I just can't buy that that was water rushing inside the cylinder. I thought I heard something else. And that chute. What came out of it?"

"Maybe Ollie took some pictures that will explain things."

Sighing, Lenny whispered, "I know this sounds crazy, but I keep thinking of feeding time at an aquarium. What if that chute was filled with some kind of food? It's probably been sitting there for decades, rotting away, which explains the stench."

Tara shivered. "Yeah, but what answered the dinner bell?"

"I wish I knew."

***

"Well, let's make it a point not to do that again," Heidi said the moment they stepped into their new island home. She kicked off her sneakers and stripped off all her clothes in the foyer. She turned to her husband. "And before you get any ideas, I have to steam everything off me. God knows what was in that water."

Steven went right to the tile counter between the kitchen and dining room and poured a glass of scotch. They'd left Marco and Ollie with Tara, who was taking care of their wounds at Ollie's house. Lenny apologized profusely, everyone accepting his apology, saying there was no way he could know that would happen.

As Heidi slipped under the shower, she couldn't help blaming Lenny. She didn't know him all that well. He seemed like a decent guy, if not a little sophomoric at times. In her mind, he did know it could be dangerous, which is why he made them take all that safety gear. What the hell were they doing in there anyway? Getting your kicks from breaking into deserted buildings was teenager stupidity, as far as she was concerned. Just because they gave it a name—urban exploration—and made it a forbidden passion for adults didn't make the whole thing any brighter.

Steven knocked on the door. "You want a drink?"

"Some wine would be nice."

"Gotcha. It'll be waiting for you."

"I want you to take a shower, too. That place was vile. And don't sit on anything, especially the bed."

Steven was silent, then he replied, "Yeah, sure. I can always help dry you off."

She knew what that would lead to and she was so not in the mood.

He couldn't see her grin when she said, "Not now."

"I think this can count as a brush with death. The only way to celebrate surviving a brush with death is by celebrating the act that can bring n-n-new life into the world."

She shut the water off and froze.

Was he saying he wanted to have a baby? Here? On the island with no doctors?

"Come again?"

He opened the door and was hit with a face full of steam. "I meant practice, n-not actually make a new life. Lots and lots of practice." He held out a glass of chilled white wine for her. Naked and dripping, she drank it down in one gulp.

She looked down at the bulge in his shorts. He was definitely ready to "celebrate life." They had been here two nights and hadn't christened the house yet. The wine smoothed the rough edges of her agitated nerves.

"Take a shower first," she said. He got out of his clothes faster than a pit crew at the Indianapolis 500.

He gave her a long kiss, his hardness pressed against her belly. "I love you," he said.

"Love you, too."

This could be fun. Maybe they could turn this into Fantasy Island, at least for the next hour. Time for a little role play. That always got their engines going full speed. She made sure to put some water by the bed. They'd need it later.

CHAPTER NINE

Ollie ached in places he didn't even know existed. He'd woken up so stiff, it hurt to yawn.

Just like that time I got jumped by those three guys outside Mickey's Bar.

That had been a world class beating, though he had gotten his licks in. The next day, when Marco was trying to get him to go to the emergency room, he remembered peeing red Kool-Aid. At least it wasn't *that* bad.

And this time, I wasn't the one that instigated the beating.

After a scalding hot shower, he lumbered over to Marco's. His friend was on the phone in his office, surrounded by blueprints and dozens of bound documents. When he saw Ollie outside the sliding glass doors, he quickly hung up the phone and ushered him inside.

"How you feeling?" he asked, fixing up a pot of coffee.

"Like I was in a mosh pit with a herd of elephants. How's the leg?"

Marco wore shorts. His thigh was wrapped in gauze, courtesy of Tara's excellent first aid attentions.

"Throbs a little but I'm pretty sure I won't lose it."

Ollie winced when he sat. "That's too bad. Having a peg leg is right in line with the theme of living on a remote island in the high seas."

Marco handed him a warm mug. "I'll settle for a parrot and an earring."

The coffee was so hot, Ollie had to suck in cool air, which made it feel like tiny daggers were stabbing his ribs.

"So, any idea what the hell happened yesterday?"

Marco slumped into his leather office chair. He looked up at the ceiling as if seeking answers from on high.

"I don't have a clue, bro. That was the most freaked out I've been in . . . shit, ever."

"Something was in there. I couldn't see it, but I felt it moving around," Ollie said.

"The surf was coming in pretty hard on the beach. The ocean is one powerful, mad bitch."

"I know. But here's the thing. The ocean has a rhythm to it. Whatever was inside that tank had no rhythm. It was almost manic, like it knew I was on the other side and it wanted to get at me."

"You know how crazy that sounds?" Marco looked down at his phone, scrolling through a message, his brows knit.

"I don't care. I know what I felt. And there was something else that bothered me."

"What's that?" He put the phone face down on top of a stack of paper.

"The front door to the lab was open. Who the hell was in there before us?"

"What does it matter?" Marco gnawed at the pink tip of his thumb. It looked painful as hell.

Ollie rubbed the back of his neck, massaging a kink that was pressing on a nerve. "I don't know. It just does."

"Look, this place has been empty for a long, long time. God knows what went on here. I wouldn't be surprised if there are people buried around the island. What better way to dispose of a body than some deserted rock in the ocean?"

If it wouldn't hurt so much, Ollie would have laughed.

"You can take the man out of Jersey, but never Jersey out of the man," Ollie said. "Always thinking like a mobster."

"It's what they call buried treasure out here," Marco joked.

Ollie put his coffee down and was overcome with the memory of the stench of whatever had come spilling out of that chute. He must have made a face because Marco said, "If you smell a fart, it's your own."

"I'm going to be haunted by the stink of that stuff that splashed into the water for the rest of my life. Seriously. I think its taken root in the membranes of my nose."

And that's exactly when things went crazy, Ollie thought.

Cause and effect? Or just coincidence?

He counted twelve taps on the side of his mug with his index finger, then cursed, making himself to stop.

"Whatever it was, it's been festering in there since the fifties. Even if it was flowers, they'd reek by now," Marco said. He turned around to check something on his computer. Playtime was over. The past couple of days had been fun, but there was still work to be done.

And the financial side of things would be a constant. Ollie felt bad about laying this burden on his friend. He had to remind himself that Marco was being handsomely rewarded for his efforts. It just felt weird having anyone working for him. He even felt guilty when the construction crew was out hammering away under the sun. Or when Lae cooked his meals or cleaned his house.

"It definitely wasn't flowers," Ollie said. "More like what I imagine chum would be like."

"Well, if it was chum, that would make sense, out here in the land of sharks."

"But why the hell would the military build a tank that tall that leads directly to the ocean underneath it?"

Knowing that also kept him up last night worrying about the structural integrity of the entire area around the decaying lab. Images of everything plunging into the ocean kept running through his head, the sinkhole marching outward, heading toward them like an unstoppable, unquenchable beast.

"You'd have to ask them. God only knows what was going on at the time. It was the Cold War. Both sides kind of lost their minds for a while . . . like three decades worth of insanity," Marco said while he scrolled through what looked like lines of debits and credits on his laptop screen. Always the multi-tasker.

Ollie finished his coffee. "I just hope it wasn't some underwater nuclear observation shit. We could be living on top of a cancer hot spot."

Now Marco turned to face him. "We already covered that when we had those special inspectors come out months ago. All background radiation is normal. Bombs were never detonated here."

Feeling like his own grandpa, Ollie held in a pained groan as he got out of the chair.

"I guess that's some consolation."

"That's a lot of consolation if you ask me. Hey, I emailed the demolition team this morning to see if they could speed up the timetable to take the lab down. No sense keeping it around."

Ollie stared out the window at the clear blue sky kissing the equally clear, aqua ocean. He was living in Eden, just fifty yards away from Tara and his friends. He had to shake yesterday off and enjoy every moment.

"Good. I can't wait to watch that thing get wiped off my island."

***

Two houses away, Lenny paced in his kitchen.

Yesterday had been a major clusterfuck. They were lucky no one had gotten killed, especially Ollie. Poor guy had really taken it on the chin not once, but twice.

The main attraction of urban exploration was uncovering mysteries, revealing forgotten pasts, stepping back in time and trying to piece that world back together. It wasn't always possible to find answers, as the truth turned to so much dust over time.

What had transpired in the lab was no ghost from the US military past.

Whatever Ollie had done up on that catwalk had woken something up.

But what?

"Was everything alright, Mr. Lenny?"

He didn't even hear Lae come in the open patio door. She blew in with the island breeze, a slim, middle-aged woman with short, jet-black hair, tawny skin, and a smile that could be substituted for a ship's beacon. She'd brought him breakfast and coffee a half hour ago. Lenny had barely touched it.

"It was fine," he said. "I'm sorry. I'm just not hungry."

"Do you want me to save it?" she asked in perfect English. He'd studied up on the Marshall Islands before he came here and was happy to learn that most people spoke fluent English. At least he wouldn't be the dumb American stumbling his way through conversations with the locals.

Then again, Lae and so many others spoke at least two languages, so he *was* the dumb American.

"That would be great. Thanks."

She went about putting his rice and eggs in a Tupperware bowl and sealing the sliced fruit in cling wrap.

"Lae, can I ask you a question?"

"Of course."

"You know that old military lab on the end of the island?"

She cleaned up his counter with a paper towel. "Oh yes. I see it every day from my boat."

"What do you know about it?"

"I don't understand."

Lenny chose his words carefully. "I mean, you and your family have lived on the next island over for a long time, right?"

"Oh yes. A very long time."

"Did anyone ever talk about what went on here after the war?"

Her smile faltered for the briefest of moments. "No. The Japanese had relocated anyone who lived on the island in the thirties. More than a thousand Japanese then moved in. When the United States took over, naturally the Japanese were removed and the island was closed off. We don't know what they did. We are just grateful they didn't set off any bombs."

She made a quick sign of the cross before washing his plate and mug and putting them in the drainer.

"Thanks," Lenny said, cleaning his glasses with the end of his shirt.

Before Lae left, she said, "You should stay away from there."

"Why is that?"

"All militaries do bad things when people can't see. Not just Americans. Leave the bad be. There's so much else to enjoy."

She left as quietly and quickly as she'd arrived.

Leave the bad be.

Lenny changed into less comfortable clothes and left the house.

No, that just wasn't his style.

***

Lenny tried to get Steven to go back to the lab with him but the mere thought of telling Heidi left the big man jittery and flushed.

"She'll kill me *and* you if she found out," he said, looking behind him to make sure she wasn't close enough to listen.

The island was too small to keep a secret.

"You're really that whipped?"

"Spoken like a true single man. Besides, why the hell would you want to go back there?"

"I want to look inside that tank or whatever it is."

"You saw how well that worked out for Ollie."

"We won't be going back there as blind as we were before."

"Count me out. I'm too pretty to die."

Lenny rolled his eyes. "What, they don't have mirrors in your house, Coots?"

"Why am I standing here talking to a crazy person when I could be swimming or getting my tan on?"

And that was that.

Tara looked for a moment like she was game, but then she thought of Ollie and Marco and wanted to check in on them. She said they were both busy doing island construction stuff today.

"Promise me you won't go there alone," she said. "After everything that happened, it might be ready to collapse."

"It touches me that you care, T-Mac."

"As a former veterinary assistant, it looks like I'm the sole medical expert on this island. I don't want to have to pull your ass from the wreckage."

"Come on, not even if it meant a little mouth to mouth?" Lenny said.

"Been there, done that, got over it with therapy."

For a second, he thought she was serious, then she smiled. "Now go put on your bathing suit and meet me at the beach later. I have a strong desire for sun and cocktails."

Sun and cocktails.

Nope. It was darkness and whatever was lurking in that tank for him.

***

He felt bad lying to Tara. But maybe he'd be in and out so quick, she wouldn't even realize he'd gone. His house was on the end of the oval, so no one saw him walk out his back door in full exploration gear.

It was a truly stunning day. Yesterday's gray cold front had knocked a few degrees off the thermometer and a cloud couldn't be seen for miles.

He didn't feel bad about wasting the day in the old lab because there would be more sunny days than he could count in his future.

Lenny had always had a stubborn streak as wide and deep as the ocean itself. He questioned things to the point of annoyance for those on the opposite end of his endless queries.

The Omega Lab left him with too many questions to be able to sit back and relax. He had to see for himself, and he hoped there might be some documents left behind in the military's mad dash to leave Grand Isla Tiburon.

He walked along the beach, comforted by the sound of the lapping surf. It was tempting to just take a fast dip with his clothes on. He knew if he did, he'd end up staying in the water.

Climbing the dune, he came upon the ugly lab complex. From the outside, it looked as if nothing had happened just twenty-four hours ago. Dozens of birds were perched on the roof. They stared down at him as he made his way to the front.

The door was closed but unlocked. Just like Tara did yesterday, he kept it open with a heavy rock. He did the same with the next door until he got to the heart of the lab.

Alone in the dark, the lab was downright eerie.

Much of the cement on the cylinder had crumbled off, revealing the drab metal work underneath. The water hadn't completely drained off. It was up to his ankles and cold.

Taking a deep, echoing breath, he grabbed hold of the ladder on the side of the tank and tugged on it. It seemed sturdy.

"It did yesterday, too."

The sound of even his voice was comforting.

He made the climb up to the catwalk as quickly as possible, avoiding the section that was mangled when Ollie almost took a nosedive.

He'd brought the most powerful flashlight he had along with a few flares. Striking one of the flares to life, he tossed it down the catwalk. The bright orange flames illuminated the observation deck. There wasn't much to see.

Were there computers back then?

Sure there were, but they were the size of tractor-trailers. There wouldn't have been room for any up here. No, this was strictly an area built to observe whatever was down in the cylinder.

Lenny lit another flare and tossed it into the tank.

He saw undulating water and nothing more.

Sweeping his flashlight around, he spotted a wide beam with a metal box and big red button. Above it was the open flap of the chute Ollie had accidentally opened.

A breath of wind spiraled up from the cylinder, whispering past the chute and toward Lenny. It brought with it the horrendous stench Ollie had spoken about.

Lenny instinctively pinched his nose closed and expelled the foul vapor from his mouth. He hesitated to inhale until he was sure the breeze had passed.

"What the hell was in there?"

Reluctantly, he stepped toward the chute's opening, daring himself to plumb its depths with the flashlight. The sloping metal was stained with rust or . . . something. He thought of slanted autopsy tables, putrid fluids pulled by gravity to the opening at the end.

What did they do with the body fluids? Did they cremate them? Toss them down the drain?

He'd have to remember to look that up later.

The smell was so bad now it made him dizzy. He was going to puke.

Bent at the waist, his muscles locking as he retched, his flashlight's beam focused on an object so unexpected, so out of place, he screamed between bouts of vomit.

CHAPTER TEN

Ollie was talking to two guys who were going to start painting the interior of the rec center when Tara came by wearing a white cover-up that did little to hide the black bikini underneath.

"Call me if you need me," he said to the men, anxious to be alone with Tara.

"How you feeling today?" she said. The handle of her wicker bag was looped over her shoulder, a water bottle poking out of the top.

"I've been worse," he said, not wanting to let on just how sore he was.

"I'm sure you've been better."

"With all of you here in this amazing place, I doubt that."

Her smile made his knees weak.

"Getting sappy in your old age," she said.

"Since we're the same age, I'm sure you'll agree we're far from old."

She peeked into the open door of the rec center.

"What's going on?" she asked. One of the workers had turned on a radio. An old Michael Jackson tune drifted down the hall.

"They're painting the game room today. Some other guys are coming in to lay down the carpet in the theater. We want to get this done fast before you all get bored."

She patted his shoulder. He hoped she didn't see the pain flash across his eyes. "After yesterday, I could use a little boredom. I'm going to plant my ass in the sand. You have time to hang out?"

"I'm the boss. I can make time."

He gave an awkward smile.

Stop being so damn doofy!

She turned toward the beach. "Walk with me. Talk with me."

He followed her like a puppy dog. God, he was being so transparent. And awkward. It was like college all over again.

They spotted Heidi and Steven in lounge chairs by the water's edge. Tara waved.

"We should probably give them their space," she said.

"Yeah, I think we need to throttle back and ease Heidi in a little easier," Ollie said, chuckling. "It's like introducing a new cat to the house."

"Be nice."

"I'm always nice."

Tara stopped and looked at him over her sunglasses.

"Well, now I am," Ollie added.

"We both are."

Of course, on Grand Isla Tiburon, it was easy not to fly off the handle because he wasn't being made fun of or surrounded by assholes.

"You know, I haven't been in the water yet," she said, pulling her cover up over her head and tossing it in the sand. "Time to rectify that."

She flipped her sunglasses to him and made a beeline for the water. Ollie caught himself staring at her with his mouth wide open.

So had Steven, who grinned like a lunatic at him.

"Come on!" Tara called out over the crash of the surf. "It's so warm. Oh my God, it's perfect."

"I'm not wearing my suit."

Treading water, she looked around. "Is there a rule about proper bathing attire I can't see?"

He also wasn't wearing any underwear, so stripping off his shorts was out of the question. He didn't want to take his shirt off and have her see his full body bruises. That would kill the mood, if there was a mood, for sure.

Ollie kicked off his sandals and placed her sunglasses in her bag. The water wasn't warm, but it wasn't freezing like the lakes back home in early summer.

"Hope you don't have anything important in those pockets," she said as he paddled out to her. Swimming had never been his strong suit, but he planned to rectify that.

"Like Lenny's head, they're empty."

Tara floated on her back, eyes closed, bobbing on the water like driftwood. Beautiful driftwood.

"Make sure I don't float too far out," she said. "I don't want to get eaten by sharks. Not yet, at least."

He was tempted to hook his finger around hers to keep her tethered to him.

You big chicken, he mocked himself. *Just go for it!*

As he reached out his hand, he spotted something breaking the surface of the ocean.

Not just something.

Lots of somethings.

"What the hell is that?" he said.

Tara didn't hear him.

Dozens of plumes of water spewed into the air as sleek, gray shapes came rushing toward them like tennis balls rolling down a hill.

Now, he grabbed Tara's hand.

"Tara. We gotta get back on the beach."

"What? How come?"

She followed his gaze and froze.

"Are those sharks?"

"No. I think they're dolphins."

"There's so many of them."

"Yeah, and they're coming right at us. We're going to get smashed if we don't get the hell out of their way. Come on!"

Tara cleaved through the water with the grace of one of the fast approaching dolphins. Ollie struggled to keep up, his legs and arms suddenly feeling as if they were weighted down with anchors.

He saw Heidi standing now, pointing. He could feel the concussion of the dolphin's bodies as they broke the surface and smashed back under, getting closer with each passing second.

Frantically dog paddling, he didn't even realize he was in shallow water until Tara reached down to help him up.

"Look at them," she said, her eyes glued to the onrushing spectacle.

Now that they were safely out of the way, it was a pretty amazing sight. There had to be at least thirty of them, the sun glinting off their slick bodies.

"Good thing I saw them," he said. "I don't think they're used to humans being in their way."

"I don't think that's it," Tara said. "It looks like they're running from something."

"Maybe there's a killer whale out there. They eat dolphins, right?"

"Land animals are my specialty, but I think they prefer seals and penguins. A dolphin might be too big for them."

"It's amazing," Heidi said. Ollie didn't even notice her and Steven coming up to them. They stood in the water up to their ankles, shielding their eyes as the dolphins made a steady march toward land.

"They have to turn around any second now," Steven said. "Dolphins don't beach themselves."

But there was no sign of them slowing down.

"Something has them spooked," Tara said. She ran back to her bag and grabbed her phone, snapping picture after picture before changing to video.

Steven turned to Ollie. "You've been here a while. You ever see anything like it before?"

"Not even a little."

Without realizing it, they had all backed out of the water. It seemed as if the pod of dolphins wasn't going to stop until they made land.

They were so close now, Ollie heard their bodies splash as they popped in and out of the water in their oceanic stampede.

Movie clips from *Jaws, Shark Night, Sharknado, Deep Blue Sea* and even *Flipper* ran through his mind. He could never help to compare real life to reel life. God help them if this was anything like what was depicted in those movies.

Heidi said, "What do we do if they—"

A dorsal fin the size of a Cadillac crashed to the surface. It was just a few feet behind the dolphins at the rear.

"Holy shit! Look at the size of that thing!" Steven shouted.

Heidi yelped, running farther onto the safety of the beach.

Now we know what's got them so freaked out, Ollie thought. *But if that's a shark, it's the biggest damn shark I've ever seen.*

"What the heck can it be, Tara?" Ollie asked, unconsciously making fists as if he could punch his way out of the situation.

She kept her camera trained on the runaway nightmare.

"It's . . . it's some kind of shark. I think. But it's way too big."

The dorsal fin was nothing compared to the wide open maw that burst from the depths, swallowing two of the dolphins. Its massive teeth chomped down, obliterating the majestic creatures to ribbons of pink and gray flesh.

The rest of the dolphins changed direction, heading east now, away from the beach.

The shark—because that's what it had to be—slipped back under the water. Within seconds, it was over, the water returning to normal as if nothing had happened. There wasn't even blood visible to mark the spot where the dolphins had been mercilessly consumed.

CHAPTER ELEVEN

Marco touched the bandage on his leg and hissed as a tiny electric shock went straight to his balls. He wanted to see what was going on under there, but Tara threatened him with violence if he so much as touched the bandage before she came over to check it later today.

Part of her was the same girl he remembered from college, but something about her had changed. He couldn't put his finger on it.

He didn't have time to contemplate the new Tara. Being in the lab yesterday had set his nerves on edge, and it had nothing to do with what happened by the tank. Marco was sure he had held his breath from the moment they opened the unlocked door until they ran from the damn building.

His stomach cramped from the ulcer he was sure had settled in for the duration.

Take your mind off it, he thought.

Looking at his email inbox, he felt a burning need for a drink.

He limped to his liquor cabinet and plucked a bottle of Grey Goose vodka, filling a glass with ice. The clear liquid burned. It was exactly what he needed.

Looking out his bay window, he saw Titus Lomon, the foreman for the small crew working on the rec center's interior, walk by carrying cans of paint. Marco waved. Titus, always grim faced but genial enough to talk to, gave a head nod.

He never realized how big this undertaking was going to be. It would only have been worse if they were doing it in the states, dealing with multiple contractors because everyone was a goddamn specialist, unions, local city laws, ordinances, the usual graft and on and on.

So yes, it was simpler here in Grand Isla Tiburon, but it was still a freaking headache and a half. He couldn't wait until everything was done. He planned to spend one year shadow boxing his liver and staring into space and see where things went from there.

Tired.

The past five years had worn him down to the nub. Ollie's windfall and unbelievable offer was the only thing that kept him from gobbling a mouthful of pills. His call had come the morning

Marco had planned to score some Vicodin from the punk teenager that lived in his rundown complex. Marco was going to get thirty pills, take a couple that night to see how they worked—if at all—and if they weren't cheap knock-offs or aspirin, he would down the rest the following day. It would be the fourth anniversary of his girlfriend Mazie's death. A car had sideswiped her on the Jersey Turnpike Exit 11 off-ramp. Her Prius flipped over the guardrail, landing on its hood.

The medical examiner said she'd died instantly from a series of mortal wounds, including the severing of her spinal cord and the crushing of her skull into mere pieces.

Everyone had been devastated. Mazie was fresh out of college, her first job landing her on Wall Street where she was an up-and-coming stockbroker. A red-haired beauty who could have easily made a living off her looks, Mazie was one of those rare people who had everything they needed to take life by the balls but was still humble and self-deprecating.

And she was so smart. Believe it or not, that was what attracted her to Marco most. He'd already gone on the hot bimbo tour. That grew tired fast. No, Mazie was different from any woman he'd ever met. His parents and friends constantly urged him to put a ring on it before he lost the greatest thing that would ever happen to him.

When Mazie died, his whole world shattered. His grief nearly broke him.

Because it was laden with a guilt so crushing, he hadn't dared speak of it to anyone.

Only Ariana, Mazie's best friend, knew where he was when he got the call.

In Ariana's bed.

Marco filled the glass with more vodka, willing the memory to cower back in the dark corner of his mind.

Ariana slit her wrists in her parents' bathtub a week after Mazie's funeral, so at least he didn't have to worry about their awful secret coming out.

His initial relief made things even worse. He felt responsible for both their deaths. If he hadn't been with Ariana, fate wouldn't have seen the need to teach him a lesson. And if Ariana hadn't fallen into bed with him (after four White Russians), she'd still be alive, probably pregnant and living in Manalapan with a man who worked in IT.

Everything just went to shit from there. Marco reveled in self-abuse, setting his sights on a true rock bottom—the bottom of a grave.

He fell into a new circle of friends, well, actually, scumbags of the highest order, hoping they'd do the job for him sooner rather than later.

Frantic banging at his door pulled him from his trip down bad memory lane.

He made sure to dump his vodka in the sink and hide the glass in a cabinet before opening it. He didn't want anyone to know that hard liquor before ten in the morning was a thing for him.

Lenny stood on his doorstep panting. He looked like he'd come face to face with a serial killer.

"Marco, where is everybody?"

"Lenny, what the hell?"

He was dressed in the same clothes he wore yesterday to go in the lab.

That damn lab.

"Ollie's not here?"

"I think he's at the beach with everyone."

"Get them." Lenny put his bag on the couch. "You have anything to drink?"

"Sure, there's water and juice in the fridge."

To his surprise, Lenny took out two bottles of Sapporo beer, ripping the top off with his bare hand. The Sapporos were not twist offs.

"Jesus, you stink," Marco said.

Lenny didn't even respond to the insult.

He stared at his hands and hissed, "Still burns." Pouring nearly an entire bottle of dishwashing liquid on his hands, he rubbed them feverishly under the running water, babbling something under his breath. When he was done, he dried his hands on the curtain above the sink.

"Thought I got it all off in the ocean," he said.

Marco was too taken aback to ask what the hell he was talking about.

Lenny collapsed next to his bag. A wet bag, Marco noticed, staining the pristine white cushion. Before he could snap at Lenny to take it off the couch, he saw the wild expression in his friend's eyes and thought better of it.

"I . . . I just need to sit for a bit and catch my breath."

"Bro, what happened?"

Lenny took a long drink. "I'll tell you all when everyone's here. Oh, and ask Tara to bring that ledger with her."

"What ledger?"

"The one she took from the lab."

Okay, so Lenny had been at the lab. What the hell had happened this time?

Oh God. He hoped it wasn't . . .

"Lenny, what did you see in the lab?"

His lips were attached to the bottle. He shook his head. "I need everyone. Now, man."

Before he left, Marco turned off his computer. His leg ached like hell as he trudged through the sand. As luck would have it, he didn't have far to walk.

Ollie, Tara, Steven and Heidi were running toward him.

***

At some point during their sprint from the beach, Tara's hand had slipped within Ollie's grasp. He only realized it now because she was squeezing him so hard, his knuckles were grinding against one another.

Marco waved them over, looking relieved to see them.

"You won't believe what we saw," Ollie said to him.

"Lenny's in my house totally freaked out about something that happened in the lab."

"In the lab?" Tara said. "We were with him."

Marco shook his head. "He went back there this morning. He's on my couch drilling beers. He wanted me to come get all of you to show you something."

Tara showed him her phone. "Wait until you see what we have to show *you* guys."

When she finally let go of Ollie's hand as they stepped into Marco's house, Ollie was overcome with an irrational wave of rejection.

Chill your hormones, dummy. There's something bigger than your ten-year crush going on here.

When Lenny saw them, he put his empty beer down and said, "You all might want to take a seat."

"Has this whole place gone insane?" Steven said. Heidi sat on his lap, his arms wrapped around her waist, pulling her close to him. She'd been unusually quiet since they'd decided to leave the beach and show Marco and Lenny what they'd captured on video.

Ollie was pretty sure Heidi was never going to dip her toes in the water again.

He wasn't sure if he'd ever go out there, either. That wasn't a good thing when you lived on an island.

Massaging his brow, Lenny asked, "What the heck happened to you guys?"

"You first," Ollie said. Waves of funk were coming off Lenny, reminding Ollie of the gunk that had spilled out of that chute. "You didn't go back up that tank, did you?"

"Uh-huh."

"Are you out of your mind? You could have gotten killed," Tara said.

"But I didn't," Lenny countered. "I know, it was stupid, but I had to see for myself what was in that tank."

Steven piped up, "I can tell you without having looked inside. Water. And lots of it."

Ollie noted the look of absolute confusion on Marco's face. Everyone but him had a hell of a start to the day. He sat on the arm of his couch, eyes roving across their faces, trying to take it all in.

"You're right about that," Lenny said. "I dropped a flare down there and looked around. But what I found wasn't in the tank."

He plucked his pack from the floor and unzipped it. The full force of the foul odor that clung to Lenny burst from the bag. Everyone pinched their noses, waving at the air.

"What the fuck, Lenny?" Marco said, rising to his feet.

"You got a towel I can use?" Lenny said. "Preferably one you won't miss."

Marco stormed into the bathroom, muttering. "Could have done this at your house, you know."

"This place needs air," Tara said, opening every window she could find.

Marco handed a bath towel to Lenny who draped it over his glass coffee table.

"I found out what was in that chute," Lenny said.

"We already know," Heidi said. "Something gross and rotten."

Lenny held up his index finger. "True. But we didn't know what had rotted in there."

He reached into the bag. They heard a squish as his fingers probed the contents. "*This* is what was in there."

The skull thunked on the table, viscera sliding off it onto the towel. With it fully out in the open, the stench was enough to make their stomachs hitch.

Steven leapt from his chair, holding onto Heidi like she was a football. "Whoa! Are you kidding me?"

Tara's body went rigid next to Ollie.

Ollie's vision wavered. Between the excitement from earlier, the horrid smell, and the grisly skull, he worried he would pass out.

We couldn't even have paradise for a week, he thought, cursing God for always finding a way to give him the short end of the stick.

"Is it, um, you know . . ." Marco said.

"Human?" Lenny said. "I think so. If it's a monkey, it's an awfully big one."

Holding her hand over her nose and mouth, Tara leaned closer to the dripping skull. It had been stained the color of dried blood, black goo clinging to it, leaking from the empty eye sockets like tears of sludge.

"It's definitely not simian," she said. "That's a person. Or was a person."

"Are you crazy touching that thing with your bare hands, bro?" Marco said.

Lenny shrugged. "When I saw it, I just grabbed it without thinking. After that, well, the horse was already out of the barn."

Ollie didn't dare get too close. "Maybe someone was messing around in there and got stuck."

"That's what I thought, too, since the lab door wasn't locked," Lenny said. He thrust his hand back in the bag and came up with another skull, this one slightly smaller but equally horrific.

Ollie had to step away. "Holy crapping Christ. Exactly how many skulls *did* you find?"

"Just these two. And a bunch of other bones, some big, some small. The rest was dumped into the ocean."

Marco wrapped the towel around the skulls. "Please put them away and get them outside. I'll have to burn this place down to get the smell out."

Lenny did as he was told, carefully placing the bundle of skulls in the sand beyond the back patio.

"What do we do n-now? Call the police?" Steven said.

"For something that happened decades ago?" Marco said, pacing. "I don't think they'll give two shits."

"Maybe call an archaeologist," Lenny said. "The lab is over fifty years old. I'm sure they would be interested in it."

Ollie thought what they saw in the water was going to be the biggest, craziest thing that ever happened on the island. How could he be proven wrong in just minutes? He said, "You don't think the US military was dumping bodies, do you?"

All eyes were on him, the silence in the room overwhelming.

It was Tara who finally said, "Why would they do that? Look, our military isn't made up of saints, but human sacrifice isn't on their agenda."

"They say the N-Nazis dabbled in the occult and sacrifice," Steven said. Ollie was beginning to think the man watched way too much television. Just because he was glued to the History Channel didn't mean it made him any more informed. From what Ollie had seen, it was mostly bizarre fringe theories wrapped around historical events.

"It wasn't Nazis," Ollie said. "Besides, the Germans were never here."

"Says you," Steven said. "The Japanese were. They could have had some Nazis with them."

"Yes. Says me."

Tara snapped her fingers. "I almost forgot. Marco, Lenny, check this out. While you were in the lab, this is what we saw at the beach."

Ollie didn't bother standing over Tara to watch the giant shark attack the dolphins like a fat man at a casino buffet. He heard Heidi's recorded gasp and their frenetic cries.

"That's a shark?" Marco said.

"No. It has to be a whale. Like one of those humpbacks or blue whales." Lenny said.

"Whales don't have dorsal fins or teeth like that. Look, there are rows of them," Tara said.

"It was definitely a shark," Heidi said. She too had refused to watch it again. "Believe us."

Marco took the phone from her and played the video back. He passed it to Lenny who swiped through the photos.

"There's no such thing as a shark that big," Marco said. "That makes the one in *Jaws* look like a goddamn goldfish."

Ollie was overcome with a sudden burst of anger. He shouted, "Okay, then what the hell is it? We didn't make it up. You can see it with your own eyes. If it's not a shark, what else can it be?"

He felt Tara's hand on his back, urging him to calm down.

How could he? He had a killer giant shark in the water and dead bodies on land. Everything was going tits up at the speed of light.

Marco looked like he was ready to tear his hair out, too. "I'm just saying. A great white on the large side is what, fifteen feet? That thing is fucking huge!"

Lenny snapped his fingers. "How about a whale shark? They get really big."

Tara looked doubtful. "Whale sharks don't move like that and are kind of like bottom feeders. They don't snack on dolphins."

"How are you so sure?" Steven asked. "Didn't you take care of cats and dogs and rabbits?"

"Don't be an ass," Tara said.

"What did you call me?"

Heidi placed her palms on her husband's chest. "We all need to settle down. Freaking out won't do us any good."

Lenny snapped his fingers. "What about those things they found at Loch Ness? There were like dozens of them."

Marco waved him off. "There are several problems with that. One, they're all dead. Some psychos took an arsenal to them and wiped them the fuck out. Two, even the largest one of those Loch Ness Monsters wasn't as big as what Tara's talking about. And three, those things were lake monsters in a whole different part of the world. If you haven't noticed, we're surrounded by the ocean, not the Scottish Highlands."

"Maybe it's a cousin to those things," Lenny replied sheepishly.

"There are n-no Loch Ness Monsters in the Marshall Islands. Enough already," Steven said, slapping Lenny's arm with the back of his hand. "You were probably right the first time. It had to be a whale shark."

Tara strode over to Marco's computer. "What's your password?"

"Why do you need it?"

"To show you all what whale sharks look like."

Marco gently nudged her aside and typed in his password, pulling up a web browser. Tara not-so-gently bumped him away with her hip and started typing. She pulled up a website that had pictures of whale sharks and a list of facts about the large, lumbering creatures.

Yes, they could reach a length of forty feet, but they were exceedingly docile. They had telltale spots, kind of like sea leopards—nothing like the gray and white monster they saw. Whale sharks were also plankton eaters, just as Tara had said.

What they saw was as much a whale shark as Steven was Brad Pitt. Sure, they were the same species, but very different animals.

She put the laptop on Steven's lap. "Now do you believe me?"

The knock at the door startled them.

Marco answered it.

Lae said, "Titus Lomon wanted me to tell you that he and his men have to leave now for more supplies. He's pretty mad at Nathan for forgetting something they really need for today. Poor kid looks about ready to cry."

Marco gripped Lae's shoulders. "Wait, did they leave yet or are they planning to leave?"

Lae tilted her head, perplexed. "No, Mr. Marco. They were headed toward the dock."

Ollie felt his blood run cold. "Crap. We can't let them go out there."

"Why?" Lae asked.

Ollie sprinted past her. There was no time to explain.

He couldn't let Titus get in that water.

CHAPTER TWELVE

Ollie ran as fast as his short legs and the soft sand would allow. He lost a sandal but not his momentum.

"Titus!"

Ollie turned to see Marco right behind him.

They made the turn around the housing complex, toward the dock. Ollie saw Titus and his two younger helpers for the day jump into the gently rocking boat. The sun's dappling reflection off the water blinded him.

Marco shouted, "Titus, hold up!"

The boat's engine rumbled. There was no way Titus would hear them over it. Ollie searched for a higher gear, his lungs burning, a stitch forming in his side.

Marco, with his longer stride, overtook him, waving his arms and yelling.

The boat veered from the dock, heading for open water.

Ollie scanned the horizon. There were no dolphins rushing about. With any luck, they'd led that shark miles away by now.

His feet slapped hard on the dock. Marco was bent over, hands on his knees, back heaving. The boat was too far gone now. Titus was a man who walked around with blinders on. When he had a task to do, he focused on it to the exclusion of everything around him.

"You think they'll be all right?" Marco asked, squinting at the rapidly departing motorboat.

"I hope so," Ollie said. He looked everywhere for that enormous dorsal fin. Just because he couldn't see it didn't mean it wasn't out there, just below the surface.

"Of all the days for them to have to head right back out," Marco said.

"Let's face it, we'd be uncomfortable as hell if they knocked off late in the day."

"True. But does that mean Lae can't leave? I don't think she'll be happy to be under island arrest."

Ollie gently rubbed his hand over his bruised ribs. Each hard breath felt like a rabbit punch. "If her husband makes it here to pick her up later, I'll feel better that the coast is clear."

"Wait, we can't just let him head out here and possibly come across that thing. I'll tell Lae to call him. Maybe it's better he waits a day."

Ollie sighed. "Uh, did you forget who Lucky Malolo is? That man loves his woman to the point of distraction. There's no way in hell he'll leave her out here if he thinks there's any danger to her."

"As long as she's on land, there isn't."

"Did you forget about those skulls?"

Marco walked up and down the small dock. "They're history. I'm not worried about that. I'm pretty sure we don't have a killer hiding on the island. And if the person who did that to them was still here, he'd be old as fuck by now. You saw them. They've been stuck in that muck for a long ass time."

Ollie wasn't so sure. He wasn't sure about a damn thing.

Looking out at the ocean, he could still see Titus's boat. "We have to call Titus and tell him not to come back."

"Agreed."

"And we have to find out what the hell kind of shark is out there."

Marco said, "I'll bet you dollars to donuts that Tara is already busy doing just that. I just hope she doesn't screw around with my files." He got a faraway look, gazing back where the houses were around the bend and over the rise. "In fact, we should go back and see what she's come up with."

Ollie was about to do just that when he saw an enormous shape leap out of the water. It headed straight for Titus's boat.

"No!"

Marco's head snapped to the same direction Ollie was pointing.

One second, the boat was there, cruising on a sunny day, the next it was gone, the giant sea creature pouncing on it so quickly and efficiently, it vanished in the blink of an eye.

Whether Titus and his men were in the ocean or the belly of the shark was impossible to tell. They were too far away for them to see.

"Do you have binoculars?" Ollie said, his senses stretched to the snapping point.

Marco stood at the end of the dock, mouth wide open, arms limply at his side.

"I don't believe it," he said.

"Marco, do you have binoculars?" Ollie wanted to see if he could spot Titus or his helpers on the water. If they were in fact alive, maybe there was a chance . . .

A chance of what?

If Ollie got in his boat and headed out to pluck them out of the water, he'd be the next meal for the shark.

What was the equivalent of the Coast Guard out here?

"I had binoculars," Marco muttered.

"Where are they?"

He pointed out across the Pacific. "I lent them to Titus last week. I forget why he said he needed them. I assumed it was to look at girls on the beach over the weekend."

Ollie eyed his brand new Pursuit tied to the next dock. He'd bought it for necessity as well as future water sports and some big time fishing once everyone had settled onto the island. It wasn't all that big, but it was comfortable and had a kick ass engine. Ollie didn't know squat about boats but he knew he liked his Pursuit. He'd named it after his mother, who had passed away when he was in high school. The *Sarah Kay* was a sweet ride and he was looking forward to taking everyone out on her someday.

He did not want to take her out on a suicide mission.

If anyone was still alive out there, they wouldn't be for long. That shark would get them way before the *Sarah Kay* could make it that far.

"Jesus, look," Marco cried.

The water churned and splashed. It must have been massive for them to see from so far away.

It only confirmed Ollie's worst fear.

"We have to get back to your place," Ollie said. "I'll talk to Lae. She'll just have to order Lucky to stay put."

***

The beast fed on the morsels of meat, along with everything else that littered the ocean. Its jaws snapped open and shut with unparalleled speed and ferocity.

Blood in the water excited it, but the food did not trigger the surge of energy it craved.

It was far from going back to the dark, dormant place, but it needed more. Something in its primitive brain knew it could not venture far. To do so would allow the darkness to come back.

No. If it wanted to grow strong, its instinct commanded it remain here.

Food was coming.

***

Marco was right. Tara had been busy looking for anything that closely resembled the shark she captured on her phone.

While she went through web page after web page, Steven, Heidi and Lenny raided Marco's refrigerator for anything cold and alcoholic to drink. Lenny kept working on the beer while Steven and Heidi had found a bottle of vodka in the freezer.

When Tara hit on an image that looked almost exactly like the shark they saw, she slumped back into her chair and rubbed her eyes.

No. It can't be that.

She blew up one of the images on her phone, the one that gave her the best, though pixilated, view of the shark's mouth. She'd captured the very last moment of life for the two dolphins before they slipped down the shark's gullet. She compared the titanic shark to the artist's rendering on the website.

Next, she did a side-by-side comparison of the dorsal fins.

It was all very inexact. For one, she wasn't comparing apples to apples. She had grainy photos, and she was comparing them to drawings, some of them quite detailed. But they were drawings, not the real McCoy.

"Is that it?" Lenny asked, his funk preceding him. She could smell the beer on his breath, which was a welcome relief over the crud from the lab.

She gave a half-hearted chuckle. "Yeah, we got a match all right."

Moving the cursor to close out the page, Lenny said, "Hold on. Let me take a look."

"Don't bother."

Urgent whispering between Steven and Heidi dragged both their attention away from the dueling shark images.

Tara and Lenny watched them step out onto the patio and then walk away, locked in a heated discussion.

"I'll bet Heidi's reading him the riot act about packing their bags now and ditching this place," Lenny said.

"I wouldn't bet against you."

Lenny had taken over the laptop, scrolling down to see more images of the giant shark Tara had found.

"How come we shouldn't bother looking into this?" he asked. "I mean, from what I can see, they're a pretty close match."

Tara leaned over his shoulder and scrolled up to the list of facts about the shark.

"Because that's a Megalodon shark, buddy. It would make sense to think I found our culprit, except it's been extinct for over two million years."

CHAPTER THIRTEEN

"We have to get the hell off this island!"

"Babe, you n-n-need to calm down. Flying off the handle isn't going to help."

"Flying off the handle? Jesus. I think I'm being pretty damn calm. It's bad enough that . . . that thing is out there, but now we have dead bodies. Dead bodies! We'd be insane to just sit around and pretend everything's okay."

"No one is saying we should do that. But we do n-need to take a moment and approach everything rationally."

"Rationally. Yeah, right. I knew we shouldn't have come here. I got caught up in the moment. What the hell was I thinking?"

"You were thinking you wanted to get away from where we lived and spend the rest of our days in safe, comfortable leisure. Anyone would go for that."

When Steven and Heidi had left their bungalow, they'd forgotten to open the windows. The trapped heat was stifling. Heidi didn't open them now because she didn't need everyone to hear them.

"Where's the phone?" Steven asked.

"I don't know. Wherever you left it. Who are you going to call?"

"I'll figure that out once I find my phone."

Heidi tried her best to calm him down. Ever since Mexico, he'd been prone to panic attacks and paranoia. Back home, in their neighborhood that hadn't seen a crime since the eighties, he'd had to do three of his so-called perimeter checks each night before coming up to bed.

Even though she wasn't crazy about being so far away from her family, she'd hoped coming out here would heal some of her husband's internal wounds. She worried about him so much and loved him more than words could express. That worry made her appear uptight to people who didn't know her. She was well aware that Steven's friends hadn't exactly warmed up to her, but she was fine with that. All that mattered was calming the voices in Steven's head.

Now, any progress they'd made had flown right out the window.

"What are you going to do, call another boat to come out here?" she said. She could hear him tearing the bedroom apart searching for his cell. "We are not going out on that water. Not today, at least."

He stormed into the living room, his head reddening, the scar pale and stark in comparison.

That scar was a constant reminder of the day that had changed Steven.

They'd just come out of a nightclub in Cabo. It was their first anniversary and they treated themselves to a kind of second honeymoon.

Drunk and anxious to get back to their room, they'd been accosted by two men wielding knives that looked big enough to chop down trees. Steven kept the agitated men as calm as possible. It was obvious they were both tweaking hard. He'd said he had no problem giving them his wallet, modulating his voice, hands held down to let them know there was no reason to do anything rash .

The problem came when he reached into his pocket and realized his wallet was gone. It had fallen out back at the club, most likely being kicked around on the dance floor.

As soon as the taller man saw Steven's hand come up empty, his eyes went as big and white as hardboiled eggs and he slashed Steven's head with the knife. Both men ran like hell when the blood started pouring from the grinning wound.

Boy, did it bleed. Heidi looked like she'd sacrificed a pig in some bizarre ritual by the time they got him to the emergency room. And the entire time, all he did was soothingly reassure her that everything was going to be okay. He even asked her to make sure they had dinner reservations at this restaurant they wanted to try the next day.

That was the last time he'd been cool under pressure. By the next morning, he was a changed man. And it wasn't for the better.

"Got it," he said, unplugging his phone from the charger by the kitchen counter.

"Can you at least sit down?"

He jabbed at the phone as if it had buttons instead of a touch screen. "Of course, I can't get any reception."

"And what happens when you do?"

"I'll call the police. The military. Everyone. And I'll find a way to get off this rock, even if I have to hire a helicopter. Ollie can foot the bill. This is all his fault, anyway."

Shouldering his way out the back door, Steven walked in circles, staring at the phone's display.

"Honey, I just need you to sit down and take a few deep breaths. Can you do that for me?"

He carried on as if he hadn't heard her.

What she saw on the water and in Marco's house had freaked her out, too. She didn't know what was worse, the skulls or the giant killer shark that might be circling the island as they speak.

But as long as they stayed out of the water, they were safe. And those skulls were old. She realized there was nothing to panic over. Now she needed Steven to realize the same thing.

"Steven, why don't you sit with me?"

She patted the lounge chair next to her.

He paced the patio, searching for bars.

"And I won't miss being called Cooter," he said, as if it were the middle of some internal train of thought, not meant for Heidi to actually hear.

She heard a distant rumble. Getting up, she looked to the sky. It was pale blue with strings of cotton candy to the east, a beautiful day.

Far to the west, there was a wall of dark clouds, rolling toward them like a tidal wave. There was a brief flash within the roiling mass, lightning zigging from one end to the other.

"Steven, are we supposed to get a storm? I thought Ollie said there was a drought."

He finally put down his phone and looked to where she was pointing. It looked like one hell of a storm, the kind people built fruit cellars to escape from.

"I don't know," he said. "It's n-not like we get the local news out here." He punched the side of the house. "Well, there goes our chance of getting out of here by air."

The island was so utterly exposed. Heidi wondered if they were sturdy enough to stand against the storm when and if it hit.

***

"Where's Lae?" Ollie asked the second he burst in the door.

Lenny couldn't take his eyes off the illustration of a Megalodon shark attacking what looked like an aquatic dinosaur. The similarity to what Tara had captured on her phone was chilling.

But Megalodons were extinct, right?

He scratched at his hands. There was a nagging itch in his palms, under the skin, right where he couldn't get. He looked at them to see if there was a rash. Maybe he was having an allergic reaction to that nasty gunk on the skulls he'd stupidly touched.

No redness, splotches, or weird bumps. Just mild scratch marks from his nails.

"I don't know. She left not long after you guys," Lenny said.

"Why? What's wrong now?" Tara said. She had brewed a pot of coffee, telling Lenny to cut the beer. They needed to be sober. A cigarette dangled out of the side of her mouth.

"It got them," Marco said. He'd gone white as a sheet, leaning against the wall.

"Titus?" Lenny said, finally peeling away from the laptop.

"All of them. It waited until they were some distance out, but it attacked them just the same," Ollie said. "It . . . it happened so fast. They didn't stand a chance."

Marco brushed Lenny aside, stomping into his bedroom.

"I have to find Lae," Ollie said, chest heaving.

"I'll get her," Tara volunteered. "You sit down and catch your breath."

"Before you come back, grab that ledger you found at the lab," Lenny said.

"Why?"

"It might have some clues. I found a few things, too, aside from the skulls."

She nodded and dipped outside.

Ollie refused to sit, pacing the kitchen, hands clasped atop his head as if he were trying to keep it from blowing outward.

"It was fucking horrible, Lenny."

"I know, buddy. Come on, at least have some coffee."

Ollie waved him off. "Last thing I need is caffeine to make me more jittery."

Marco emerged with a rifle. Ollie's eyes went wide.

"What the hell?" he spat.

Marco slung the rifle's strap over his shoulder. "Being the only outsiders on a remote island, I had to make sure we were protected."

"A rifle? Really?"

"It's an AR-15 semi-automatic rifle, to be exact. Now I wish I bought some extra magazines. I only have the one. Guess I'll have to make every shot count."

Ollie exclaimed, "Have you lost your mind? Where in the name of all that's holy did you get that? It's not like you could have stowed that in your carry on when we flew here."

Marco shrugged. "I bought it during an island excursion. It wasn't easy. Not a lot of guns out here. But just like home, money talks."

Lenny would bet his left nut that Marco had never fired anything remotely like it. Odds are, he'd shoot himself before any intended target.

"What are you planning to do with that, Mr. Seal Team Six?" Lenny asked.

Snarling, Marco said, "I'm not just gonna sit here and watch a fucking fish pluck us off. I'll find a way to lure it closer and shoot the goddamn thing between the eyes."

"Do you know how crazy that sounds?" Lenny said. And how the heck did Marco plan to lure the massive shark?

"Crazy is cowering inside here."

Ollie went to touch Marco's shoulder but he shrugged it off. "That rifle is a pea shooter next to that thing out there," he said.

"You guys might want to take a look at this," Lenny said, showing them the image of the Megalodon.

"That's it!" Ollie said. "That's exactly what we saw."

Marco's lips pulled back in a tight, grim line.

"There's only one problem," Lenny said. "The Megalodon shark disappeared off the face of the earth millions of years ago."

"It looks like the shark census missed one," Marco growled.

"So if that thing isn't a Megalodon, what the hell is it?" Ollie said.

"I don't have a clue," Lenny said. "But I do find it awfully coincidental that it shows up right after we had that mishap in the lab. If we can find out what the hell the military was doing out here, we might have a better understanding of what we're dealing with."

Marco huffed. "The military hit the bricks over sixty years ago."

"Megalodons supposedly all died a lot longer than that," Lenny countered. "I'm not saying there's a definite correlation, but it is a possibility."

"You guys can have fun talking about possibilities. I'm going to do something about it."

He stomped out of the house, slamming the door behind him.

"I've never seen him like that," Lenny said.

"He was pretty close to Titus," Ollie said, standing by the window, watching Marco head toward the beach. "We should probably follow him and make sure he doesn't do anything stupid."

"We will, once Tara and Lae get here. Until then, maybe we should look at some of the other stuff I crammed into my pack."

Ollie followed him out the back door to get his backpack. The western exposure gave them a full view of the oncoming storm.

Lenny said, "Where the heck did that come from?"

Ollie kicked a seashell. "Are you kidding me? It was supposed to miss us entirely. When I first heard about it, I watched *The Perfect Storm* just to freak myself out, I guess. It felt safer knowing it wasn't going to happen here."

"What are you talking about?"

"If that's the storm I think it is, it's real bad news. We're talking hurricane winds, torrential rain and massive flooding. Last I saw, it was supposed to carry on south of us and die somewhere in the middle of the ocean. This island normally doesn't get drizzle, much less a super soaker like this."

Lenny's mouth went dry. "How much soaking are they talking about?"

Ollie stared up at the black and gray storm clouds. "No clue. I just hope it's not more than the island can handle."

CHAPTER FOURTEEN

As luck would have it—not that there was much going around at the moment—Lae was tidying things up in Tara's house. Trying to keep as much of a poker face as possible, she said Ollie and Marco wanted to talk to her back at Marco's house.

The older islander saw right through her. "Something terrible has happened."

Tara's instinct was to lie and tell her no, everything was fine.

Then she thought about all those dark days at the vet's office when she had to tell pet owners that their beloved dog or cat was gone, or that there was no saving them and it was time to put them to sleep. It was the worst part of the job. The first few times she had to deliver bad news, she cried, having to be consoled by the grieving pet owner in one case.

Through it all, she did learn one thing.

You can't sugarcoat death.

"Yes," she said.

Lae remained calm, apologized for not finishing making her bed, and said she would be back.

Tara was pretty sure no one would be worrying about making beds today.

Lae lit a fresh cigarette, took a hit and stubbed it out. It was funny, Tara smoked when she was relaxed. For some reason, if she was amped, smoking only made things worse.

That's one tough lady, Tara thought.

Life in the Marshall Islands, Grand Isla Tiburon excepted, wasn't easy. People like Lae had to develop thick skins and strong constitutions. It made what Ollie was doing out here all the more important, if only to give them an opportunity they normally wouldn't have had. The money was being put to good use.

She found the old ledger, emptied her beach bag and carefully placed it inside, worried it would fall apart. After everything that had happened, she hadn't even thought to leaf through it.

Stepping outside, she pulled up short when a cool breeze whispered past her. She shivered. It was downright cold, almost like walking past an air conditioner. The past few days were marked by varying degrees of heat and humidity, her skin constantly dotted with sweat.

She waited, hoping to catch another breeze.

"Weird."

Before going to Marco's house, she was compelled to return to the beach. She couldn't explain why. Morbid curiosity, maybe. If there was a chance that Titus or his men had evaded the shark's ire, they could be out there right now, treading water and praying for help.

Of course, if they were out there paddling away, odds are the shark would find them before she could ever get to them.

And how are you supposed to rescue them?

It's not like she knew how to operate a boat. She didn't even have the key to start it.

Rounding her house, she saw what had caused that cooling wind.

Off in the not too far distance was a whale of a storm. The dark clouds churned like smoke trapped in a bottle.

"Jesus."

She didn't know squat about trade winds and ocean currents, but she hoped to hell that somehow it all pushed away from the island. It looked nasty, bordering on sinister.

Tara walked as far as the ebbing and flowing water line, afraid to immerse herself further than the tops of her feet. It was a clear shot of sunny skies and sparkling blue water, the storm brewing off to her left.

The seemingly endless view made her realize why people once thought the earth was flat and one could sail right off the edge. When a place like this was your sole viewpoint, that's exactly what it looked like.

When the massive dorsal fin appeared several hundred yards away, the gray triangle cleaving the water like the periscope of a submarine, she darted out of the water. The shark could never swim in shallow water, but its awesome yet alien presence chilled her to the bone. It was like being terrified of her grandmother's dark, musty basement all over again.

Except in this case, the monster was real.

The fin dipped below the water, popping up a hundred yards away in such a brief flash of time, it defied logic.

How fast can it swim?

Its tail fin must be enormous to propel that much weight through the water.

Tara went numb, watching the creature surface and submerge over and over again in a widening circle. It was as if it were searching for something.

"Or spinning a web."

Now why had she said that?

Because next to that thing, they were powerless houseflies, trapped in the center of the web, Grand Isla Tiburon, the big bad spider in no rush, knowing there was plenty of time. They would be there when its hunger was too great to ignore.

***

Marco hoped Ollie wouldn't follow him. The guy was in love with Tara. Not that he'd told him in so many words, but you had to be deaf, dumb, and blind not to see it.

No, Ollie would wait for Tara to return. This was Ollie's chance to shine. To be her protector.

He just hoped he hadn't overplayed his hand and looked so distraught that his friend would feel he had to come out and talk him off the ledge.

Watching Titus go down like that had shaken him to his core. Titus was a good man, a little rough around the edges, but honest. And a damn good worker.

Marco had brought him some cold beers one night after an exceptionally productive day when the sun was doing its best to fry them like ants. He and Titus sat in a pair of lounge chairs on the beach, watching the sun go pink, the horizon purpling. This was back when Titus and his team stayed on the island—in Lenny's bungalow—so they could get an early start and late finish.

Tight-lipped Titus had loosened up after a few beers, talking about his wife who had passed five years earlier, his regret at never having kids. His wife was afraid their child would have some of the maladies that were being passed down the generations since the atomic bomb tests. Her family had been close to the Bikini Atoll during those dark years. Her mother died young of cancer, and she herself had never been the picture of health. She was terrified of passing down that horrible legacy.

"I kept telling her our child would be half of me," Titus said, staring far away into the distant past. "I'm strong. My half would have healed hers. But she said no one was stronger than the poison they spread. It was Biblical to her, the sins of the father being carried upon generation after generation of sons."

Marco had a vague recollection of the passage. The Bible wasn't his bag. Even as a kid, he'd cut Wednesday afternoon Bible school as often as he could. He did like that Thomas guy, the one who doubted Jesus's resurrection.

That was a guy he could have a beer with.

Faith was for suckers.

Show me, motherfucker.

He spotted the lab, and the oncoming storm, and checked his watch.

They could be there now, for all he knew. It was early, but it's not like these scumbags adhered to a timetable. He'd spotted them once in the pale light of day, scurrying into the lab, lugging a dozen or so boxes. He assumed the pickup happened at night.

Creeping up to the side of the lab, he set the AR-15 against the outer wall. The last thing he wanted to do was spook them if they were here and get caught in a shootout. Marco wasn't Gary Cooper. If he was going to shoot them, it was going to be when they least expected it and didn't see it coming.

He felt no shame for thinking that way.

Marco may have been a fuckup, Mazie's death just exacerbating his natural penchant for fuckupery, but he wasn't an idiot.

Peeking inside the lab, he thought that might be up for debate.

The lab was empty, but the stench that Lenny had dragged into his house was especially strong out here.

Maybe, just maybe, they'd been swallowed up by the storm. He'd followed the NOAA storm reports closely, only unclenching his ass cheeks when he heard the storm had veered to the south, away from Grand Isla Tiburon.

With everything that had happened in the last twenty-four hours, he hadn't had time or the frame of mind to check again.

Lightning flashed in the upper reaches of the oily clouds.

This could be a good thing. It might work to his advantage.

If he could keep them from coming ashore, they would be doomed to heading back out to sea. Let Mother Nature do the rest. Or better yet, that freaking monster shark.

Once the storm passed, he'd have to get out to New Jersey fast, set things right. The storm wouldn't take care of everything for him, but it could buy him time.

Marco's stomach clenched. Acid gurgled in the back of his throat.

He should have taken his parents with him. But they were so set in their ways.

Dammit, you should have forced them!

Right, that would have worked. He could have just trussed them up like Hannibal Lecter and wheeled them onto the plane.

Yeah. That would have worked.

Rifle in hand, he positioned himself on the ocean side of the old lab, finding a corner where he couldn't easily be seen, either by the smugglers or his friends.

Smugglers.

As Ollie would say, holy crapping Christ.

He'd lived through it and he still couldn't believe he'd gotten mixed up in this shit. Maybe everything that was happening was a sign. Things were changing . . . fast. He could be the force of change on this particular front.

If the smugglers were still coming, he wanted to be here to either send them packing or have the satisfaction of watching them go down like modern day Jonahs, only this time they wouldn't be *living* inside the giant sea beast.

Marco chuckled, his nerves jangling.

"How's that for Biblical?"

A tiny smudge on the clear section of the horizon got caught in his periphery.

Something was definitely headed their way.

He looked for any sign of the dorsal fin, humming the theme to *Jaws*. He thought Ollie the movie lover would appreciate it.

Poor fucking Ollie. Marco had let him down big time, just like he'd done to everyone else. Except this time, the stakes were huge. Too big for him.

But not too big for that shark.

Marco had a nose for when things were about to go sideways. It's what made him a master of the stock market. He was the gambler with an almost preternatural edge, always knowing just when to dump a slew of stocks just before they went tits up.

Things were coming undone on the island.

He couldn't trust the smugglers to just drop their drugs or money or guns or ivory, for all he knew, and run. Something was in the wind. The canary in the coalmine had died on its perch.

If fate was on his side for once, it would send those men into the waiting maw of that shark.

If not, he would have to force them to the dinner table.

Because if he didn't, that something that itched at the back of his brain told him they were going to die. Nature was nudging those dangerous men to one of two choices—suffer at the wrath of that shark from Hell, or push toward safety on the island, where the smugglers would discover they were not alone.

You had to pay attention to the signs. Ignore them at your peril.

Maybe he was just being paranoid, a state of mind he was well versed in during his years as an addict.

But he didn't think so.

"Come on, big guy. There's a nice meal coming your way."

CHAPTER FIFTEEN

"It figures the one thing I find is a folder of receipts and logs of visitors. Though there are a ton of doctors listed here. That definitely points to some secretive medical shit going on here . . . but what exactly was it?" Lenny said, exasperated.

He and Ollie stared at the small pile of mildewed pages strewn about Marco's kitchen table. The ink was badly smeared on most of them, but it was apparent that there was nothing to be gleaned from the trash that had been left behind.

"Maybe we should go back to the lab and look around more," Ollie said, hands gripping the edge of the table, hovering over it like a gargoyle. He had gone past frightened and confused and was feeling a familiar friend nudging closer and closer: anger.

He walked around the table, counting the revolutions.

One-two-three-four-five. Stop.

Shit. Now he was back to counting again.

How dare all this happen when all he wanted to do was make people happy!

They should have had the fucking lab demolished before they ever set foot on Grand Isla Tiburon.

Although, there had been signs.

Grand Isla Tiburon translated to Shark Island. It made sense at the time, since it was surrounded by a shark sanctuary. How the hell was he to know it would also be home to the biggest damn shark anyone had ever seen?

And why hadn't anyone lived on it since the military left? Oh sure, it wasn't toxic. It just had dead bodies crammed into metal chutes and an aquatic killer patrolling the water.

When he'd first come up with the idea of creating a place where he and his friends could live, he considered building a kind of compound in a state like Tennessee where the winters weren't so brutal. He could find a lake, build some houses around it and have a hell of a time.

No, he had to go big or go home. It was an island or nothing.

Maybe I really am Alligator Arms—reaching for things I can't get.

Lenny scanned the pages, absently rubbing his hands on his shorts. "Hold the wedding. What do we have here?"

Towards the back of the file, a folded slip of paper had been crammed between the fragile pages.

"It's some kind of note," Ollie said. "Hard to read, though."

The ink had bled over the page. Lenny carefully lifted it to the dining room table, under the bright overhead lamp. His lips moved as he silently pored over the note.

"It looks like it was written by Seaman Chet Hardy," Lenny said.

"Seaman is like a private in the Army," Ollie told him. He caught Lenny's eye and said, "Before you say anything stupid."

Lenny smirked. "Not today, Raging Bull. Anyway, from what I can read, it appears Seaman Hardy was kinda peeved." He pointed at a blurry line of text. "It says, 'Can't believe we have to work with these guys. My father died killing them, yet I have to.' I can't read what comes after."

Ollie traced a finger down the page. "'Just trying to get through this and come home. I wish I could tell you everything. Science fiction has nothing on this place.'"

"He's got that right," Lenny said.

"Does that look like the word shark?" Ollie asked.

Lenny leaned over her shoulder. "It could be. Or it could say sharp. Or shit. We could just be seeing what we want to see. I guess Seaman Hardy was planning to send this note home but something happened before he could stick it in an envelope."

"And I'm sure it wasn't something good," Ollie added.

"I think at this point we have to hit the lab again. If this note was written in the mid-fifties, I'll bet the guys Chet is referring to are Germans. Nazis to be more specific. Or they could have been Japanese," Lenny said. "Now what the hell was our military doing with them way out here? I can't help thinking they're directly linked to that big-ass shark."

Ollie held back from saying, *no shit, Sherlock.*

There was no such thing as coincidences. Just a long series of interrelated clusterfucks.

There was a knock at the door. Ollie let Lae inside. She looked worried.

What did Tara say to her?

"Mr. Ollie, your friend said you and Marco wanted to talk to me," she said, adding, "Did you see the storm?"

He grabbed Marco's phone from his computer desk. "All the more reason for you to call Lucky and tell him to stay put. We're going to have to batten down the hatches."

The quizzical look on her face told him she had no idea what the phrase meant.

"We'll have to stay together and ride out the storm," he clarified.

Lae nodded. "Yes, that would be best. I hope you don't mind my being here."

He gingerly touched her shoulder. "Lae, we're more than happy to have you. Yours and Lucky's safety is the most important thing. Give him a call."

The storm was something even pragmatic Lucky could see and respect. Lae could be clued into the whole shark business later.

Lae walked off to a corner of the living room by the big bay windows overlooking the beach to make the call. The skies were still blue from that vantage point.

To Ollie's surprise, Heidi came back. She had changed into cargo shorts, a T-shirt and sneakers.

"Where's Steven?" Lenny asked.

"At the house freaking out," she said. "He's calling everyone he can find to tell them about the shark and the skulls. He's desperate to find a way off the island right away."

Ollie bit the inside of his mouth so hard, it hurt. "That's crazy. No one will come out in this storm."

"I told him that. He's beyond listening to me."

"He talk to any cops? Is the Coast Guard out around here?" Lenny asked.

"Who knows? Reception is a disaster. He's just doing a lot of cursing and staring at his phone. I'm hoping he'll calm down on his own. I got the feeling if I stayed there, I'd just make things worse. He needs to find out for himself that we're going to have to stay put."

Ollie offered her a cup of coffee, which she eagerly accepted. "I don't get it. I never saw Cooter . . . I mean Steven, panic, not even the day before finals and he hadn't studied. I always thought the reason he pulled through was because he could stay calm no matter what."

"A lot has changed since you last met." A glimmer of sadness shimmered in her misty eyes before she looked away.

Ollie didn't know what to do. Heidi's hands trembled, drops of coffee splashing over the side of the cup. Should he put his arm around her? Was that off limits because she was married to his friend?

Tara burst in, breathless.

"It's still out there," she said.

"Where?" Lenny asked.

"Not that far out. It's just circling, like it's waiting."

Heidi nearly dropped her coffee. "Waiting for what?"

Tara shrugged. "Since the dolphins are gone, I assume more people like Titus in slow-moving boats."

"Fuck!" Heidi shouted. She sat in a chair at the kitchen table staring at the note Lenny had spread out.

Lae stared at them while she talked to her husband in hushed tones. Ollie could tell she was very, very confused, as well as a bit frightened. He prayed Lucky was being reasonable and wouldn't attempt to put his toe in the water. If the storm didn't get him, the circling shark surely would.

Tara showed them the ledger. "Maybe this will help."

Lenny eagerly took it from her. Ollie cleared a space on the table so he could crack it open. Old papers scattered all over the floor.

"Crap," Lenny blurted. "Now this really makes sense." He flipped to the front of the ledger, a name listed on each line along with the date, time of entry and departure. "Look at those names."

Ollie swallowed hard. Lenny was right, most of the names were doctors. They were right there in black and white.

Dr. Knoop

Dr. Schmidt.

Dr. Mueller.

The list of German names went on and on.

"Fucking Nazis," Lenny whispered. "We have to get back to the lab. There has to be more stuff like this hidden around."

"Where's Marco?" Heidi asked.

"He took off with a rifle," Lenny said, nonchalantly. "He'll be back."

"A rifle?" Tara said.

"He thinks he's going to pull some great white hunter, Hemingway shit," Lenny said, flipping through the pages.

Ollie stood close to Tara, feeling her body heat. "With the storm coming, we should think about getting everyone in one place until it passes."

Tara nodded. She took her pack of cigarettes out of her pocket, eyed it, then threw it in the garbage.

"Oh man!" Lenny exclaimed, slamming the book closed. "We've got all the culprits right here."

Tara swiped the book away from him. "Maybe we can track down the names and find out who they were."

"You could start by Googling Nazi war criminals," Lenny said.

Tara ran to Marco's laptop and quickly became dejected. "Internet's down."

"Of course it is," Ollie said.

Heidi stood up and said, "So maybe now we concentrate on this storm. We can deal with killer mutant sharks and crazy skulls later."

"She has a point," Tara said. The sky had darkened considerably.

"I'll get Marco," Ollie said. "Heidi, you take Lenny and talk Steven off the ledge. We'll meet in my house. Grab anything you think is essential from your places."

Heidi nodded.

Lae was still on the phone.

Ollie leaned close to Tara.

"You mind making sure Lae gets to my house?"

Tara squeezed his arm. His overreaching alligator arms.

"No problem. Did you tell her about the shark?"

"Not yet. I figured the storm would be enough to ground her husband. But it doesn't look like it's going so easy. Nothing is easy today," Ollie said, chewing at a nail.

Rodney Dangerfield in *Easy Money* popped into his head, as inappropriate a flick as he could conjure at the moment.

If only life were as uncomplicated and silly as a comedy.

Stepping outside, Ollie was struck by a nasty gust of wind. The storm was, at best, less than an hour away.

Less than an hour until he found out if all this work could withstand a tempest.

He shuddered, thinking that the lab that had withstood the elements for six decades might end up being their only hope.

***

Steven threw his phone on the bed. It bounced once, twice, and landed on the floor.

What was the point?

They were screwed.

Even the few calls that had gone through were so garbled, neither side could understand the other. It was like living in the fucking Stone Age.

"Now what?"

He stood in the middle of his bedroom, hands on his hips.

And where the hell was Heidi?

Sure, he'd been a bit of a dick, but that was no reason for her to desert him.

She's with everyone else, he thought.

Most importantly, she was with Marco.

They'd been role players right at the start of their relationship. It was the one thing that turned Heidi on. Literally, the instant he mentioned getting into some role play, she was wetter than Niagara Falls.

Last night, when he was going down on her, she'd told him she wanted to pretend he was Marco. In the heat of the moment, he didn't give it a second thought. He was harder than a Redwood, she was grinding against his mouth, the tang of her juices on his tongue. He didn't care if she wanted to call him his father's name as long as he made her come and got to slip inside her, filling her with his seed, shaking from head to toe as she groaned with unmitigated ecstasy.

He'd been so worn out afterwards, he hadn't even thought about it until now.

They'd indulged each other in their fantasies, pretending they were fucking friends, strangers, celebrities, and porn stars. It had become second nature. Part of their love-making ritual.

Steven always assumed it was the best way to keep their relationship fresh and exciting. Like daydreaming about killing someone when you were pissed at them, it was a way of exercising the id so you didn't have to act out on it in real life.

But out here on an island where Marco was one of only three other men, it didn't seem so cool.

"I bet she's hanging on his every word right now," he said. "She'll expect me to bang her brains out later, calling out his name. Maybe I should call her Tara while I do it."

He shook his head. He'd had his go-around with Tara back in the day and had no desire for a repeat. She was a nice girl, but just not his type. He'd wiped her out of his spank bank a long time ago.

What the hell is the matter with you?

How had his mind wandered so far off topic?

They weren't having sex tonight. Between the storm, the shark, and God knows what with the skulls, sex was a pipe dream. And there was nothing he could do right now. As much as he hated to admit it, he had to suck it up and sit tight. Once the storm passed, he'd get a helicopter out here to get them back to Majuro where they could hop a plane to the states. Ollie would be footing that bill, whether he liked it or not.

Steven was glad he and Heidi hadn't sold their house just yet. He'd acted responsibly, not throwing everything away to live out here. You always needed a safety net. He knew Ollie and the rest of them expected him to be the same hard partying, reckless goofball he'd been in college.

That version of Steven Combs was long gone. He'd buried Cooter the day after graduation.

Now he hoped he wouldn't be buried out here in the middle of nowhere.

CHAPTER SIXTEEN

"Sir, I think you should see this."

Captain Robert Powell was in the sonar room. His back was killing him. Chewing on several Tylenol had done little to ameliorate the pain. That put him in a less than hospitable mood. His crew sensed it, and they were giving him a wide berth.

"What is it?" he snapped, grabbing the tablet from the officer. The kid was steely-eyed, but Powell could tell he'd rather be anywhere but here at this particular moment.

"Intercepted cell phone communications," he said, his posture more erect than the Empire State Building.

Powell wasn't in the mood for chatter gathered by the tentacles of the NSA. That department was the head of this goose chase. Sure, there was valuable intel they stumbled upon, but it was usually enmeshed in a goulash of babble. Most of it came in handy only after the fact, hindsight making it very easy to put all the pieces together.

When Powell saw the origin of the calls, his back pain suddenly disappeared.

"Are they sure about this?" he asked, not expecting an answer. None was mercifully supplied.

Grand Isla Tiburon.

What the hell was going on there?

It couldn't be that thing. It had been in cold storage so long he wondered if it was even still alive.

The Pacific Ocean was prime breeding ground for numerous black-ops projects. It was far from prying eyes and the shores of America. The theory was, if something were to go wrong, knowledge of the event, and more importantly, any serious repercussions, weren't going to be felt in the US.

That was why they had sent the *Maximus*—a super-secret, black-budget submarine—down to this quadrant of the Pacific. After the explosion of prehistoric chimaera fish off the coast of Miami two years ago, several live specimens had been captured by the US Navy for further examination and testing. They were held in a special containment unit off the coast of western Australia.

Powell was here to check on things and make sure there was no chance for the giant ghost sharks to escape. The scientists in charge of the lab said the creatures were growing, which seemed impossible, considering they were already over fifty feet long. It might be time to put them down like rabid dogs. The captain didn't like the thought of any of those demonic fish swimming in the land of the living. They needed to be eradicated with extreme prejudice, not studied.

Just thinking about the sea battle that was waged against the horde of ravenous beasts made his gorge rise. They'd lost a lot of good men and women that day.

And now there was this.

They would have to head north to the Marshall Islands. That was all he'd been told so far.

But he knew it couldn't be good.

What the hell had gone wrong on that dead, deserted island?

***

The storm seemed to be picking up speed, gobbling up the blue skies like a starving man.

So was the boat skipping across the water like a flat rock.

Marco settled behind a stack of driftwood, the rifle resting steadily atop it, keeping the boat in the crosshairs as he watched it approach.

Am I really going to shoot them? I've sunk low, but this is a new bottom.

He banged his head against the wood, the pain centering him.

Yes, he'd fucked up royally, but this was a chance to start making things right.

He should have never taken that gig cooking the books for Donovan Bailey. But he wasn't thinking straight, his fentanyl addiction in total control. The soul-deadening narcotic was the only thing that got him through life after Mazie. With so many people overdosing on the stuff and it making headlines—especially after a celebrity like Prince died from it—the stuff got harder and harder to score.

His bank account tapped out and brain itching, he told his dealer he'd do anything they asked of him to get a steady supply of his precious fentanyl. His dealer, a low-level piece of street grease who went by the name Scoots, knew Marco had once been a Wall Street hotshot. He took great delight in mocking him for his fall from grace.

Scoots passed the word up the line, and somehow it reached Donovan Bailey, the head of the Jamaican Mob for the entire northeast. Marco had never met the man, but he'd heard plenty of stories, like how Bailey gouged the eyes from his wife's head when he found her looking at another man. Or the time he had an entire village in Ecuador executed just to show the local drug lords that there was a new man in charge, his trade in America no longer enough to satisfy his desire for money and power.

He was never mentioned in the papers. He kept it that way on purpose. He saw how well being a celebrity worked for the Italians. The Mafia was a shell of its former self, its days of glory gone, never to return.

Donovan Bailey had no intention of letting his empire collapse. Not while he was still alive.

Aside from drugs, guns, human trafficking, and other unsavory revenue pipelines, Bailey had his brutal hands in dozens of legitimate business. Naturally, most of them were in place to launder his ill-gotten gains. Word had it that once he heard he could have a legitimate Wall Street player in his pocket, his previous money manager disappeared . . . for good.

He'd supply Marco the fentanyl he desperately needed at the start, but he needed him clean. So, Bailey paid for Marco's rehab in one of the finest centers in New York. It was all part of Bailey making Marco indebted to him. And Marco truly was, at least at the start.

Marco knew what he was getting into. If the drugs could no longer kill him, he'd be just as happy to let Bailey do the job for him.

And then Ollie came along. Ollie with his friendship and money and generosity. It was the promise of a new life.

Marco's plan was to take his parents, his only relatives, and move them down here, well out of Donovan Bailey's sight. They'd simply disappear.

But somehow, Bailey had gotten wind of the change in Marco's circumstance. He probably had Marco's damn apartment bugged.

Once he knew that Marco would be living on a remote island, Bailey quickly came up with a way to taint the whole thing. Grand Isla Tiburon would be a kind of way station for various associates – a place to drop things off and pick them up.

In return for use of the island, Bailey wouldn't behead Marco's mother and father.

"Where the hell is that shark?" Marco hissed, hoping the beast would take his burden from him. But of course, it was nowhere to be found. The boat was almost ashore now.

Marco's finger tightened on the trigger.

Being in charge of Ollie's money, he'd found a way to hide a few million dollars from his friend who'd trusted him. It wasn't much, just enough for Marco to grab his parents and disappear if the moment ever presented itself. Ollie would understand, not that Marco ever planned to face the music. He wasn't man enough for that.

With everything going to hell at the same time, this was that moment.

The rifle was just supposed to be a backup. He'd counted on the shark.

It would eat Bailey's men, the storm would blow through, and Marco would rush back to New York and smuggle himself and his parents away in a small town in Canada he'd picked very carefully.

The boat stopped, dropping anchor. Six men loaded into a dinghy, headed for the lab.

Sweating so much the salt burned his eyes as it ran down his head in steady rivulets, Marco tensed.

You can do this. You can do this. You can do this.

He couldn't tell if any of the men had guns. Why hadn't he bought a scope?

The dinghy hit the beach and the men scrambled out.

Marco looked past them to the waiting boat.

No massive dorsal fin.

The storm loomed in the shrinking distance. The wind picked up, pelting his face with grains of sand.

The men were carrying full gunnysacks, running up the beach. They wanted to dump their shit and get back on the boat, peeling away from the storm.

But Marco knew that wouldn't happen. He felt it like a fever, burning his brain to cinders. They would never get back in that boat. No, they would be stuck here, a band of very bad men who would do terrible things to Marco and his friends.

The signs were there.

In the past, they screamed at Marco, *SELL!*

Now, they shouted, *KILL!*

Marco pulled the trigger, aiming for the bearded guy in the lead. The crack of the rifle echoed, piercing the whistling of the escalating winds.

A plume of sand shot up near the man's foot.

"Shit," Marco murmured.

The men dropped their gunnysacks.

All of them had formidable-looking guns.

Marco didn't even flinch as he pissed himself, hoping they couldn't see him.

INTERLUDE... 1952

"It's getting too damn big!"

Dr. Lancaster slammed his fist on the table, glass bottles jumping, several breaking on the floor.

"We can't keep feeding it. We can barely control it. What happened yesterday should be all the proof we need that the entire project needs to be shut down. And I mean immediately."

His face was so red, Dr. Laughton worried he was on the verge of a stroke. He'd worked with Lancaster for a long time and was alarmed by the growing stress the man was under.

Maybe stress wasn't quite the right word. They were all stressed.

No, his bookish contemporary was angry. Livid.

"You need to calm down," Dr. Laughton urged. "Here, sit down and have a drink."

"What's the point? We can't drink our worries away."

"I'm not implying we do that. But it wouldn't hurt to take the edge off."

Obeying his own orders, Laughton knocked back two fingers of scotch. He barely felt the burn.

He'd been rattled since yesterday's test run with the Megalodon. It was their fourth Operation Hansel and Gretel and it had been a complete disaster.

Using pieces of irradiated bodies that had been loaded into a submarine, the Navy had doled out small portions to the shark—just enough to keep it fully functioning, but not enough to get it even close to a quarter strength. The sub released the "food" in stages, like breadcrumbs, leading the Megalodon to the target, which in this case was a scuttled destroyer off the coast of Australia.

The idea was that once they got to the destroyer, they would give the shark a heavy dose of its special food and observe how it attacked the vessel.

Dr. Laughton and the other scientists knew that once the Megalodon was allowed to get to a certain level of consciousness, it would destroy everything around it.

Operation Hansel and Gretel was filmed extensively so footage displaying the potential military might could be sent to Washington.

That would then lead to a greater influx of funding, which they were blowing through at an alarming rate. Resurrecting the Megalodon and maintaining it was as costly as it was miraculous.

No one said miracles came cheap.

What they hadn't anticipated was one of the "breadcrumbs" being jettisoned too close to the previous. The Megalodon, infused with a fury of energy, not only smashed the sub in two, it also attacked a fishing trawler on the surface. The ship and everyone on board was devoured in minutes.

They had to wait for the shark to sate itself, and for its adrenaline levels to flat-line, before they could send a retrieval unit out to corral it back into its cage.

All in all, seventy-three men had been lost, including the civilians on the trawler.

Of course, no one was to ever know what became of the trawler. It would be just another ship lost at sea.

Dr. Laughton's stomach churned, curdling the scotch. Dr. Lancaster paced the room.

"If we tell them unanimously and in no uncertain terms that the Megalodon cannot be controlled, they'll be forced to put it down," he said, just under a shout. "The key is, we have to be unified."

"It's gone too far to turn back now. Besides, there'll still be Mueller whispering in their ears. He's the genius to end all geniuses. Our aquatic Dr. Frankenstein. Except this mad doctor has a host of organizations behind him, along with more money than you or I could spend in fifty lifetimes."

Dr. Lancaster slumped into a chair. "Then we'll just refuse to work."

"They'll replace us with someone else . . . or make us disappear."

Lancaster's eyes went wide. "You don't think they'd actually do that!"

Laughton nodded. "I do. Look how many men they sacrificed yesterday. Are we any better than them?"

"No, we certainly aren't," Dr. Lancaster sighed. "We helped unleash this demon. We don't deserve to breathe the same air as those brave men."

Dr. Laughton pushed away from the table. "Come with me."

They walked to the central lab, ascending the stairs until they stood atop the observation tank. Powerful lights above and below the water illuminated the slumbering giant. Every time he came up here, Dr. Laughton's knees grew weak.

When they had first brought the Megalodon back to life, there had been unbridled exaltation. They had defied the laws of death and perhaps redefined the future of man and beast.

Several years ago, the Megalodon had been half the size it was now.

At just under sixty feet, the massive creature was terrifying to behold, even as it floated in its cage, dreamless and motionless.

The catwalk around the observation tank was lined with soldiers. Bright lights shone down into the dark water, illuminating the slumbering beast. Dr. Laughton found it laughable that the creature that could consume the lab and island with unmitigated ferocity needed guarding by puny humans.

In a low whisper, Dr. Laughton said, "We could always inject Dr. Mueller with poison and feed him to his damn creation."

Just picturing throwing the Nazi scientist down the tank gave Laughton a shiver of pleasure. Those had been hard to come by lately.

Dr. Lancaster chuckled. "It would make for a fitting ending to this whole debacle."

The Megalodon twitched in its sleep, its tail fin banging against the cage.

"*You stare into the abyss, the abyss stares back,*" Laughton said.

"I'd happily believe in God if Mueller and his pet somehow come to a tragic end before more lives are lost," Lancaster said.

Laughton looked around to make sure no one was listening to them. "Let's just hope we're still around to see it if it happens."

CHAPTER SEVENTEEN

Nacho didn't like the look of that sky. The weather report called for one motherfucker of a storm. All he wanted to do was make the drop and get the hell off this place.

Hitting the water with the heavy sack on his back, he felt the need to itch the ropy scar on his face.

Trouble was brewing.

It sounded ridiculous, but that itchy scar had saved his ass more than once. In fact, most of his luck had run bad until the day he'd been bequeathed the scar from the end of a British gangbanger's blade. It had flayed his face practically in half. There went any hopes for a career in modeling.

He never had a "woe is me" moment, even during his initial recovery. In his line of work, a scar like that only made him look meaner. It gave him an edge.

And now it was telling him to be very careful.

It could just be the storm. He didn't need a lucky itchy scar to tell him things were capable of going sideways real fast.

A heavy breaker crashed into his back, almost knocking his gun out of his hands.

If things got worse, they would have to get everyone off the boat and spend the night in the abandoned building. But where would they moor the boat?

One problem at a time.

Nacho scanned the empty beach, the wind kicking up the sand and limiting visibility.

"You see anything?" he asked Mofongo in Albanian. It was the one language everyone who worked internationally for Donovan Bailey had to learn so they could communicate with one another. He didn't know why Bailey had picked Albanian and didn't care. The entire crew went by nicknames, all of them based on food from their native countries. Mofongo hailed from Puerto Rico and had eyesight like an eagle. He had the breath of a diseased cow, so everyone tried to stay upwind of him. In this wind, his putrid breath was snatched away the moment it left his mouth.

"Where?"

"Around the building, pendejo."

They waded cautiously through the water.

"Nah, I don't see nothing."

"Anything," Nacho corrected him. "You don't see anything."

"That's what I fucking said."

Nacho gritted his teeth and sighed. He couldn't wait to get cycled off this crew. Bunch of retards.

Right now, he just wanted to drop off the bow and blow the hell out of here.

He turned to the men at his back. "Bami, Akara, Cambuulo, Escargot, keep alert."

Akara, the dark skinned Nigerian, said, "For what?"

"I don't know."

Nacho scratched his scar as they walked onto the beach, dropping their hefty gunnysacks.

"See, I told you there was nothing," Mofongo said.

A shot rang out. Nacho flinched. The sand at his feet exploded.

"We've got a shooter!" Nacho yelled. All of the men brandished their weapons. For all they knew, a rival group had been lying in wait this whole time. There was a fortune in cocaine in those bags. Cocaine most likely headed for America, where the real money was.

If they lost that coke, they were as good as dead.

Knowing that didn't leave room for fear of the shooter.

But Nacho would make him very, very afraid.

***

When Ollie heard the first sharp crack, he instinctively ducked and covered his head, thinking it sounded like a tree branch breaking.

"You idiot."

The nearest palm tree was fifty yards away. This wasn't like walking the streets of Minnesota after an early snowstorm, most of the leaves still on the trees, laden with heavy snow, straining each and every limb to the snapping point.

He stopped, his body buffeted by the wind, getting a face full of sand. It actually hurt. It was like being pegged by hundreds of sharp tacks.

Something definitely broke. He just couldn't tell where the sound had come from.

He jogged to the dock, expecting to find Marco there, rifle trained at the ocean, waiting for the shark to get close enough so he could take his shot.

Ollie found the shark, the imposing dorsal fin popping up and disappearing quickly, too close for comfort. Marco was nowhere to be found.

Where the hell did he go?

Maybe he'd met up with Steven. He could be at the rec center, making sure everything was secure. The last thing they wanted was half the building supplies to spread wings and end up in the Pacific.

The rec center was empty. It looked like Titus had stowed things away before he left. For a contractor, he'd been exceedingly tidy. Or maybe he'd sensed the weather reports were wrong and the storm was going to take a turn their way. Islander intuition.

"Marco!" Ollie shouted against the harsh breeze.

The storm's front only seemed to make the humidity worse. Ollie's shirt clung to him like a second skin.

Grand Isla Tiburon wasn't so big that Marco could simply lose himself. They'd only built on half of the island so far, deciding to leave the other half alone and let nature keep its hold.

He had to be back in one of the bungalows.

Marco's was deserted.

Steven stepped outside his bungalow before Ollie could knock.

"What's wrong now?" Steven asked. Ollie must have looked as ragged as he felt.

"Have you seen Marco?"

A tense darkness washed over Steven's face, but just for a moment. "N-no, I thought he was with you."

"He left a while ago . . . with a rifle."

"A rifle?"

Ollie shrugged. "Yeah. I had no idea he even had one."

"What the hell is he planning to do with it?"

"Shoot the shark I guess. But he's not at the beach."

"Where's Heidi?" Steven asked.

"She was with Lenny. They were supposed to take you to my house. We're all going to stay there until the storm blows over."

Steven slammed the door behind him. "Wait, you're telling me my wife is gone? And Marco, too?"

"And Lenny," Ollie added. Steven was acting strange. He kept rubbing his bald head, eyes squinted, jaw clenched.

"So where the hell is everybody?" Steven asked.

"That's what I'm trying to find out."

The jarring pop of rapid gunfire jolted them.

Ollie looked past the beach where the dock was located, out to where the lab lay.

"Why is Marco out there?" he said, more to himself.

"That's n-n-ot just one person shooting," Steven said.

Pop! Pop! Pop! Pop! Pop! Pop!

He was right. That sounded like an awful lot of guns. But who the hell was shooting them?

Ollie's skull felt as if it were going to go full Vesuvius.

What the fuck else is going wrong?

"Do you have a gun?" Steven asked.

Ollie stared at him, flinching with each gunshot. "Why would I have a gun?"

Steven pointed over his shoulder, toward the epicenter of the unseen shootout. "To deal with that, for one."

***

As soon as Ollie left to find Marco, Lenny and Heidi headed out to her house, telling Tara they'd meet her and Lae at Ollie's in a few.

Things weren't working out as planned. That seemed to be the order of the day.

"Something's wrong," Lenny said.

Heidi spun around. She had to practically shout over the wind. "What?"

His right hand, which had been itching like the devil before, now felt as if someone was taking a blowtorch to it. He'd jammed it deep in his pocket, afraid to see what the heck was going on with it. The idea was to deal with it later, hope that Ollie had cortisone cream or Benadryl, because he was definitely having some kind of allergic reaction to whatever sludge he'd touched on those skulls. He cursed himself over and over again for being stupid and careless. A flare-up of curiosity had gotten the better of him. He knew better than that.

"My hand," he said, bringing it into the fading light for them both to see.

Heidi gasped.

"Oh man, that's not good," Lenny said, feeling his legs turn to tapioca.

He'd had a hard time extracting his hand from his pocket. Now he knew why. It had ballooned to twice its normal size. His flesh had turned a startling pink with brown lines, like veins but more haphazard, zigzagging from his palm to his fingertips.

And it smelled. If it were a cartoon hand, Lenny imagined there would be stink lines waving around it.

"What did you do to it?" Heidi said, trying her best to remain calm.

"It was real itchy before. In just the last minute, it started to burn." His stomach flip-flopped. He put his hand down. If he looked at it any longer, or kept it close to his nose, he was going to pass out.

Heidi, her eyes wild and desperately searching, suddenly screamed, "Tara!"

Tara and Lae had left Marco's house, heads bowed against the wind.

Heidi waved them over, arms flailing like one of those inflatables at a used car lot.

"What's wrong?" Tara said.

Things had come to the point where they all assumed any new development was bad.

That's one assumption that's absolutely correct, Lenny thought, trying to keep his mind from fixating on the burning and rotten funk.

"It's Lenny's hand," Heidi said.

When Lenny showed it to Tara, she stumbled back a bit. Lae was horrified.

Recovering quickly, Tara said, "Quick, let's get to Ollie's house. I'll check his place for something that might help. You having any trouble breathing? Dizziness?"

The biting sand felt like piranhas gnawing on the tender flesh of his hand. He tried to put it back in his pocket but it would not longer fit. If they didn't take care of it soon, it was going to pop like a balloon.

"Dizzy," he said. "But for good reason."

Tara grabbed him by the elbow, leading the way. "Just try and stay calm."

"Sure, no problem. I'll pretend my hand doesn't look like something from a John Carpenter movie."

The tropical storm was morphing into a sandstorm. They had to shield their eyes to keep from being blinded. The walk to Ollie's seemed to take forever.

Lenny tried flexing his fingers, but it was if they were made of wood. The pain got worse and worse with each passing second. By the time they walked into Ollie's door, he was screaming and cursing.

His broiling hand had gone nuclear meltdown. He wished it would explode already and give him mercy.

***

The only thing keeping Marco alive was the storm. It was impossible for the men to see him. All of their shots had been way off the mark.

But they were getting closer.

He had to abandon his position. That would mean he'd be out in the open for at least twenty yards before he could slip behind the lab. Twenty yards was nothing unless you had six armed men gunning for you. It might as well have been a hundred acres.

Thwang!

A bullet kicked up sand as it sank into the driftwood. Marco dropped his rifle, cowering.

He dared not pop his head up. The men had fanned out, hands over their eyes like visors, shooting indiscriminately. Sooner rather than later, one of them was going to make a lucky shot.

Not lucky for Marco.

Bracing himself, Marco picked up the rifle and darted from the dwindling safety of the pile of driftwood. He sprinted to the lab, afraid to look over his shoulder, his back tingling as he expected to feel the impact of a bullet any second.

Chips of brick scattered ahead of him. It was either a random shot, or one of the swarthy men had a bead on him. He dove, hitting the sand so hard, the breath was knocked out of him. It took a few seconds, seconds he didn't have, to recover. He crawled on his belly around the corner of the building.

Only then did he dare to stand, leg muscles jittering, threatening to go on strike and leave him in a helpless pile.

Peeking his head around the building, he saw the six men in the same position, still shooting in wide arcs. One of them raised a hand, and they all stopped. It was clear they were listening for him, though the whistling wind wasn't going to make that easy.

Now what? I should have shot up the dinghy while it was still in the water. Maybe if they flopped around enough in it, the shark would have come.

There was no point now playing the "shoulda, woulda, coulda" game.

Marco may have been a shit heel, but he couldn't lead these smuggler assholes back to the bungalows. He'd have to find a way to hold them here . . . holding meaning kill them, or at best, get them to decide vacating immediately was in their best interests.

Take out the leader. It was common sense. It worked with people as well as it did with animals.

The one with the beard seemed to be the big man in charge.

Marco raised the rifle, trying to steady his arms so he could get a clear shot.

Mr. Beard was accommodating, standing perfectly still, trying to see through the swirling sand.

Getting his breathing under control, Marco took a deep breath, let it out, finger wrapping around the trigger.

Something hard and heavy landed on his shoulder.

The rifle swung low just as he fired, the round tunneling harmlessly into the sand.

The six men looked his way.

Marco froze, knowing that whoever had crept up behind him wasn't going to let him exist in the land of the living for much longer.

CHAPTER EIGHTEEN

Tara rifled through Ollie's medicine cabinet. Thank God he'd stocked up. She guessed he had to prepare for just about anything, knowing there were no drug stores just around the corner.

"Hold on, Lenny," she called out. His screaming two rooms away was so loud, it was as if he were wailing directly in her ear.

Considering what was going on with his hand, she couldn't blame him.

She dumped what she needed into a bath towel and ran to the living room.

Lenny was on the couch, clutching his right arm but not touching his hand. Heidi stood over him, holding on to his shoulders, trying to calm him down. Lae sat aghast in the chair opposite him.

"Okay, I'm going to—"

When Tara saw his hand, she completely forgot what she was going to say. In just the past thirty seconds, it had swelled even more, his discolored skin splitting in multiple places.

Tears streamed down Lenny's face.

"Please don't touch it," he begged.

His hand was turning gray, parts of the palm blackening. It looked like it was necrotizing right before their eyes.

Tara held the bottle of peroxide and knew it was going to be less than useless.

This wasn't an allergic reaction.

"Do something!" Heidi snapped.

Tara could barely close her mouth, much less think of what to do. She wasn't sure a doctor would even know how to handle this.

"I, I . . . take him to the kitchen. Now!"

Heidi helped Lenny up. His knees buckled once, twice, but he managed to walk.

"Lenny, put your hand in the sink," Tara said. "Heidi, hold onto his arm. I need to see if there's anything caught in his hand that's causing this."

She turned on the tap. The second the water touched his flesh, Lenny howled like a wounded werewolf.

"Jesusfuckshittingfucker!"

"Hold him steady," Tara said, bending over the sink to get a closer look. Heidi struggled to keep him from flailing. Lenny was twice her size, but she was determined.

The rupturing wounds were now leaking black—black!—pus. The smell coming off it was so bad, Tara almost puked. With her hand over her mouth, she went to touch it.

"No! Don't touch me!" Lenny shouted. "Don't get it on you!"

"Get what?"

Lenny's arm shot straight up. Heidi spun away. Lae squealed.

"God, it burns! Oh my God!"

Tara didn't know what to do. She tried to corral Lenny, but he was too strong, bouncing around the kitchen, gripping his forearm.

"I can't take it anymore!"

He slammed his hand down hard on the edge of the counter. A jet of viscous goo hit the ceiling as the back of his deformed hand split like a hot dog in a deep fryer.

"What are you doing?" Tara said, trying to keep her voice from hitting the hysterical range. Heidi was beside her, crushing her arm with both hands.

"I have...to get it...off!"

Lenny smashed his hand again and again, the flesh bursting at the seams, horrid fluids splattering the kitchen. Tara pushed Heidi back. The last thing she wanted was for that stuff to land on either of them.

And the stench. It was inhuman. If she hadn't experienced it herself, she'd swear it was impossible for that smell to come out of a living creature.

"Get off! Get off!"

To her horror, Tara saw that Lenny was close to accomplishing just that. His hand was hanging on by a few strands of tendons, the wrist bone cracking like walnuts.

He's going to bleed right out.

She looked over at Ollie's stove and turned on one of the burners, grateful it wasn't an electric range.

There was no point urging Lenny to stop now. It was best that he got the infected limb off.

Each time his hand hit the counter, Lae and Heidi screamed.

Which was nothing compared to Lenny's cry of agony and victory when the pulped hand finally broke free. His eyes rolled to the top of his head.

Heidi rushed past Tara and somehow managed to prop him up, directing him to the stove.

"You're not really going to do that, are you?" she said to Tara, eyeing the blue flame.

Tara looked for a clean spot on Lenny's arm. He was seconds away from passing out. She yanked his arm forward. His flesh sizzled. The hairs on his arm burned away. If the strange rot seeping out of his hand was bad before, it was even worse roasted.

Heidi gagged, a long line of thick spittle stretching from her mouth to the stovetop.

Tara's senses spiraled.

It was unreal.

Lenny went completely slack. It was as if he'd gained a hundred pounds in a nanosecond. He was too heavy for Tara and Heidi to keep propped up. He fainted, landing on top of Heidi.

The impact knocked the wind out of her.

Tara watched in horror as Lenny's arm flipped backwards. A stray drop of ichor sailed from the charred stump of Lenny's wrist, landing right on Heidi's tongue.

***

"Grab his gun!" Steven snapped, trying to keep his voice down.

Ollie managed to grab the barrel as a stunned Marco brought it up to shoot them. He instantly regretted it. Even over the howling wind, he could hear his skin sizzle. The barrel felt hotter than a pizza oven.

"Ollie? Steven?"

Marco looked like a sleepwalker who had been abruptly woken up.

"What the hell is going on?" Ollie said. "Who are those guys and why are you shooting them?"

The three of them took a quick look at the men who appeared ready to charge their position, guns drawn.

"Because they're shooting at me," Marco said. "I can't explain it all right now."

Ollie wasn't sure how much more he could take. First sharks. Then skulls. A tropical storm that wasn't supposed to be here. Now a half dozen dangerous looking guys with guns. What else could possibly go wrong?

We can all be dead, he thought.

A shiver ran down his spine.

"Ollie, we need to grab the girls and get on your boat," Steven said. His gaze was wild to the point of feral.

"We can't do that. The storm will swallow us up in minutes, if not seconds."

"Don't forget the shark," Marco murmured. "The storm is nothing compared to the shark."

As if on cue, the first drops of cold rain started to fall.

Ollie grabbed Marco. "What have you done, man?"

"It's a long story and you're not going to like it," Marco said.

"We don't have time for long stories," Steven said.

Marco pushed Ollie's hands away. "The only chance we have is to take them all out right now, while they're out in the open. Are either of you good with a rifle?"

Ollie wanted to smash his friend's head into the wall. "Are you kidding me?"

"No. I've never fired a rifle before. I'm missing them by miles."

"Don't look at me," Steven said, palms up. "And I'm certainly n-n-not going to start target practice with people."

Ollie snatched the rifle from Marco's hands. "We can't let them get to the women, if they're really out to kill us. They are, aren't they?"

Marco avoided Ollie's gaze. "I . . . I don't know. I'm not even sure they knew the island is inhabited. It's just supposed to be a drop off for them."

A drop off? All part of the long story that would have to wait.

"But I get the feeling that they won't stop until they make sure there's no one left to talk about what happened here," Marco added.

"Just fucking great," Ollie spat.

Thunder rumbled long and low.

Ollie dared to look around the corner again. This time, he spotted a boat not far from shore. It bobbed violently as the ocean grew more and more restless. The men on the beach, the definition of a ragtag crew of ne'er-do-wells, slowly made their way to the lab.

He thought of every bad guy extra he'd ever seen in movies with Caribbean thugs. One of them even looked a little like a younger Danny Trejo when he was in that Harrison Ford stuck-on-an-island movie, *Six Days, Seven Nights*. He'd been one of the smugglers out to kill Ford and Anne Heche.

But these smugglers or whatever they were hadn't taken a shot since he'd stopped Marco.

Was Marco the bad guy here? Were they only defending themselves? If Ollie shot them, would he be shooting innocent men, even though they looked far from it? And why were they here in the first place?

He rubbed some grit from his eyes.

No. They were all bad guys, Marco included. He knew Marco had run into hard times, but he never thought it was something like this. Whatever the hell this was.

One of the men at the rear shouted something, pointing at the water.

Ollie motioned for Marco and Steven to look as well.

The shark was back.

The dorsal fin circled the jouncing boat, the tip of the fin level with the highest point of the ship. In fact, the fin alone was almost bigger than the entire boat.

And Ollie knew there was so much more just under the surface.

A man with a long wiry beard shouted something and they all ran toward the water. The boat headed eastward, trying to get away from the shark. Ollie saw a few men on the boat running around the deck. He couldn't hear them, but he could imagine the rising panic in their voices.

The beached men followed the retreating boat, a few of them taking impotent shots that were sucked up by the turgid Pacific.

"They're leaving," Steven said.

"But not for long," Ollie said. "They're sure as hell not getting on that boat. Which means they'll be stranded here . . . and pissed."

"Just like I knew . . ." Marco said.

"What?" Ollie said.

The giant shark suddenly breached the surface, the top half of its massive silver and gray body in full, terrifying view. Its mouth opened wide, massive teeth even visible from their vantage point, gums red and raw.

"Holy Christ!" Steven exclaimed as they watched the forward half of the boat disappear into the shark's mouth. It clamped it jaws down on fiberglass, wood and steel, snapping it as if it were kindling.

Ollie thought he spotted men jumping overboard into the blackening sea.

The remaining half of the boat tilted upward, its grasp on the surface shifting quickly.

The shark slipped under the water.

Ollie gasped when it leapt seconds later like a dolphin, using its body to smash the boat and everyone clinging to it to splinters. They watched in revulsion as it swam back and forth, like a man mowing the lawn, devouring everything in sight.

Steven tugged on the back of his shirt. "Come on, we have to go back while those guys are preoccupied."

He looked to Marco, who could only hang his head in shame.

"He's right," Marco said to the sand at their feet.

The rain kicked into another gear, coming down in sheets. The temperature had dropped at least five degrees in the past few minutes. Ollie shivered, but he was pretty sure it was from shock.

"Steven, go to my house and make sure you lock everything up. Stay away from the windows and keep the lights out."

"What are you guys going to do?"

Ollie ground his molars, counting to five until the pain made his eyes twitch. "There isn't any choice. We're going to clean up Marco's mess."

***

The beast felt the changes in the ocean as the storm raged overhead. The charged atmosphere excited it, confused it.

But nothing could match its hunger and need to feed.

There was more meat and foul substances floating and swirling around the ragged bits. The beast masticated them all without prejudice.

Its olfactory senses scanned the water for any sign of what it craved above all others. There could perhaps be more farther out, but its brain would not let its body go past the boundary of the island.

For now, there were still the withering remnants of fresh blood. They would have to do.

CHAPTER NINETEEN

Steven ran into the biting wind, lungs burning, the skies opening up and dumping what seemed like decades of hoarded rain on the island. The cold realization that there was no way off Grand Isla Tiburon hit him hard.

They didn't just need to find a way to wait out the storm.

Now they had to avoid being spotted by those men. Who the hell were they?

"Damn you, Marco," he spat, water spraying from his lips.

That fucking Jersey wheeler-dealer had screwed them all. It was one thing when he messed with his own life. But now...

The door to Ollie's house was open.

He stepped inside to another nightmare.

Lenny was passed out on the couch, covered in a sheen of sweat. What looked like a torn up sheet was wrapped around his right hand. The sheet was stained red and black.

Heidi sat in a chair, her head between her legs, Tara rubbing her back. There was a bowl at her feet. Heidi kept spitting into it.

Lae stood apart from them, hands clasped together in what he could only assume was a silent prayer.

"What the fuck happened?"

The women looked up at him, startled. Heidi sprang from the chair and threw her arms around his neck.

She tried to speak but her sobbing made it impossible to understand her.

He looked to Tara who was the only one not shocked or in hysterics.

"Lenny's hand was infected," she said, looking down at him.

"Infected? With what?"

"I don't know. Whatever it was, it basically devoured his hand. He...he...it's gone. We had to cauterize it, and he passed out."

Her eyes drifted to the kitchen. He followed her gaze, biting his tongue when he saw the blood and other dark, cancerous stains painting the walls and cabinets.

"Is Heidi okay?"

She trembled in his arms, her face pressed to his rain soaked chest.

Tara crouched next to Lenny to inspect the makeshift bandage. He noticed she was careful not to touch it.

She replied, "Yes. I...I don't know."

Heidi took a deep breath and pulled away just enough to look into his eyes. She sure as hell didn't look all right.

"It got in my mouth," she sputtered.

He held her head in his dripping hands.

"What got in your mouth, honey?"

She pointed at Lenny. "The stuff that was in him. Oh God, I think I'm going to be sick."

Lae broke her prayer, scooped up the bowl and handed it to Heidi, who made quick work of filling it up. He couldn't help but stare into its contents as if they were tealeaves, foretelling the future of his wife's health. It was just a pink and tan froth of meals past and bile.

With everything that he'd walked in to, he'd forgotten why he was there in the first place.

"Tara, Lae, you n-need to turn out the lights and lock the doors. Now!"

"Why? Where are Ollie and Marco?" Tara asked.

"There are men on the island. Men with guns. I don't kn-know who the fuck they are or why Marco was shooting at them."

Lae hurried about the room, snapping the lights off.

"Wait," Tara said. "Marco was shooting people? That doesn't make any sense."

Steven lifted Heidi into his arms as if she were a wounded child and carried her to the bedroom. "Yeah, well add it to the list of things that don't make sense on this fucked up island," he said as he stormed off.

***

Ollie was nothing but a tight ball of rage.

Rage at his friend Marco, the man he'd given a second chance to and had used it to spit in his face—in all their faces.

Rage at the strange men and the threat they brought with them.

Rage at the giant shark that had swum from the depths of hell to ruin their paradise.

Rage at yet another atrocity left behind by the US military. What had the Marshall Islands done to deserve the hand that had been dealt them?

And rage at God himself for sending this storm their way. The rain was coming down so hard, he could barely see ten feet in front of him. He had to keep blinking to clear the water from his eyes. He couldn't hear a damn thing over the rain and wind. He knew that Marco was still behind him because he could feel his hand on his shoulder.

They crept along the beach, now hiding behind a small dune. He couldn't see where the men had gone.

A torrent of questions swirled around his brain, questions Marco could answer, but he didn't want to shout them on the off chance the men would hear him.

"No worries, all you have to do is kill six men and everything will be fine."

"What?" Marco said, his lips close to his ear.

Ollie shook his head, waving him back.

He worried that if Marco pressed him, he'd ram the butt of the rifle in his face.

Checking to make sure they were clear—at least as far as he could see—he slipped out from behind the dune, running in a crouch. He took a quick glance at the water, gray skies melting into a gray ocean.

Somewhere out there, that shark was munching on what was left of the men and that boat. The storm meant nothing to it. He wondered if it could still be hungry, or if it would move on.

Fat fucking chance.

***

"Heidi's still throwing up," Steven announced.

I don't blame her, Tara thought.

She would have to keep an eye on her. After what happened to Lenny, she couldn't imagine ingesting that goo being benign.

"Is everything locked?" he asked.

"Just the door, Mr. Steven," Lae said. "There aren't locks on the windows."

Tara was surprised there was even a lock on the door. Realistically, what would have been the purpose?

"Lae, close the blinds and get the hell away from the window," Steven said.

Poor Lae put her hands on her head and went about shutting blinds and shades.

"Steven, did anything happen to Ollie or Marco?" Tara asked.

"N-n-no. They're fine."

"So where are they?"

"I think Ollie was going to try to take those guys out."

"Go back. Who are *those guys*?"

"How the fuck am I supposed to know?" Spittle collected on the corners of his mouth. He looked about ready to break. Tara made it a point not to push him.

"Okay. Okay. So there are guys with guns. Are they headed this way?"

Steven stalked the room, breathing heavy. "They will eventually. There's just so far you can go here. That goddamn shark ate their boat and everyone on it."

Christ. Tara was hoping the Megalodon had decided to head for deeper waters and more plentiful food sources. She knew it was insane to think there was a prehistoric Megalodon out there, but until she was proven otherwise, she was sticking with it.

Besides, it didn't matter what she thought.

Whatever it was, it was bigger than anything anyone had ever seen, hungry as hell, nasty, and apparently territorial.

As if that wasn't enough to worry about.

The windows shook as the storm kicked up its assault on the island.

"I hope to God they didn't skimp on the building materials," Tara said.

Steven stopped his pacing, clenching and unclenching his fists. He parted the blinds just enough to stare out the window, the day turning to night in the blink of an eye. "We're gonna find out real soon."

Tara went into the kitchen, wrapping her hands in dishtowels. She rifled through the drawers.

"What are you doing?" Steven asked.

"If we have strange men out there with guns, we need to find something to defend ourselves with. Kitchens have knives. Knives kill."

She found a meat cleaver, butcher knife and several steak knives in a drawer.

She carried them to the coffee table.

"Lae, Steven, take one."

Steven was quick to grab the cleaver. Lae was far more tentative, taking a steak knife.

"No," Tara said to her. "You take the butcher knife. I'll find something else."

Which she did. It was a meat tenderizer. It wasn't much, but it would have to do. She slipped a couple of steak knives in her back pocket, just in case.

Be careful when you sit, she thought.

"The rain is really coming down," Steven said, peeking between the blinds. Tara took a look for herself.

She'd never seen anything like it, at least in real life. This was the stuff of cataclysm movies.

"The tide is coming in really high," she said, watching the beach get eaten away second by second. If this kept up, they'd be flooded within the hour. "Lae, what do you do when storms like this hit?"

Lae fiddled with the meat cleaver. "We have a shelter on higher ground. My home has had several devastating storms over the past ten years. We've lost many, many homes."

"Is there higher ground on this island?" Steven asked.

Lae looked down, shaking her head. "Maybe not high enough."

"Ungh, what's happening?"

Lenny stirred on the couch. Tara wished she had some painkillers on hand. He'd need them once he came fully awake.

She left the window to sit beside him.

"Try to go back to sleep. We're taking care of things."

When he tried to sit up, a wave of agony washed over his face. He looked down at his bandage-covered stump as if he were just remembering what had happened.

"Does it hurt?" Tara asked.

He was still sweating profusely. "Not as bad as it did before."

She didn't think she'd ever get the image of Lenny smashing his hand to wet pieces out of her memory.

"Why is Steven holding a knife and looking like he's about to shit himself?" Lenny asked.

Tara almost laughed.

"It appears we've ended up in one of the deeper levels of hell," Tara said.

Lenny moved his arm and slammed his eyes shut, biting down on the pain.

Heidi came stumbling back into the living room. A line of vomit stained the front of her shirt.

"Steven?" she mumbled, looking like she was about to pass out.

Her skin had gone from pale to a disturbing jaundice.

"Heidi, why don't you sit down," Tara said.

The house shook as an exceptionally violent gust of wind roared like a lion. Tara gritted her teeth at the sound of chunks of the roof breaking loose. A window in another room shattered. It was like standing too close on a platform as a train barreled past.

Lenny grabbed onto her arm with his remaining hand.

The wind kept coming and coming, until she was sure the house was going to break apart under the huffing and puffing of the Big Bad Wolf.

CHAPTER TWENTY

The storm was getting harder and harder to fight. A couple of times, Ollie was pushed backward, slamming into Marco, who was never far behind. They couldn't stay here much longer.

"We have to go back," he said to Marco.

"Okay."

His only hope was that the storm would wash the men out to sea, where the shark would then take care of the rest. It wasn't too much to ask, was it?

Maybe he'd used up all his luck when he won the lottery.

It sure as hell seemed like it.

Marco patted his shoulder excitedly. Ollie almost elbowed him in the throat. Marco wasn't high on his list of favorite people at the moment.

Instead, he looked to where Marco was pointing.

Through the steady sheets of rain, they saw the six men turn from the beach. The water was creeping closer and closer. Pretty soon, there wouldn't be a beach.

Pretty soon, there won't be an island, Ollie said to himself.

The rain had turned into a deluge. Noah would have shaken in his boots if he were here right now.

They watched the men trudge deeper into the island in single file, keeping close enough to grab onto the man in front if needed.

They're headed right for the bungalows!

Ollie's chest tightened, his blood chilling.

He couldn't let that happen.

"Let's go," he said, grabbing hold of Marco's collar. His friend nodded resolutely, sticking close.

It was hard going, the storm trying to push them back to the derelict lab. Taking the shorter route, they made it to their custom-made civilization before the interlopers. When Ollie finally spotted the small complex of houses, his heart caught in his throat.

Bits and pieces of each of the small, comfortable bungalows were breaking loose, violently sucked up into the storm. He watched in horror as all their hard work was yanked into the vengeful sky.

It figures. Why not finish us off entirely?

"No!" Marco shouted.

He ran ahead of Ollie, kicking up wet sand, headed straight for Ollie's darkened house.

Ollie looked about before following, making sure the strange men weren't close by. If he couldn't see them, odds were they couldn't see him.

They both arrived at Ollie's door at the same time, crashing into it, panting. Marco pounded on the door with his fist.

"Open up! Open up!"

He just wants to save his own skin, Ollie thought, sickened by his former friend's cowardice.

Tara flung the door open.

Ollie was never happier to see someone in his entire life.

She looked equally relieved and happy to see him.

"Get in!" she shouted, slamming the door behind them.

The storm howled at their back. Ollie leaned against the door, trying to collect himself.

Tara melted into him. "Thank God you're all right."

"They're...they're coming," Marco blurted.

"Who?" Lenny asked. He looked like two weeks of warmed dog turd.

What's wrong with his hand?

"Shit," Steven barked, slamming his fist into a wall.

The house shuddered. Ollie could feel the foundation weakening as the storm blared on. He wasn't sure how much more the structure could take.

"What do we do?" Tara asked. He looked into her pleading, emerald eyes and wanted to melt. There was no way he was going to let anything happen to her.

"The lab!" Ollie exclaimed.

"The lab? We just came from there," Marco protested.

The sound of crashing glass and roof tiles being pried free by the wind helped Ollie's case. "Yes, it's the most solid thing on the island. Plus, there are no windows. It's the safest place to be."

"That's what you fucking think," Steven said. Heidi looked like she'd been run over by a train. She rose weakly from her chair and joined her husband's side.

"He's right," Lenny said. Sweat rolled off his face as he sat up. "That place is solid as can be."

Tara looked at him. "You think you can make the walk?"

Lenny shrugged, getting unsteadily to his feet. "Not like I have a choice."

Ollie opened the door, searching for any sign of the men. They weren't here yet. Or they could be a dozen yards away. He couldn't tell through the curtain of rain.

At least at the lab, they only had to secure and guard the one door. With the way things were progressing, Ollie's little dream house would be nothing but kindling in a few hours. Let the armed men who had trespassed on his paradise enjoy the bungalows while they lasted.

Ollie gripped the rifle, biting down on his lower lip so hard, he tasted copper.

"Okay, we're going to the lab. Everyone has to hold onto the person in front of them. I'll take the lead. I saw the way those guys were walking. We'll just skirt around them. Let them find refuge in one of the houses. It'll be a short-lived shelter."

As if on cue, a jagged crack zigzagged from the top of one of the living room walls right down to the floor.

"I don't want to go back there," Heidi said. She clapped her hand over her mouth, holding back a wave of nausea.

"We don't have a choice," Ollie said. The first thing he'd ask once they secured the lab was what had happened to Lenny and Heidi.

Steven jabbed a finger towards Lenny. "Just keep him away from her."

Tara narrowed her eyes at him. "It's not his fault."

"Bullshit!"

Ollie got between them. "Stop! We don't have time for this. I'll get flashlights and candles." Darting around the bungalow, he gathered them up and tossed them in a canvas bag. It was an oversized bag from Aldi supermarket. He'd brought it along with him as a little memento from Minnesota. Money had always been tight and Aldi was the cheapest place to shop in the state. It was a reminder of where he'd come from.

He only had two flashlights, but the dozen candles would come in handy. He also threw in two lighters and a pack of matches.

Tara said, "Marco, help me with Lenny."

Marco was still as a statue, staring off into space and gnawing on his thumb. A line of blood rolled down the digit. Ollie nudged him with the rifle. "Help her, asshole!"

Marco and Tara each took an arm, ushering Lenny forward. Steven, Heidi and Lae were right behind them.

"Get ready," Ollie said. He took Lae by the hand. She squeezed him tight. "This isn't going to be fun."

***

The rain came down so hard it hurt.

Lenny tried to shield his face with his good arm but it was useless. It felt like being pelted with BBs. When the rain hammered his stump, the pain spiked even more, which seemed impossible to believe it could get worse.

It was probably a good thing. Without the pain, he just might pass out. His legs didn't feel attached to his body. He moved, willing his legs to put one foot in front of the other, but it was like watching everything from a distance. Thank God Tara and Marco were holding him up.

As they abandoned Ollie's house, he thought he spotted a dark figure moving swiftly to their right.

The top half of a palm tree tumbled past them, nearly clipping Steven.

The figure was gone.

If that was one of the men Ollie was talking about, they'd gotten out with seconds to spare.

The trek to the lab felt like hours. So much rain was coming down, he worried he would drown if he were to open his mouth too wide. As it was, he sucked in deep, pained breaths between his teeth. He didn't even know they were near the lab until they were right outside the open door.

Lenny looked down. The shoreline was now just a couple of feet away. Small rivers branched outward, searching for more land to claim. Where had the beach gone? How could at least fifty yards disappear so fast?

He spotted an olive bag floating nearby. Where had that come from? Whatever was inside looked bulky. There was another one on the little bit of beach that was left. If he felt any better, he would check it out. As it was, he could barely stand.

"Are you fucking kidding me?" Steven shouted.

A momentary break in the curtain of rain revealed a giant shark fin slicing through the encroaching water. It was too far away to be a threat, but way too close for comfort.

"Everybody inside," Ollie said, standing beside the doorway, rifle at the ready. He waved them in. Marco and Steven had to help him shut the door against the wind.

Tara guided Lenny to a wooden chair. His stump hit the side of the chair, making him cry out in agony.

"I'm so sorry," Tara said.

"Not your fault." His eyes rolled in his head and for a second there, he thought it was lights out.

The second the door closed, they were encased in utter darkness.

Heidi whispered something. Lenny couldn't make it out. When he moved his feet, he heard water sloshing.

A square of blue light penetrated the pitch. Steven had turned his cellphone on, holding it over their heads, shining it down on them. Ollie dove into the bag he'd put on the reception counter. He handed a lighter to Lae who lit a few candles. They were the fat ones in glass jars that gave off scents that always gave Lenny a headache.

Headaches were the least of his worries.

At least those candles could burn for hours and hours. It might be a long while before they left the lab.

His entire right arm had gone numb. He wondered if the infection was spreading up his arm, zeroing in on his heart.

There was no way he was going to look. What was the point?

Now that they had light, they could see the steady stream of water seeping under the door.

"We have to secure it," Ollie said. "Steven, Marco, find anything you can and we'll pile it up."

Ollie used the bag to tie around the handle, securing the other end to something protruding from the wall to keep it closed.

Lenny wished he could help, but it was taking great effort just watching them toss chairs and tables and file cabinets against the door. The constant splashing of their feet as they ran to the adjoining room and back was almost hypnotizing.

There was pressure on his left shoulder. "Stay with us, buddy."

Tara smiled at him, but it did little to mask her worry.

"I wish I knew what the hell was all over those skulls," he said.

She looked past him, to where the heart of the lab waited in the darkness.

"Yeah, well I don't think we should go in there to find out. Whatever weird shit they were doing in the fifties is going to remain a mystery."

"But maybe if we find out what it is, Heidi and I can be saved."

Heidi stiffened at the sound of her name. She was no longer threatening to throw up, but she looked terrible. Dark circles rimmed her eyes. Her cheeks were dotted with little pink dots – busted capillaries from all that power vomiting.

Lae cupped a candle in her hands, held just under her bosom. Her eyes were glassy, distant. Lenny wouldn't be surprised if she was in shock. He nodded his head toward her.

Tara said to Lae, "Are you all right? Come on, why don't you sit down?" She tried to usher her to the remaining chair in the room. The padding was most likely riddled with mold, but beggars can't be choosers.

The Marshallese woman didn't budge.

"It's Lotano," she whimpered. Tears sprang from her eyes, running down her cheeks like rainwater.

Tara tried to console her. "I'm sorry, honey. What's Lotano?"

As her hands shook, the light from the candle quivered. She tried to speak but nothing intelligible came out. Everyone circled her but Lenny. He wasn't sure he'd ever get up out of the chair.

"Lae," Lenny said as loud as he could muster. He held up his ruined arm. "Did the Lotano do this?"

She shook her head.

So much for uncovering the mystery of what's killing me . . . and Heidi, he thought, frustrated.

Lae looked to the pile of junk against the door.

Composing herself, she said, "Lotano is the, the slave of the ocean goddess Mannanu. When she is displeased, she can control the winds and the clouds. She calls forth Lotano to set things right."

"What the fuck is she talking about?" Steven said, hands on his hips, staring down at the distraught woman.

Lenny understood. Closing his eyes, feeling his pulse beating against the charred end of his arm, he said, "She means the shark, dumbass. That shark is Lotano."

Lae nodded vigorously, dropping the candle. Tara took her in her arms.

Sighing as he contemplated giving in to the unrelenting pull of bleak, blessed unconsciousness, Lenny said, "Well, at least we know what to call it."

There was a tremendous crash in the belly of the lab. All eyes turned to the open door, unable to pierce the gloom into the adjoining sections. The floor rumbled.

It appeared Lotano knew they were here, and it was making its way to the cylinder to get them.

CHAPTER TWENTY-ONE

"Empty," the Jamaican, Bami, reported breathlessly.

"All of them?" Nacho said.

Bami nodded.

This island was supposed to be deserted. Now, not only did they have someone trying to kill them, but it appeared people were actually living out here.

In one way, it was a small relief. Regular people defending their home were a lot easier to kill than other men like himself.

Oh, and he would kill whoever had shot at them. He would kill them all.

But where the hell had they gone?

Nacho still couldn't wrap his mind around the creature that had destroyed their boat. It had been so startling, they had forgotten all about their coke-laden gunnysacks.

That it ate the crew didn't bother him a bit. They were all next to worthless. None of them would be missed.

That whale, because what else was that big, had eaten their only means of getting off this hell. And with the coke probably washed out to sea, they'd need something seaworthy and big enough to get them way the fuck away from here, or anywhere close to civilization.

Retirement had come earlier than he expected.

The roof groaned as a heavy gust slammed the bungalow.

"What happened in here?" The Somali, Cambuulo, waved them into the kitchen.

"It smells like the devil's shit," Escargot, the dusky Frenchman said, waving his hand in front of his nose.

There was black muck and blood everywhere. Nacho spied a lumpy mass on the floor.

"Is that a hand?"

Mofongo peered over his shoulder. They both kept a good distance from the vile-smelling room.

"It kinda looks like it. I think I see fingers. But look at it. Even Akura's skin isn't that black."

Nacho's scar felt as if it had been dipped in poison ivy. He worked at it until he could feel the flesh split.

What the hell was going on in this place?

The bungalow shook violently.

"This place is going to collapse!" Bami exclaimed.

Nacho looked out the window as an uprooted palm tree speared the front of the nearest bungalow. Next, the roof peeled away like an orange rind.

"We're getting the fuck out of here," Nacho growled.

"Where the hell are we gonna go?" Escargot asked, his usual calm demeanor cracking from the wild turn of events.

Nacho spat onto the kitchen floor. "The only place stronger than this storm."

***

Ollie was so amped, he felt as if his bones were about to leap free from his skin. He took a few deep breaths and stood before Lae, trying his best to exude a sense of calm in the literal storm.

Everyone's attention was fixated on the hub of the lab.

It wasn't as if the shark could pop out of that big tank and wriggle its way in here. The Land Shark was a Saturday Night Live skit, and there was nothing funny at all about what was going down on his damn island.

"Lae," he said, taking her hands in his. "You've seen that shark before?"

With downcast eyes, she slowly shook her head. He gave her hand a gentle squeeze.

"So how do you know it's this Lotano?"

That got her to look up. It seemed as if everyone in the room was holding their breath. The tension in the room was denser than lead.

"A shark that big can only be Lotano, Mr. Ollie," she began. "The heavens are angry. This happened before, in my parents' time. It was not long after the war, when they were testing their bombs. Lotano returned after a century's long slumber. He terrorized the islands. Many, many people went out on the water and never returned. Then a great storm came, washing away whatever Lotano couldn't reach. When it was over, Lotano disappeared."

Steven slapped the sides of his head. "This is crazy."

Ollie ignored him. He noticed Marco had broken away from the group, hovering by the piles of office furniture jammed against the door, his thumb in his mouth like a child.

"So this shark is no stranger to these waters," Ollie said. He looked to Tara. "You think it's a mutated shark from all the radiation the military poured into the atmosphere and water? You know, like Godzilla?"

She rolled her eyes. "I seriously doubt that Megalodon is Godzilla. If it were the end product of nuclear fallout from the fifties, there just hasn't been enough time for a mutation that extreme to have enough generations to cause it to grow that big."

"Maybe the military spread the old myth around to keep people away from the island," Heidi said. Her contribution surprised Ollie. A few seconds ago, she barely looked capable of coherent thought. Sealing themselves off from all of the madness and taking a moment to catch their breath was helping settle her down.

When he moved a candle closer to her, he had to stifle a gasp. She looked horrid. The skin on her neck was bruising, as if someone had tried to strangle her. Bloodshot eyes stared back at him.

"But then what about the missing people?" Tara said.

Lae went quiet.

Steven said, "That's easy. They off a few here and there to make the story seem real."

Ollie vehemently shook his head. "Look, I know terrible things were done here, but I honestly believe it wasn't intentional. Hindsight is 20/20. They had no idea of the long-term consequences from radiation. I can't see our military willingly offing innocent civilians just to prop up a cover story."

"Don't place so much trust in them," Steven said. "They sold this bridge to you, didn't they?"

Ollie bit his tongue. Steven had him there.

Lenny coughed, then hissed in pain. He cradled his right arm against his chest.

"Maybe the *nuclear testing* was the cover story," he said.

"Come again?" Ollie asked. Lenny wasn't well. He was probably delirious. Ollie didn't want to dismiss him and make things worse.

He tried to sit up but ended up collapsing back into the chair. "I'm not saying all those nukes were a cover story. But maybe there was more going on here than history tells us. Just think. We snagged all those Nazi scientists in Project Paperclip and put them to work on jet propulsion, nuclear energy, biochemical weapons, you name it. Most of these guys were straight eggheads, only interested in progressing science, whether for the Nazis or the Americans. It didn't matter to them so long as they had a place to do their work and financial support."

A racking cough stopped him. Ollie noticed the bandage at the end of his arm turning red. Tara noticed it too. She quickly went to his side, examining it without touching it.

"Take it easy, buddy," she said.

When Lenny settled down, he resumed his theory. "But there were other, more esoteric guys who came here. We saw in the ledger that the place was crawling with Germans. Some of those Nazi freaks were into eugenics and altering genetic lines, mixing it with the occult and paranormal. Maybe, just maybe, they found a way to bring back the Magalodon. Why? To weaponize it, of course. But something that big can't be controlled. Not to a large extent. It gets loose, a storm hits, and an old myth is reborn. That might explain why this lab is one giant fortress. They didn't want anyone seeing inside. I just can't figure out where the shark went all this time and why it's back now."

Steven, who had been pacing in the dark, said, "Because six dipshits decided to make this place a home and woke the damn thing up. It doesn't take a genius to figure that out."

Ollie snapped his fingers. "Cooter, you may be right. When I hit that button on top of the tank, remember all those sounds and the place rumbling? Then those bones and goop spilled into it."

"So it was in suspended animation?" Tara said.

Shrugging, Ollie said, "I don't know."

"You rang the dinner bell," Lenny said. "Woke it up and fed it. I'll bet whatever was on those bones was some kind of Megalodon chow they cooked up in the lab. It would explain why it was so…so wet. If it had been up there for decades, everything would have dried out by now."

Lae raised her hand as if she were in a classroom.

"Lotano is not something from a science lab. It lives deep in the ocean . . . in every ocean."

The lab vibrated again. They heard a tremendous influx of water spill over the cylinder two rooms away. It could have been a gust from the storm.

Or not.

"Guess it doesn't like us talking about it," Heidi said.

"You think it can hear us?" Ollie asked.

"I'm no shark expert, but I'd say no way," Tara replied. She smoothed some sweaty hair from Lenny's forehead.

Lenny said, "With the storm brewing, there's nothing around for it to eat. So it's coming back to the place where it was trained to get its reward."

"I don't know what's crazier—a genetically resurrected Megalodon, or a vengeful creature sent by an angry goddess," Ollie said.

"Who gives two shits?" Marco blurted. He kicked something small and metallic across the room. "Either way, we're fucked."

Tara motioned for him to be quiet. "The name of this lab was . . . it was . . . Let me think—Deep Sea Rebirth. Holy crap. That's what it said on the ledger. It didn't make any sense to me before. If Lenny's right . . ."She lapsed into silence.

So much water began to run under the sole door to the outside, it sounded as if the place had sprouted a creek.

Ollie put his arm around her. "And here we are, locked in a giant tomb with a killer shark below us and a half dozen killers outside."

His mind ran through so many possible scenarios, his temples throbbed.

He was going to find a way to get them all safely out of this.

Judging by the steady flow of seawater spilling into the lab from both sides, he was going to have to think awfully damn fast.

***

Steven closed the door to the other room so they couldn't hear what was going on deeper in the lab as much. Each splash of water or thud had them jumpier than neurotic cats.

He'd been acting like an ass all day, but Tara was grateful he did it. The way things echoed in the empty lab, she was imagining all sorts of things going on in there. She kept picturing the massive shark shattering the tank, ramming through each section of the lab until it swallowed them whole.

Sure, it would die from being out of the water, but only after they had suffered one of the worst deaths imaginable.

Wrapping her arms around herself, she checked on Lenny and Heidi. Lenny appeared to be rallying. Some color had come back into his face. Or was it just a trick of the poor, flickering light?

Heidi sat next to Steven on the floor with her head between her legs. She'd started to wheeze and was disturbingly quiet.

Tara could only imagine what that poison was doing to her. She wished there was a way she could help them both, other than to sear a limb closed and wrap a bandage.

She crept to the entrance, careful not to trip on the legs of the chairs the guys had thrown into the pile. The storm raged on outside, battering the door, water sluicing in between the cracks.

"When the hell is it going to let up?"

"I wish I remembered to bring the radio," Ollie said, cursing under his breath. The rifle was slung over his shoulder. Every few minutes, he gave it a thorough once-over. Normally, Tara would have brought it to his attention so he could stop his obsessive behavior. Right now, it was wisest to make sure the rifle was okay, as it was their only means of defense if those men decided to seek shelter in the lab.

The men.

They'd been so obsessed with the Megalodon, or Lae's Lotano, no one had bothered to ask Marco who had invaded their island.

"Marco," she said. "Who were those men you were shooting at?"

Keeping to the shadows, it was hard for her to see his face, but it looked like he sneered at her. "Does it matter?"

"Hell yes, it matters," she snapped.

Ollie came up next to her. "She's right, Marco. Everyone in here has a right to know. All of our lives are in jeopardy because of you."

For a second, in the silence, Tara thought Marco was going to deflect and put their attention back on the shark or the storm. To his credit, he didn't.

He balled his fists, looking like he wanted to fight them rather than tell the truth. Then he shook his head, heaved a great sigh and leaned against the reception desk.

"You guys should know I've been nothing but a total fuckup."

"We figured that," Steven said, cradling Heidi's head in his lap. Black vines crept under her flesh, reaching toward her cheeks and mouth.

"College was it for me, man," Marco said. "It was supposed to just be the last rung on the ladder until we were set free and really made something of ourselves. And for a while, it was. Then I threw it away. And what I somehow managed to hold onto was taken from me."

Staring at the floor, he recounted in agonizing detail everything from his rise in business to the love of his life, Mazie. A love he dishonored by cheating on her the very night she died. It was all a fast run downhill from there. Tara didn't know whether she wanted to hug him or throttle him. The brash New Jerseyan with the sharp wit and formidable IQ she'd briefly dated in college was gone. She couldn't find even the tiniest spark left in her old friend.

Both hands on the rifle, Ollie said, "So you're saying these guys are goons that work for this Jamaican crime boss, Donovan Bailey?"

Marco shook his head. "The smugglers may work for someone else who is just doing business with Bailey. It was all on a need-to-know basis. I didn't need to know and I didn't wanna know."

Ollie suddenly attacked Marco, grabbing him by the collar and driving him to the floor. Tara and Lae rushed to break them up.

"You fucking son of a bitch!" Ollie spat. "I trusted you. I sank everything I have into this island, into our futures, and you . . . you tainted it!"

Rearing back, Ollie punched Marco in the face.

Thwack!

Then again. And again.

Tara tried to grab his arm, but it was too powerful, too fueled by rage for her to stop.

Marco didn't even raise an arm to defend himself.

More and more blood poured from his nose and mouth as Ollie pummeled him, cursing the day he ever met him.

"Steven, help me!" Tara shouted.

Lae fell onto her rump with a loud cry after she lost her grip on Ollie's shoulders.

"Fuck him," Steven shot back, pulling Heidi closer.

Lenny rose unsteadily from the chair. "That's enough, Ollie," he said, though not loud enough for a raging Ollie to hear.

Ollie jumped to his feet, panting, Marco's blood dripping from his fists. Tara stumbled backwards, falling into Lenny. They collapsed into the chair. Somehow, it didn't break.

Instead of walking away, Ollie pointed the rifle in Marco's face, the muzzle inches from his nose.

"Tell me why I shouldn't kill you right here!" he shouted.

Tara extricated herself from Lenny and the chair. "Ollie, don't."

When he turned to her, she stopped. There was a fire burning in his eyes she'd never seen on another human being.

"Stay back," he ordered her. The rifle moved oh so slightly in her direction before he trained it back on Marco.

"Tell me now, Marco! Beg for your worthless life!"

Marco groaned, turning his head from side to side. His nose was in ruins, several of his front teeth hanging on by a thread.

"Just kill me," he sputtered, blood frothing from his cracked lips. "Do it, Ollie. You're right. I *am* worthless. I'm tired of hurting. Please . . . kill me."

Marco tumbled into uncontrolled sobbing, crimson bubbles blowing from his nostrils, popping and dripping down his face.

Ollie's arms trembled, or was it a trick of the candlelight?

Steeling himself, Ollie let out a cry that froze Tara's heart.

Lenny reached out for her, trying to get her behind him.

"Fuck!" Ollie screamed, pressing the rifle hard into the pulp of Marco's nose. Marco didn't flinch. He just kept crying.

With one last grunt, Ollie threw the rifle away. It clattered into the shadows. His legs buckled, and he collapsed next to Marco's prone body.

Tara realized she was crying. No one dared move or speak.

Marco's sodden bawling echoed in the musty room.

Ollie trembled, his voice shaking between ragged breaths. "You . . . ruined . . . us."

Tara crept toward Marco, leaning down to get a better look at his face. It was bad. He'd need multiple surgeries to repair his nose, dentures, and maybe even a plate in his cheeks if they were fractured. She hoped to God there wasn't any internal bleeding.

"Can you sit up?"

He tried to push her away.

She cupped her hands behind his neck and pulled slowly. "I don't want you sucking in all that blood."

She fought against her nurturing side, telling herself that Ollie was justified in beating him to a pulp.

A hand touched her shoulder. It was Ollie.

"I'm sorry," he said.

She gripped his hand.

In just a few hours, they were all broken, the island coming apart around them.

There was so much water on the lab floor. She imagined this sealed place filling up like a fish tank in no time.

Something knocked heavily on the door. Broken furniture shifted, scraping against the floor.

"Where's the rifle?" Ollie said, getting up to look for where he'd thrown it.

The banging continued.

It wasn't the wind.

Donovan Bailey's men were here.

INTERLUDE 1954

Even within the sealed fortress that was Deep Sea Rebirth—
Omega Lab, Dr. Laughton could hear the howling wind outside. The
sound of the ocean crashing furiously within the tank echoed
throughout the heart of the lab.

The Category-5 hurricane hadn't even touched down yet, and
already the island was in danger of being swallowed up.

The very air was charged with barely controlled panic. Men
were shouting, orders were being given and there was chaos
everywhere.

Dr. Laughton leaned against the doorway watching everything
unravel with calm indifference.

First, he was simply too sick to have the energy to get worked
up. In fact, all of the scientists that had been here since the start
were dying from radiation poisoning. They'd learned a lot about safe
handling of radioactive material in their time here, though too late to
save themselves. It didn't help that Dr. Mueller's toxic concoction
was deadlier than any plague known to man, reducing men to
screaming puddles of viscera in days if they touched it directly.

*And to think the Magelodon eats men infected with it to no ill
effect*, he thought. *In fact, it only makes it stronger. How can we
maintain dominance over a being like that?*

We can't, of course.

He wished Dr. Lancaster was able to get up to see everyone
running around like chickens with their heads cut off. The poor man
was confined to his bed, no longer capable of standing on his own
two feet. His body had finally given out two days ago. They'd learned
that there was no going home from here. The island would be their
grave, and they would take their secrets with them.

"You look quite content."

Dr. Laughton turned to find Dr. Mueller beside him, leaning on
his cane. He'd lost so much weight, he ironically resembled a death
camp survivor. His skin was a disturbing yellow, with red sores on
his arms and face.

"And you look like death warmed over . . . twice."

"They're evacuating the island," Dr. Mueller said. "Military
personnel only."

"I'm not surprised."

"I've had assurances they will come back once the storm passes."

Laughton laughed. "Mother Nature's given them the perfect excuse to finally pull the plug on your nightmare. They're never coming back."

Mueller coughed into his hand, his palm glistening with blood.

"They will . . . someday, when science catches up with our great achievement."

"You really think what we've done is a boon to mankind?"

"You Americans never had the mettle to strive for anything beyond your limited imaginations."

Laughton huffed. "Yes. Morality will do that to you."

"Morality is the panacea for the weak and feeble minded."

"Unlike your master race?"

Mueller scowled at him.

Taking a deep rattling breath, he headed toward the stairs that led to the top of the observation platform.

"Where do you think you're going?" Dr. Laughton called after him.

"If I'm going to die in this cursed tomb, I'll do so beholding my creation."

He watched the frail Nazi slowly make his way up the stairs. Laughton offered a silent prayer that the man's heart would simply give out, denying him his final wish.

But as Dr. Laughton had suspected long ago, there was no one to hear their prayers.

The ground trembled and water sloshed from the tank. Laughton caught snatches of conversations from the scrabbling seamen. All eyes avoided his gaze. They felt guilt knowing he was to be left behind. He wanted to tell them there was no cause for their shame. He was perfectly willing to die here. Sure, he'd give anything to be surrounded by his family just one last time, but he knew he was toxic. Any selfish intention to be with them would only curse them later.

Not that the military was in the habit of granting wishes.

He did hear that a tidal wave was heading their way and speculation that the entire island would be underwater before the hour was up.

Would the lab collapse?

He hoped to hell it would.

Breaking from his ruminations, he looked up to see Dr. Mueller had made it to the top. He took something out of his pocket.

It was a hypodermic needle.

No!

"Mueller, don't!" Laughton shouted, his voice too fragile to be heard.

He's injecting himself with the serum. Good God, he's going to unleash the creature!

Laughton grabbed a soldier as he ran past him.

"Son, I need you to shoot Dr. Mueller," he said, pointing to the top of the tank.

Dr. Mueller had completed the injection, throwing the needle aside.

"What?" the soldier, a kid who looked barely out of his teens, said.

"Shoot him now. He can't get into that tank."

"Sir, I can't just shoot a man."

Lashing out, Dr. Laughton went for his rifle. The move startled the man so much, he was able to pluck it from his hands.

A scientist, not a marksman, Dr. Laughton had seconds to take as many shots as he could before the soldier reclaimed his rifle.

He aimed it in the doctor's direction and pulled on the trigger again and again. Bullets pinged off the tank and the metal gangway.

Dr. Mueller looked down at him with a wolfish grin.

The rifle was ripped from Laughton's hands. He fell hard, the back of his head smacking into the wall.

He watched in horror as Dr. Mueller waved at him, toppling into the tank and out of sight.

"You're all going to die," Laughton said.

The soldier stood over him, hopping from one foot to the next as if unsure what to do.

Laughton saved him the trouble. "If you go with the evacuation team, you'll die." He saw the name patch on the soldier's jacket. HARDY.

"What's your name, son?"

"Chet . . . Chet Hardy."

Something thundered underneath the lab. The muted sound of twisted metal screeched from within the tank.

"Sir, I have to go."

Laughton grabbed hold of the man's pant leg. He gripped it with the remaining strength he had left.

"Please, listen to me. The Megalodon is breaking free. That goddamn Nazi has condemned you all. I don't know if the lab will withstand the storm, but it's better than being in the water when the creature is loose."

Chet Hardy's mouth screwed up tight. They were the only two people left in the main lab.

"You've seen what it does," Laughton said.

Hardy gave a solemn nod.

"Don't go in the water."

Laughton's hands grew too weak to hold the boy any longer. After everything that had happened these past five years, it was going to come down to saving one life. This stranger, a mere boy he had seen but never acknowledged before, would have to be his final act of grace.

If man had a soul and there was such a thing as judgment, would this be enough?

"I don't care about my damnation," Laughton said.

"Excuse me, sir?" Hardy said, leaning down to ease his eyelids open.

A great flood of water erupted from the tank, hammering them both. It knocked the wind out of him, his mouth filling with water.

Be safe, Chet Hardy, he thought, too weak to paddle his arms, drowning on sea water.

Be safe.

CHAPTER TWENTY-TWO

"Tara, Lae, you think you can get everyone into the other room?" Ollie barked. He stared ahead with the rifle aimed at the door.

The steady pounding at the door matched the beat of Lenny's frenetic pulse in his ears. "I'll be able to walk on my own."

Lae and Tara were having trouble getting Marco to his feet. Steven carried Heidi as if she were a bride about to be brought over the threshold.

"It's six against one," Tara said. "You can't stay here and hold them off."

"Watch me."

Everyone went into the adjoining room except Lenny. "I'm not going to leave you."

Ollie softened his stance. "Buddy, you're not well. Go."

Lenny found a piece of rebar on the floor. "But I'm not dead." *Yet.*

"If you stay here, you'll just get in the way," Ollie said. "You can barely stand as it is. How do you expect to fight guys with guns off when you—"

Lenny smirked through the throbbing in his right arm. "Have only one arm? I'm not exactly Conan, am I?"

"Hell, I'd take a Minion over you at this point." For a moment, Ollie smiled, but he quickly turned serious. "Look, I have the element of surprise. It's dark as hell in here and I'll bet they don't know I have a gun. I don't want to accidentally shoot you."

The door shuddered, opening just a crack as the pile of chairs shifted.

"Crap," Ollie spat, running toward the door. He looked at Lenny, who held the rebar high. "You're really not going to listen to me, are you?"

"Why start now?"

"Maybe I can discourage them. You think you can put your good shoulder into the door and try to wedge it shut when I give you the signal?"

Lenny looked for an opening amidst the tangle of furniture. "Yeah, I'm good."

Ollie peered through the slit in the door. The pounding increased. It sounded like the men were using their bodies as battering rams, picking up the pace now that they saw it was working.

"Just a little bit more," Ollie said. He bit his lower lip so hard, blood trickled down his chin.

He pressed the muzzle into the opening.

The door shifted, opening just a little wider.

"Get the fuck off my island," Ollie whispered, shoving the barrel through the gap.

He pulled the trigger.

The sound reverberated in the cement room. Lenny couldn't believe how loud it was.

Outside, men started shouting. One man screamed in agony.

Trying to catch his breath, Lenny said, "Jesus, Ollie. You just shot a guy."

"At least I hope I did."

He took the rebar from Lenny and jammed it as best he could in the slight gap between the door and the floor. Water continued to pour inside.

The pounding stopped.

They put their ears to the door. They couldn't hear anything other than the roar of the wind and the crash of waves.

"Maybe it's five to one now," Ollie said.

"If we're lucky, they'll head back to the bungalows."

"If there's anything left to head back to."

They waited ten minutes, silently listening for any sign that the men were still outside.

Lenny muttered, "I think they're gone."

"We're not that lucky."

Lenny looked down at where his right hand should be. How could it be that just twenty-four hours ago, he had two hands and was living in a paradise?

"We should head deeper in the lab," Ollie said. "This room is too big and there's no cover if they do come back."

"You join the military after we graduated or something?"

Ollie stepped away from the door. "No, but I watched a hell of a lot of war movies. I'm a big fan of *Kelly's Heroes* and *The Big Red One*."

"Yeah, well remember, this isn't a movie. You shoot people, they shoot back. And no one is going to yell cut just to save your ass."

Ollie slipped an arm around Lenny's waist. "Let's go."

They were about to open the door to the next room when the front door exploded in a hail of gunfire. Ollie dropped them to the ground. Lenny's stump hit the floor. He saw stars and galaxies and was almost swept into a black hole.

Bullets whizzed over their heads, pinging into the walls.

Through the haze of pain and fear, Lenny looked toward the door just as it came apart. A swirl of wind powered rain cascaded into the lab.

Behind it, the silhouettes of the men appeared, guns drawn. Two of them carefully stepped over the detritus.

He felt Ollie tugging at him.

"Time to get the hell out of here."

The meager light coming in from the gray world outside wasn't strong enough to reach to their end of the room. Ollie opened the door just enough for them to slip into the next room. He closed it as quietly as possible.

The room was empty.

***

Escargot's head was gone.

"Shit," Bami cried.

Nacho didn't care much for the Frenchman. That was why he'd made him try to get into the building first.

"Looks like we'll have to do this the hard way," Nacho said.

The people inside were shitting themselves. He felt it in his gut. Right now, they were probably scurrying like rats, scared by the sound their rifle made.

"Shark," Mofongo shouted, pointing.

A fin the size of a billboard cruised past them. So, it wasn't a whale that had destroyed their boat and eaten the crew.

"That's one big motherfucking shark," Mofongo said.

There wasn't much left of the beach. If they didn't get in there soon, they were going to be chum.

The five remaining men aimed their automatic weapons at the door.

Nacho screamed over the howling wind, "Fire!"

***

The moment they heard the gunfire, Steven forced everyone into the center room of the lab complex. He wanted to put as much distance between them and the men with the guns as possible. Tara resisted at first.

"We have to make sure Ollie and Lenny are okay!"

When she let go of Marco, who was riding the line between conscious and delirious, he slipped from Lae's grasp and hit the floor hard.

Steven managed to hold onto Heidi and latch onto Tara's arm, preventing her from opening the door.

From the sound of things, Steven was pretty damn sure Ollie and Lenny were as far from okay as they were from their real homes back in the states.

"Don't you dare," he hissed.

She struggled to break free from his grip.

"Get the fuck off me!"

"You want to get us all killed?" He tried to keep his voice down. "If they're still alive, they'll be right behind us. N-n-now, we have to get the hell out of this room. Maybe, if we keep going, we'll find a way out."

Heidi mumbled something. He looked down at her and had to keep himself from crying out. Her skin was bruising at an alarming rate. Her flesh was beginning to puff up, as if fluids were building up just under the surface.

Was she bleeding internally?

Putting his hand to her face, he recoiled. She was burning up.

"You have to do something," he pleaded to Tara.

The shooting outside had stopped.

"I don't even know what's wrong with her. I'm not a doctor."

Lenny had maybe saved himself by taking off his infected hand. Heidi had ingested whatever vile disease was created in this godforsaken lab. What the hell could Steven cut off her to save her?

Unable to speak without crying, Steven tugged Tara into the next room. "Please, help her," he said.

Without waiting for Tara's reply, he darted into the other room and grabbed Marco, Lae right on his heels.

"Hand me that flashlight," he said to Lae.

He shined it at the door. There was a deadbolt on the door. It was rusty, but he managed to slam it into place.

"It's better than nothing," he murmured.

Marco sat beside Heidi, his head resting on his drawn knees. What a fucking lot they turned out to be. If those men got in here, they were as good as dead.

"I'm going to look for a way to get to another room," Steven said. "Maybe there'll even be something they left behind that will explain what the hell is happening to Heidi."

Tara cradled Heidi's head to her chest. He noticed she was careful not to touch any of his wife's exposed skin. "Don't count on it. Whatever they were doing out here, they wanted it to remain a secret."

Steven punched the tank just above her head. Tara didn't flinch.

Pain rocketed up his arm.

"We have to try. At the very least, there has to be another way out."

"Well, you have fun looking for it," Tara replied sharply.

He took one last look at his blackening wife and ran along the tank.

The floor shook violently, knocking him off his feet. A great wave of water spilled from the top of the tank, soaking him to the bone.

If the gunshots were bad, the pummeling coming from inside the tank was far worse.

Somehow, the shark knew they were in here.

Lae's scream echoed in the lab.

There was another enormous concussion. A web of cracks etched along the floor. He scooted away from them, the flashlight's beam illuminating the disintegration of the structural integrity of the lab.

The Megalodon was coming for them, and it appeared nothing was going to stand in its way.

CHAPTER TWENTY-THREE

The creature had grown ravenous.

Yes, it had feasted on meat it found both in the darkened depths and dazzling bright surface. But they hadn't been enough.

The taste wasn't right.

Neither was the effect the food had on its body.

It had slept a long, long time. It needed to gorge to make up for the vast space of nothingness it had endured.

It knew it couldn't go far. Not now in its weakened state.

So it waited.

And waited.

And still, nothing came.

So it grew angry.

Ravenous.

Delirious.

***

Ollie was surprised when Lenny broke free from his grasp and ran alongside him to the other door. They trudged through ankle deep water. Pretty soon, it would reach their calves. He caught a glimpse of water running from a crack in a wall.

It was more like a mini waterfall.

"Feeling better?" he asked Lenny.

"For the moment. Funny how dudes coming in blazing with guns will get your ass moving."

Ollie wrapped his hand around the doorknob and pulled.

It didn't budge.

Lenny thumped the door with his remaining fist. "Guys, it's us."

Ollie was about to join in, his heart hovering somewhere near his tonsils, when it felt as if a bomb went off under the lab. They ended up on their asses.

"What the hell was that?" Lenny said, holding onto his bad arm.

"That seems to be the question of the day."

A series of concussions got them scrambling back to their feet. Ollie pounded the door with the butt of the rifle.

He knew what was making the lab quake. The last time he'd heard that sound was when he was dangling from the top of the tank.

"Open the fucking door!" he shouted, no longer concerned whether the men in the next room heard him.

"Hold on," he heard Tara say.

There was a dull scraping coming from the other side. He took a quick look behind them to make sure they hadn't been followed . . . yet.

Maybe that little shockwave got them to rethink going any further.

God knows, if he didn't have to join his friends, he'd have no desire to go in the next room.

The door was yanked wide open. Lenny nearly spilled into the room. Lae managed to catch his fall.

A wave of relief swept over Tara's face.

She pulled Ollie inside. "I didn't think..."

He held her face in his hands. "I wouldn't have either. We don't have long. Those guys are going to head in here eventually."

"He shot one of them," Lenny said.

"You what?" Tara said.

"Just trying to even the odds."

The shark slammed into the side of the tank. A chunk of concrete crashed to the floor next to Marco, waking him from his fugue. He rolled away from the tank.

"Where's Steven and Heidi?" Ollie asked.

Tara spun around, eyes searching. "Heidi? Heidi, where are you?"

"Mr. Steven went to find a way into another room or a way out," Lae said. The poor woman looked like she was ready to pass out. She'd lived her whole life in the Marshall Islands without having her life threatened seven ways to Sunday.

At least until Ollie and the Americans had come along.

Ollie arced his flashlight around the lab. The shark continued to beat itself against the tank.

Wherever he went, something very bad was desperately pounding to get at them. Ollie had to restrain himself from firing impotently into the side of tank. As if that would deter the shark.

Lenny grabbed onto his shoulder, causing the flashlight's beam to pivot upward.

"Heidi!"

Was that really Heidi?

She didn't even look human anymore. Her skin was as dark as a pool of oil, her body bloated to twice its size. If not for her clothes, he never would have mistaken the terrifying creature for Steven's once-gorgeous wife.

Her blood-red eyes caught his gaze for a second before she continued climbing up the ladder. It was like looking into the eyes of a demon.

"What the fuck is happening to her?" Marco spluttered.

Lenny looked down at his right arm, unable to hold back the look of fear.

"Heidi, you can't go up there. It's unstable," Ollie said. He knew that more than any of them.

He grabbed the nearest rung and took a tentative step.

"Don't!" Heidi shrieked, glaring down at him.

The shark thumped right near them. The ladder shifted, part of it breaking loose from the tank. Ollie held on, chest pressed to the tank, thinking he could feel the vibration of the enormous shark churning the water through his ribcage.

"You're sick," Tara pleaded. "Please, come back down. You're only going to hurt yourself."

"There's nothing you can do for me," Heidi said.

Tara kept her flashlight trained on Heidi. Ollie cringed when he saw a tear leak from her eye. It was deep red and thick as ketchup.

"You don't know that," Tara said. "Look at Lenny. He's okay."

Ollie carefully climbed closer to Heidi.

"Maybe for now. It's inside him." She looked down at Ollie and resumed climbing. "You all have to go. Don't let Steven come back for me."

Despite her condition, she was moving pretty quickly. Ollie watched helplessly as she put some distance between them, the shark refusing to let them forget it was dangerously close.

She suddenly stopped, head thrown back, and started to wail.

"Oh God! Oh God! Oh my fucking God!"

Bile as black as bat wings spilled from her mouth. Ollie had to let go of the rung with one hand so he could angle away from the stream of toxic porridge. He cast a quick look at the ground to make sure Tara avoided the mess. He breathed a sigh of relief when he saw her jump clear.

"I'm melting inside!"

The door jounced on its hinges.

Lenny shouted, "They're here!"

Can we catch a goddamn break? Ollie cursed.

"Heidi, I need you to come with me right away. We don't have a second to waste," Ollie said.

She took a flashlight from her pocket. "You have to leave me here. I'm dying. It hurts so bad, Ollie. Give me this one last thing before I go. Maybe I can save my husband and all of you."

A bullet poked through the door and into the tank. That only seemed to agitate the shark. The ladder made a ball-shrinking groan.

"Now go," Heidi said. "Take care of Steven for me."

There was no time to negotiate with her. Those guys were going to shoot their way in any second now.

Ollie scrambled down the ladder, glad to be away from the shark.

He grabbed Tara's arm. "We have to go."

"Not without Heidi."

"We have no choice."

More bullets punched the corroded metal door.

Lae and Lenny didn't need any further provocation. They hustled past Ollie and Tara. "Come on," Lenny said.

Tara looked up at Heidi who had stopped trying to get up the ladder. Heidi gave a feeble wave. She was a nightmarish vision perched on the side of the tank.

Marco took her other arm.

"Now it's my turn to carry you," he said, his busted nose and mouth making him sound like an entirely different person.

Together, he and Ollie practically dragged her to the other end of the lab where they found an open door. Lenny and Lae had waited for them before entering the next room.

The shark went berserk. Huge chunks of the tank broke off.

Ollie heard the escalating fire and the door collapse.

He asked God to please let Heidi know how sorry he was.

What's going to happen to Steven when we tell him?

Like everything else today, it wasn't going to be pretty.

***

Nacho's rage was making him reckless.

The interior of the abandoned building was dark as night and they didn't come prepared with flashlights, other than the one Bami had swiped from the bungalow before it was blown to splinters by the storm. The bastards squirreled away in here had a high-powered weapon. They could be hiding anywhere.

He didn't give two shits. He continued screaming at his men, urging them to plow through the next door. They were going to be an unstoppable force, just like that impossibly enormous shark.

Mofongo put his hand to the rusty knob.

"No, you idiot," Nacho grumbled. "We need to put the fear of God into them. Like this."

Nacho pulled the trigger, riddling the door with holes until it blew apart.

***

Heidi almost lost her tenuous grip on the ladder's rung when the door exploded. It didn't help that the shark was doing its best to smash the tank to little bits and pieces.

The burning in her organs was blinding. She closed her eyes for a moment, trying to will back the pain. She ground her teeth so hard, they popped, the sound reminding her of her days back in grammar school when they used to stomp on empty juice boxes.

Oddly enough, the decimation of her teeth wasn't painful at all. At least not in comparison to what was happening to the rest of her body.

Opening her eyes, she saw the men spill into the lab.

There were five of them – wet, filthy and looking exceedingly pissed.

Her heart stopped for a moment, restarting erratically. It stole her breath.

Hold out for just a little more.

"Guys, they're here!" she shouted as loud as she could.

Five heads tilted her way.

Good. She wanted their full attention.

It looked like there was only one flashlight between them. Even better.

"Don't go out the hatch without me," she said, resuming her climb.

Taking a quick peek, she was encouraged to see one of the men take to the ladder. He had a deep scar that bisected his forehead. He looked like the storm had given him his first shower in months.

The damn shark chose that moment to throw itself against the tank. He stopped climbing.

She continued to pretend she was talking to her friends. At least, they might have become her friends if there'd been time.

"I'm almost there. I'll need someone to help me up."

The man went back to climbing. Once he got further up the tank, he was joined by another. Heidi continued all the way to the top, grunting as she heaved herself onto the broken platform.

She dropped to her knees, another wave of nausea producing a torrent of burning liquid she was careful not to let cascade down the ladder. She didn't want to discourage them from following her.

How much more can I take? Come on you bastards. Hurry the hell up!

Heidi staggered to her feet, standing by the lip of the tank. She didn't dare flash the light onto the surface. Despite the horrible creature she'd become, she was terrified to behold the shark. She'd be with it soon enough. There were no extra points for bravery for looking your death in the eye.

"Hurry, they're almost here," she said, but her voice was weak. There was no way it could be heard over the commotion in the tank.

She leaned her hip against the tank, each stuttering breath feeling as if it would be her last.

The man with the scarred head popped into view. He jumped up quickly, aiming his gun at her.

She didn't have the strength to feign surprise or fear. She just kept her flashlight pointed at him, luring him closer.

The second man appeared and that was it.

There was no worrying about that now.

Heidi's inflamed stomach dropped. She'd hoped to get them all to follow her.

"Where the fuck is your friend with the gun, puta?" Scar Head spat.

They couldn't see her, what she had become. She was grateful for that. She wanted them up here, not fleeing for their sanity.

She thought of Steven and the life they had just started to build with one another. There was so much ahead of them. They could have lived a life they'd never even dared to dream about.

"It would have been wonderful," she croaked.

"What did you say?"

Heidi felt something give way in her core. It was like going down a steep drop on the roller coaster, only this time, she felt everything inside her collapse into her bowels.

She leaned over the lip of the tank, balanced on her liquefying side.

Black sludge dripped from her mouth, nose, eyes and ears into the water.

The moment it hit the water, the shark went into a frenzy.

Heidi took her last breath, running into the void and away from the pain.

***

The woman, if that's what she truly was, was surely dead. He'd never seen anything like it. Nacho wondered if perhaps he had died when they first hit the beach, for surely this was hell.

Cambuulo whispered, "Monster."

Nacho was inclined to agree with him. The melting, blackened corpse was a far cry from human.

The catwalk swayed violently as something stirred within the tank.

Nacho and Cambuulo lost their balance. It was like standing on the edge of a great geyser.

They didn't need to see to know that something enormous was barreling up the guts of whatever this thing was. When it broke to the top, they were able to make out something gigantic and gray swallow up the woman and her flashlight.

With it came a spray of water more powerful than a jet from a fire hose. It hit them hard, spilling them across the creaky catwalk and over the edge.

They screamed all the way down.

CHAPTER TWENTY-FOUR

Ollie's hand was crushed by Tara's when they heard all hell break loose in the tank room. The door they'd closed behind them bent in the middle. Water splashed around the edges.

It was as if a dam had burst in the other room.

"I think that tank just bit the dust," Ollie said, moving them away from the door.

He cursed his choice of words. It was crass, especially considering Heidi had been there when it happened.

"Heidi," Marco muttered, mirroring his thoughts. "I never meant for any of this to happen. You have to believe me."

Ollie said, "I do, Marco. I do."

His friend looked so helpless, he couldn't call up the rage he'd felt for him just moments before.

This particular section of the lab was remarkable for its complete emptiness. There wasn't a stick of rotted furniture or scrap of paper. The military had cleared it of everything but the stagnant air.

Whatever secrets had been created here, they did their damnedest to keep it unknown.

"Steven!" Ollie called out.

The low-ceilinged room was as wide as it was long. He could imagine a setup like Mission Control in here at one time.

His voice echoed back to him.

"Where the hell can he be?"

"There has to be a way out," Lenny said. He was looking pale. Then again, they all were. Fear had drawn all of their blood to their vital organs, fight or flight in total control.

"He wouldn't just leave Heidi behind," Tara said.

"No, he wouldn't," Ollie said. "Which means he must be on to something and not very far. We have to keep going and hope we run into him. I don't know how much longer that door is going to hold."

The only good thing was the hope that all the smugglers had been killed when the tank burst.

"Mr. Lenny, you're bleeding," Lae said. She shined her light on his bandages.

"The skin must be rupturing," Tara said. "It's no wonder with everything that you've gone through."

What no one dared mention, including Lenny, was the color of the blood staining the bandage.

It was the same cancerous black that had leaked from Heidi.

"We can rewrap it later," Ollie said, not sure if that would do any good.

Marco took off his shirt and tossed it to Tara. "You can use this."

They just started to run when a tremendous bang sounded behind them. Ollie flinched as something whizzed past his left side. It clanged ahead of him in the dark distance.

He looked back.

The door had broken and shot forward like a bullet from a gun, the water being the gunpowder. A deluge raced behind it, foamy water churning toward them.

"Go, go, go!" Ollie screamed.

"Marco!" Tara shouted.

When Ollie turned, his legs went weak.

The bottom half of Marco was still standing. The rest of him from the middle of his stomach up was gone.

The door had sliced him clean in half.

This time, Ollie's legs did go out. He splashed into the water, his face going under long enough to suck in a salty lungful.

Tara pulled him up by the back of his collar.

His chest hitched as he coughed up the water, desperate for air.

"Are you hurt?" she shouted.

It took him a second to process the question. Yes, he was hurt, in more ways than he could count. He thought of the possibility that Marco's blood and internal juices had been mixed with the briny water that had invaded his mouth, nose and lungs. It took what little willpower he had left not to throw up.

He could only nod at Tara.

"Then move your ass," she commanded, not letting go as she ran.

Ollie was grateful he couldn't see much of the water boiling around them. What if he caught a glimpse of Marco's torso? Or a limb? Or his head? How much more would it take to shatter him? To shatter all of them until they simply couldn't go on?

He kept running.

Forward momentum was easy to maintain as the tide propelled them onward whether they liked it or not.

"In here!" he heard Lenny shout.

A pair of double doors swung wide open as the current pounded against them. Ollie and Tara caught up to Lenny and Lae as they spilled into what looked to have once been a storage room.

"Up there, Mr. Ollie," Lae said, pointing to an open window just above their heads. Sheets of rain blew inside.

For once, luck was on their side. Sturdy looking crates lay scattered everywhere. In an instant, he knew Steven had been here, since several of them had been stacked under the window.

"He really left her," Ollie said, briefly wondering if there was a way Heidi could have survived the explosion of the tank and was still clinging to life.

"Ladies first," Lenny said, helping Lae step onto the first crate.

"You go before me," Tara said. "I'll be right behind you in case you lose your balance."

He didn't look to have the strength to argue.

"I'll try not to fall," he said, wincing when his stump nudged the edge of a crate.

Ollie guarded their backs. The water continued to rush in and was now up to his chest. At this rate, it would be over his nose in seconds, not minutes.

Lae was almost out the window, Lenny close behind and Tara now balancing on the rickety crate staircase.

"Take my hand, Ollie," she said, reaching down for him.

He went to grab her hand, coming up short.

Damn you, alligator arms!

He'd never once called himself the derogatory name. He'd always left that for the insensitive jerks around him. At this moment, he hated his genetics more than all the morons he'd ever come across combined.

"Take the rifle," he said, shoving it toward her. "I'm coming."

The water level touched his chin. He started paddling, finding purchase on the submerged crates.

He scrambled up the crates. Tara slipped through the window. There was a heavy splash.

A splash?

Lae was screaming.

Ollie felt the crates shift under him as the water nudged the pile sideways. He jumped toward the window. His fingers grabbed onto the lip of the sill the moment the crates tumbled away.

He tried to pull himself out of the window but his muscles wouldn't obey his command. Instead, his arms shook like they were attached to a man in the throes of the DTs.

Lae continued to scream.

"What the hell's happening?" he shouted.

His only reply was the howling wind and pounding rain.

The water in the room buoyed him up as it inched closer and closer to the window. Freed from his hanging body weight, Ollie was able to flop through the window like a sea lion skipping across a rock.

He dove into an ocean that had devoured his island.

CHAPTER TWENTY-FIVE

Tara sliced her arms through the turbulent water, kicking her legs furiously.

Where the hell had terra firma gone?

The entire island had disappeared while they were in the lab. The storm was too much for Grand Isla Tiburon, inviting the ocean to claim it for its own.

"Lae!"

She heard the woman screaming but couldn't see her.

Lenny had managed to paddle his way onto the roof of the lab, Tara helping him up. She'd lost the rifle in the process.

And where was Ollie?

"Lae, where are you?"

Something tugged on her leg.

She gave a wild kick, panicking.

It touched her again.

She splashed toward the building, forgetting all of her swimming skills. "Lenny! Help me!"

A hand grabbed her shoulder.

"It's me," Ollie said, coming up for air.

"Jesus, I thought you were the shark."

"Aaaaiiieee!"

"Where's Lae?" he asked.

"I don't know."

"And Lenny?"

He dogpaddled as best he could, his head slipping under every few seconds. She remembered that he wasn't a good swimmer. If he kept this up, he'd drown, his body exhausting itself.

"He's on the roof. You need to get up there, too."

"Not until we find Lae."

And what happened to Steven? she thought. He had left to find a way out. Had he been swept out to sea just as the island was swallowed up?

Tara still believed in things like Heaven and Hell. For Steven's sake, she hoped he was in Heaven now, holding Heidi's hand, free from the pain and madness that had been the final day of their lives.

The gray-black skies made it seem liked the dead of night.

When is this fucking storm going to end?

It felt as if it had been pummeling them for days when it only must have been a couple of hours at the most.

"Don't make me have to save two people," Tara said. "You can't swim. Now get on the roof."

They spotted the dorsal fin thirty yards away. Pointing at the shark, Ollie sank under the water for a moment.

When he surfaced, Tara was reaching for him.

"We have to get out of here," she said, gasping and spitting water.

They reached the edge of the roof at the same time, pulling themselves up and flopping onto their back.

Ollie tried to catch his breath as the rain hammered his face, snaking into his mouth.

"Lenny?" he called out feebly.

His friend stood over him, wavering.

"Did you see it?" Lenny asked.

"Is it still there?" Tara said.

She sat up. It took Ollie a few seconds to muster the strength to do the same.

Lenny said, "It dipped below the water just as you were coming up here. I don't know where it went."

Ollie took in the carnage. Everywhere he looked, there was water. Only the tops of the lab buildings were above the ocean now.

Everything he'd dreamed of, washed away.

All that was left was the damn Megalodon or Lotano, waiting patiently for them to jump in its pool.

"How much longer you think we've got?" Tara said.

"Not long," Lenny said.

Ollie wondered if he meant them or himself. He saw dark tendrils snaking up Lenny's arm like some kind of tribal tattoo.

Lae's urgent screaming stole their attention.

"Where the hell is she?" Tara said.

Three pairs of eyes scanned the turbulent, watery horizon.

"There!" Ollie shouted, pointing to their left.

A sideways palm tree bobbed on the surface.

Lae clung to the side of the tree, screaming for help over and over again.

"I'm going in for her," Tara said.

"No fucking way!" Ollie said, getting ahold of her before she could dive off the roof.

He spotted a long metal pole on the roof. It looked like the old fashioned rods they used in his grammar school to open and close the windows. It even had a small metal nub like a hook on the end.

"The tide is pushing her this way," he said, hefting the pole. "I'll try to hook the tree and get her closer. Then we can pull her up. Tara, hang onto me."

He leaned over the roof. The water was only a couple of feet below him, but he was terrified of stepping into it for even a second. He wasn't sure if there was enough water to conceal the Megalodon, but he wasn't going to take a chance.

Tara latched onto his waistband. He angled out as far as he could.

"Help me! Help me!" Lae screamed when she saw him. "Mr. Ollie! Help me!"

"Just hold on," he said.

He swung the hook toward the tree. It missed by a foot. The tide swelled. He tried again.

Thwack!

The nub buried itself in the sodden trunk. He pulled with all his might. Lenny used his good arm to help Tara rein Ollie in. They tugged hard, drawing him, and the tree with Lae, closer.

His feet back on the roof, Ollie used the pole to keep the tree beside the lab.

"See if you can grab ahold of Lae," he said.

Tara and Lenny reached down.

The second Lae saw them, she let go of the tree and waved her hands wildly.

"Lae, you need to calm down," Ollie shouted over the storm.

Tara and Lenny kept missing her as she fought to both stay afloat and get rescued.

"Ms. Tara, Mr. Lenny, help!"

Fuck this, Ollie thought. He let go of the pole and jumped in next to Lae.

She struggled against him and for a terrifying moment, they both went under. Ollie held on, but he couldn't tell which way was up.

Somehow they broke through. The first thing he saw was Tara and Lenny's petrified faces. They thrust their hands out to them.

"It's okay, Lae. It's okay. They'll get you on the roof."

He wrapped his arms around her waist and guided her to them.

Lae went limp. Lenny and Tara each took a hand and pulled.

CHAPTER TWENTY-SIX

Lae was as heavy as an old time safe. Tara was strong, having spent the better part of her unemployment at the gym, but she was no power lifter. It didn't help that poor Lenny only had the one good arm and that poison running through his system.

"Pull!" Tara shouted, straining until she saw spots dance at the corners of her vision.

She felt Lae's body break from the embrace of the ocean and dared to look down.

The woman's face had gone from raw panic to absolute serenity.

Then something red and wet fell from Lae onto Ollie's face.

"Oh my God!" Lenny screamed.

Lae's legs were gone. Where her waist should be was just a jagged mess of torn flesh and ropy bowels.

How the fuck was she still alive?

Ollie struggled to stay afloat while her gore rained down on him.

"Hurry, hurry," Tara said to Lenny.

Lae slipped over the lip of the roof. They quickly turned her onto her back.

"Thank you," Lae said, her mouth going slack. Tara watched her life drain from her body, her eyes going milky as her chest deflated.

"Ollie," Tara said, running back to the edge. He was still there, the blood washed away by the rain and ocean. She helped him up.

Lenny lay on his side, next to Lae.

"Is he..."

Tara felt the pulse beat on Lenny's neck. "He's alive. He must have passed out from the exertion.

They looked down at Lae's ruined body.

"You think the shark did that?" Ollie asked.

"It had to. That damn thing could swallow us all in one bite. You think it could have spared her the pain."

"If this keeps up, we're going to find out how merciful it is toward us soon."

He bent over and looked like he was about to vomit. She went to touch his back but he waved her off.

"What just happened is going to haunt me forever," he said, looking down at a cord of intestine poking out from Lae. "But I can't let it overwhelm me now."

Tara peered over his shoulder and moaned.

The dorsal fin emerged, closer than before. Only this time, they could see its massive body as it skimmed just under the surface, its tail fin fanning back and forth as it patrolled the sinking lab.

Dozens of other, smaller shark's fins swam about, keeping their distance from the Megalodon. They were as afraid of it as the humans.

"What the hell does it want?" Tara said. "It has a whole ocean to explore."

Ollie dropped to his knees, eyes glued to the shark. "This is its home. It's almost like it's waiting for something."

Tara shivered just thinking what that something could be. The Megalodon had been resurrected for a very specific purpose. What the fuck had the crazy assholes who had done the impossible been thinking? Was it their goal to unleash it on Russian surfers during the Cold War? Or did they create this monstrosity just for the sheer fact that they could?

If the story about Nazi scientists being recruited to better the American quest for military dominance was true, anything was possible, no matter how insane it seemed. History more than showed the Nazi's penchant for the grotesque and absurd.

"What do we do now?" Tara said.

The waters were still rising, Lenny was dying, and there was no place else to go.

"The only thing we can do," Ollie said. "Pray the storm ends soon."

"Have you seen any sign of Steven?"

Ollie shook his head, water dripping from his hair. "He's gone."

Lenny groaned, but they couldn't wake him up. Maybe he was better off that way. The black gangrene or whatever the hell it was had inched its way up his right arm, ending just past his elbow. Pretty soon, he'd be just like Heidi had been.

Even if she had the proper medical supplies, it probably wouldn't help if she amputated the entire arm. The poison was in him, racing through his bloodstream, killing him with each passing second.

The Megalodon leapt out of the water as if it were some trained orca at Sea World. Tara grabbed Ollie's hand, skittering back from the end of the roof.

In the second or two that it left the bonds of the ocean, they were given a glimpse of its full, gigantic form. From nose to its tail fin, it had to be seventy feet . . . if not longer. She couldn't help thinking it was a living, breathing battleship.

If the American military could harness and control the Megalodon, just the sight of it would send any naval force in full retreat.

Or was Lae right, and Lotano had come to set things right once again?

She felt the concussion of the splash in her chest as the zombie shark slammed into the ocean.

Tara realized there was no way out.

The Megalodon's dorsal fin pointed straight at the building. It sped toward them, heedless of the depth of water.

"How does it know we're up here?" Ollie said.

"It can't. It just can't. Sharks can't see well."

They braced for impact.

Ollie's grip was so tight, the bones in her hand ground against one another painfully.

She hoped Lenny would remain unconscious and never know the agony they were about to endure.

"Shit, shit, shit," Ollie muttered as the shark came closer.

And then it disappeared.

The gray triangle sank beneath the water.

"Where did it go?" she wailed.

Ollie ran the perimeter of the roof, scanning the roiling ocean. "I don't see it."

Tara looked down at her feet.

She knew exactly where it had gone.

The center building was to their left. The building that had housed the tank.

The tank that was a direct pipeline to the ocean.

It was the first time she was grateful they were stuck on the roof of one of the lower buildings.

But how long would it remain down there in its private, murky lair?

"Fuck your fucking mother's sister."

Tara and Ollie turned to Lenny, who was now sitting up and holding his right arm like a baby.

"We're not dead yet?" he asked.

"I'm afraid not," Tara said, checking his forehead. He had a low-grade fever.

"Where's the shark now?" Lenny said.

"I'm pretty sure it's under the lab," Tara said. "It was coming right toward us before it dipped out of sight."

"Ollie, I want to thank you for a wonderful and interesting trip, but I'd like to go home now. If we get a plane today, I'm pretty sure we'll be in town for the Mets season ender against the Marlins."

Ollie stood over Lenny with his hands on his hips, eyes on the sea. He smirked. "I promised you a lifetime in paradise, buddy. We're not done yet."

"I think my new idea of paradise is Minnesota in the winter. Preferably somewhere not even close to water. I'm including ponds, too."

Tara rubbed his cheek. "This is what we get for bitching about the cold and snow back in college."

"I can't believe I used to love those *Sharknado* movies," Ollie joked. And why not? It was better to go down laughing than screaming.

They broke into uncontrollable laughter, tears mingling with the rain as it poured down their faces. Lenny paused every now and then to note how the laughing was making his arm throb, then started all over again.

A spray of water kicked up beside Lenny.

Then another.

He got to his feet, standing beside Ollie.

"What was that?"

Ollie's head jerked to the main lab.

A man looked down at them, his handgun drawn.

"How in holy hell did he survive?" Ollie said.

They couldn't hear the gunshot, but they saw another small geyser of water explode in front of Tara's foot. She skipped back.

She looked around the roof.

There was no place to hide.

The man paused. It looked like he was reloading.

***

Mofongo couldn't steady his trembling arms enough to take a good shot. No matter, there wasn't anywhere for those assholes to run. Even if he closed his eyes, he'd eventually hit them.

When the tank exploded, he'd been back near the entrance, making sure they hadn't missed anyone lurking in the shadows during their mad dash inside. Nacho's anger and bloodlust had left them vulnerable to an attack from behind. He'd heard the tremendous explosion, then the distinctive sound of Akara screaming. A heavy wave blasted through the building, slamming Mofongo square in the back. It pushed him right out the door, dragging him across the meager beach, the sand grating away several layers of flesh.

Stunned, he could only sit and watch as the water poured out, knowing that everyone inside had to be dead.

No crew. No coke. No boat.

He was completely screwed.

And out there was a killer shark so big, it defied logic.

The Pacific ate the island rapidly as the storm raged.

There was nowhere to go but back inside the building. If he could make it to the roof, he'd be on the highest ground. Maybe there was a chance he could ride it out.

What he'd do after he survived was anyone's guess.

Praying that the integrity of the structure was still intact, he dashed back inside. He found a narrow stairway in the middle building with the demolished tank. It was set against the far wall on the opposite of the room. He trudged through water and concrete and steel that went up to his hips. He also assumed that bits of Nacho, Bami, Akara and Cambuulo were in the swill as well.

Mofongo cried out with joy when he discovered the stairs led to the roof. Using the butt of his rifle, he smashed the lock and opened the trap door.

And then he saw the three people on the rooftop below.

How the hell had they survived?

No matter. Whatever divine luck they'd had had run out.

There could be no witnesses.

***

"Sir, there's something up ahead."

Captain Powell looked over his navigator's shoulder. He had to bite the inside of his cheek to keep what he wanted to say to himself.

"Something that big shouldn't be able to move that fast," his navigator said.

"You just keep your eyes on it," Powell snapped.

Mother Nature had gotten her tits in a twist up top. That was nothing compared to what was pinging their sonar. That little asset gone rogue was the mother of all shit storms.

To make matters worse, he'd been expressly ordered not to frag the fucking thing. That would be too easy and make too much sense.

The *Maximus* was to find a way to subdue and contain the asset. For the life of him, Powell couldn't fathom how exactly they were supposed to do that. His CO was to get back to him shortly with a detailed plan.

His ass had been rubbed even rawer when he was informed that Grand Isla Tiburon was no longer deserted. Civilians, American civilians, now called the worthless stretch of sand home.

"Dumb bastards," he mumbled.

"Skipper?"

Gary Leuis, his XO, stared at him as if he were waiting for an order.

"Nothing. Just thinking out loud."

The new administration didn't know their assholes from a knothole. They were blinded by their ultra-liberal quest to dismantle the very ideals that had built America. To this president and his cabinet, the military was the enemy. Military spending had been slashed to the extent that Powell worried about his country's future as a super power.

They had basically ignored the debriefing that had been given to them, especially when it came to projects that dated back to the 1950s. To them, it was all Cold War nonsense, real Stone Age bullshit.

Due to the very secret nature of what had been birthed at Grand Isla Tiburon, even presidents were not made fully aware of the details. All were told in no uncertain terms that the island was a no-go zone. Military officials in the know had counted on the specter of possible nuclear contamination being enough to keep prying eyes, even the president's, away from the island.

It appears that someone in the administration had sent a team from the EPA down to Grand Isla Tiburon to see if it was indeed as bad as they'd been told. And of course, they'd found it to be perfectly clean.

Because the real problem was down below.

And now some dipwad had taken it upon himself to sell the island to some lottery winner who had vowed to improve the lives of the nearby islanders in exchange for a lowball price on the island.

Very kumbay-fucking-ya.

It was just the sort of peace and love nonsense those liberal pantywaists lived for.

Naturally, no one had told Admiral Keyes, the man in charge of keeping watch over this sector, about the reckless and idiotic sale of the island. And because the military had been so weakened over the past three years, it had flown under their radar . . . until now, when it might be too late.

"You receive a protocol yet?"

"Not yet."

"We might want to give it a wider berth until then. Don't want to get its attention."

"Circle the perimeter for now."

Leuis was one of only a handful of people aboard *Maximus* who knew what was down there with them. He had every right to be sweating. There wouldn't be a need to grit through this if they were able to nuke the damn thing. The civilian casualties would be chalked up to an acceptable loss. Not that the general public would ever be made aware of it. He was told there were possibly ten people on Grand Isla Tiburon, including any laborers from nearby islands.

Sure, keep the killer shark alive, but eliminate the innocent witnesses.

It made him sick to his stomach, though the logic was ironclad. Something like this was too big to let slip.

Oh, but that damn thing had slipped, all right.

He'd wondered more than once if the Megalodon would have been an asset in the fight against the behemoth ghost sharks off the Miami coast a few years ago. That is, if they'd ever found a way to control the prehistoric shark.

More than likely, it would have joined the masses of killer fish and turned the tide in their favor.

"You might want to see this," Leuis said, handing him his tablet.

While he read, Powell gripped it so tight, the screen started to crack.

CHAPTER TWENTY-SEVEN

Ollie found a crumbled bit of concrete and threw it at the man on the roof above. He hoped the smuggler was so concerned with loading his gun that he wouldn't see it coming.

It didn't matter. The projectile missed him by a country mile.

"This is why we didn't let you pitch when we played Wiffle Ball," Lenny said.

The gallows humor was coming in a steady stream. That only stressed the increasing certainty that they were all going to die.

"Keep moving," Ollie said. "Keep your heads down and get over there. The angle will be bad for him. He may not be able to see us."

Ollie and Tara carried Lenny between them.

Something sizzled across Ollie's shoulder. He almost dropped Lenny. Adrenaline kept him moving. They collapsed in a pile, hitting the ledge while bullets peppered the wet roof around them.

"I think I'm shot," Ollie said. Even that didn't stop him from making sure he hadn't gotten any of the black horridness leaking from parts of Lenny on him. A bullet was a fair tradeoff over getting infected with whatever had caused Lenny and Heidi to rot from the inside out. He felt guilty think that way, but survival instincts didn't give five farts about guilt.

The man kept on shooting, but Ollie had been right. They'd managed to find the one spot on the roof that didn't offer a clean line of sight for the smuggler.

Tara leaned over Lenny. "Where do you think you were hit?"

Ollie tilted his shoulder toward her, not anxious to see for himself.

"Take off your shirt."

He cowered as a bullet whooshed just over his head. It hurt to pull his arm out of the sleeve. Tara prodded his shoulder. He looked down and saw the blood.

"You're lucky," Tara said. "I think it just grazed you. Can you move your arm?"

He moved it just a bit, careful not to give the smuggler something to aim for. Rotating his shoulder hurt like a motherfucker.

"Good," she said.

"Or as good as it gets," Lenny added. "Any chance this asshole is going to run out of bullets soon?"

Thunder rumbled.

For the first time since they'd exited the lab, the rain seemed to be letting up. Ollie no longer felt like he was being pelted with thousands of ping-pong balls.

"This isn't a *Rambo* flick. He can't have an endless supply," Ollie said.

As if the man heard them, the shooting stopped. The thunder sounded as if it were departing, like the ominous footsteps of a retreating giant in a children's story.

"We can't just sit here," Ollie said.

"I'm going to disagree with you on that," Lenny said. His breathing was starting to sound raspy. Not a good sign.

Ollie grimaced. "I'm tired of running like a chicken with his head cut off."

"We've kind of had valid reasons to run," Tara reminded him.

"Stay right here."

Tara snatched his hand when he tried to stand up, dragging him back down. Of course, she had to grab the hand attached to the shoulder that had been shot. Ollie saw a few stars.

"What the hell do you think you're doing?" she hissed.

"I'm going to find out if he's really out of ammo or not."

"How? By offering yourself as a human target?"

"In a way, yes."

Ollie extricated himself and scooted away before she could regain her hold.

Sure, he'd been Alligator Arms and was shorter than most of the women he met, but there was one thing he'd always been that he wasn't ashamed of—fast.

When he played Little League baseball, he couldn't hit to save his life, but he learned to hang back and let inexperienced pitchers walk him. Once on first, his speed would have him on third base in no time.

Ollie sprinted to the other side of the roof. He looked back to make sure he got the smuggler's attention. The man brought his gun hand up, taking aim.

Making a sudden zig left, the bullet plowed into the roof on his right. Ollie changed direction, the next bullet hammering harmlessly behind him.

As he dodged bullets, he started to laugh, recalling the scene in the movie *The In-Laws* where Peter Faulk and Alan Arkin ran 'serpentine' to avoid being shot.

It's finally happened, he thought. *My life has become a movie!*

Running haphazardly around the roof, it took a while before he realized the shooting had stopped.

Ollie looked at the man on the neighboring rooftop.

With the dying rain, the skies had lightened considerably.

The man stared down at him with murder in his eyes. He had a scraggly, black beard and his shirt was torn, exposing a flat, wiry chest. Ollie thought he saw blood on the man's neck.

Fuck you, Ollie seethed. *Fuck you and your dead friends.*

He'd gotten into more than his share of tussles over the years, but he'd never wanted to kill someone before.

Until now.

There was nothing he could do about that Megalodon or Lotano, the other half responsible for his burning hate.

But he could satisfy his need for retribution with the smuggler.

He scanned the distance between them. There was a two-foot gap between the buildings. He saw a connector, but he'd have to climb down to get to it. And that would take time.

There were, however, irregularities in the crumbling building that would make for perfect hand and footholds. Especially if one had small hands and feet.

"Ollie, what are you thinking?" Tara said.

He didn't realize Tara and Lenny had been staring at him.

"I'm thinking it's time to tie up one loose end."

The pole he'd used to hook into the palm tree was just a few feet away. But he wouldn't be able to hold it and scale the building.

Screw it.

He didn't want an implement between him and the bastard. He wanted to tear him apart with his bare hands.

Ollie ran, leaping over the edge of the roof, ignoring Tara's shouts for him to stop. He landed hard on the side of the building, frantically scrabbling for a crack to slip his fingers within.

Sliding down several feet, his foot caught on an exposed section of the building, stopping his descent. A jolt of pain went from his ankle to his jaw.

He struggled to catch his breath. For a second, he thought he was going to fall into the water. And that would not be good.

Just climb!

Channeling his inner Spiderman, he clambered up the side of the central lab. It was actually easier than he thought. Not that he was thinking much. He was on pure animal instinct mode now.

He couldn't make out what Tara was saying and didn't want to. She'd been through and seen enough. She didn't need to witness what he planned to do.

Just a few feet from the top, he looked up, expecting to see the smuggler waiting to stomp on him.

All he saw was gray clouds.

Ollie's shoulder crackled with pain as he pulled himself closer. Fresh blood seeped from the wound when he reached up, a few drops spattering his face.

When his hand curled around the lip of the roof, he cried out, pulling himself up and over, expecting to be attacked.

He landed with a splash on his side.

The swarthy smuggler stood ten feet from him. He flicked a butterfly knife opened and closed with his left hand. Ollie sneered, slowly getting to his feet.

"You think you're in *Tomb Raider* or something?" he said to the man. "Lara Croft made butterfly knives look cool, but you're gonna need something bigger than that."

He noticed a jagged cut on the man's neck. He wondered if shrapnel from the exploding tank had nicked him, the way the door had sliced Marco in half. Judging by the amount of blood leaking from the wound, it had to have weakened him.

And all he's got left is a knife that looks menacing in a movie but is only good for carving initials in park benches. All those visits to the knife show in St. Paul had finally paid off. Ollie wasn't intimidated.

Ollie's fury was so vast at the moment, the man could be holding Conan's sword and he wouldn't back down.

"You speak any English?" Ollie said. It was hard for him to tell the man's nationality. He may have been South American. He was definitely one-hundred percent scumbag.

The smuggler spat, a glob of crimson phlegm splattering on Ollie's foot.

"So much for any witty exchange," Ollie said, balling his hands into fists and charging.

The man squared his body, the knife's blade pointed straight out to stick Ollie somewhere soft and meaty.

At the last second, Ollie hit the deck, wrapping his arms around the man's ankles and twisting him onto the ground. The smuggler gave a painful shout when his wounded neck made contact with the soaked yet unyielding surface.

Ollie scurried from beside the man and leapt onto his torso. The knife flashed upward, catching Ollie's chest. He felt the butterfly knife slice through his left nipple.

For the moment, he didn't feel any pain.

He punched the man in the face, catching him on the bridge of his nose. The cartilage of his nose gave way with a satisfying crack. Ollie brought his other fist down on the same spot.

The smuggler squirmed under him, but Ollie pressed his thighs together, keeping him pinned. He rained blows on the man's face, blood splattering up his arms. He counted each blow, his OCD telling him he couldn't stop until he'd reached the nice round number of twenty.

Ollie was beyond speech or coherent thought.

There was only the orgasmic sensation of his knuckles crunching against the man's skull.

And the steady count—*four, five, six, seven*—his inner mantra that blocked out everything but the need to fulfill the goal he'd set in his mind.

The building rumbled hard, throwing Ollie off-balance. He slipped sideways, rolling off the smuggler. Spiraling away from the man, a sudden burst of pain flared from Ollie's thigh.

He stopped his roll and looked down.

The butterfly knife was buried up to the hilt in the meat of his thigh. He hadn't even felt it go in.

The smuggler, his face a ruined mess, had somehow gotten back on his feet. He wiped a gob of blood and snot away with the back of his hand. He raised his fists, waiting for Ollie to do the same.

Ollie had to give him credit. The man could take a beating. And now they were even in the seeping wound department. He left the blade in his thigh, recalling numerous movies and TV shows where medics talked about people bleeding out when extracting knives and other projectiles.

It hurt to put pressure on his leg.

He went rigid when he saw another man pull himself through a trap door in the roof. This one had a huge scar on his face. The second smuggler staggered onto the roof, his legs as unsteady as a landlubber on the deck of a dinghy in a storm. Rivulets of blood ran down his face. He must have taken a good whack on the head.

Ollie brought his arms up.

"I don't think your friend is going to be much help," he said.

The scar-faced smuggler growled, "The shark ate your ugly bitch. She died like a piece of bait."

He then said something to the man Ollie had been fighting in a language he couldn't pin down.

The smuggler looked at him and laughed, his gaze lingering on Ollie's arms.

Ollie saw red.

And then the building exploded.

CHAPTER TWENTY-EIGHT

The creature smelled the ripe scent of more food . . . special food.

Only it wasn't in the water.

The shark swam beneath the place that had been its home, its prison, senses heightened by the nearby presence of sustenance. Not being able to find it was driving it insane with desire.

If not below, then it had to be above.

And above meant through that hole in the ocean, the one that led to the other world where it had seen many small beings peering down at it.

Using every ounce of lust-fueled strength in its muscled body, the creature rocketed toward the hole.

It would find its food, even if it had to die trying.

***

Tara called Ollie's name over and over again but he wouldn't stop climbing. Once he slipped onto the roof above, it was as if he'd simply disappeared.

"What the hell is he trying to prove?"

Lenny shifted his back against the edge of the roof. Each exhalation sounded like it was being blown through a bowl of water.

"You didn't call him Raging Bull for nothing," he said. "He's beaten guys up just for making wise-ass remarks about his size." He swept his hands around them. "Someone has to pay for this, and it's going to be that asshole."

"That asshole has a gun."

"I think Ollie did a good job making sure he wasted his ammo. At least I hope he did."

They sat listening for the sound of gunfire. Drifting thunder made it hard to hear anything, though she was sure she'd be able to hear a gun go off, no matter how loud the departing storm got.

She looked over the roof and deflated.

Even though the worst of the rain had come and gone, the water was still rising. It wouldn't be long before she'd somehow have to get Lenny up onto the other roof. Either that or wade in the water and hope the Megaladon had finally left for good.

Lenny nudged her with his leg. She could feel the heat radiating off his skin.

"He'll be all right," he said.

"How can you know that?"

"Because there has to be a balance. You can't have all this shit go sideways without a little something going your way."

And what's going to go your way? Tara thought. The whites of Lenny's eyes were shot through with thick, red lines. Even worse, some of them appeared to be turning black.

She couldn't even begin to imagine what he was feeling inside. Heidi had said she was melting. What sick bastard could dream up a poison like that?

The same one who thought bringing a Megalodon back from extinction would advance both science and military might.

For all she knew, there was more than one of those men up there waiting for Ollie. He'd been through the ringer. They all had. How much could he have left in the tank to fight them off?

Tara wanted to make her way up there and help, or at the very least see what the hell was going on.

But Lenny needed her. She couldn't leave him here to die alone.

The building shook. She grabbed hold of Lenny.

"Not this. Not now," she moaned.

The lab was old and had been left to rot for decades. The ocean was doing its best to knock the whole thing down.

The thought of being in the water terrified her. She'd rather be shot than eaten alive by the shark.

"We should move away from the edge," Lenny said. "That'll be the first to slide into the Pacific." Tara put out her hand to help him up.

"It's probably best you don't touch me," he said. "I'm getting worse. The infection is everywhere now."

Tara didn't protest, feeling terrible about it.

They staggered to the middle of the roof.

She still couldn't see Ollie.

"That building had to have been compromised when the tank went," she said. "If this one is starting to go, that one can't be far behind."

"Ollie!" she shouted with her hands cupped around her mouth.

The rumbling under their feet intensified. She'd been through a minor earthquake in Japan when her father took the family to Sapporo in the nineties. He had been transferred to the Sapporo office for six months, with an allowance to bring his family for one all-expenses-paid trip. The earthquake shook the apartment they were staying in on their first night there. Even though nothing happened other than a picture falling off the wall and some plates clattering off a shelf, Tara had spent the rest of the trip asking when they would go back home.

Even though it hadn't been much in the way of earthquakes, it was just enough to demonstrate to her the full power and amoral wrath of nature.

"You going to be all right to swim, Stump?" she said.

"Looks like I'm not going to have a choice, T-Mac," he said with a pained grin.

Zigzagging cracks snaked across the roof.

Expecting to fall through the roof and into the water any second, Tara was blown backwards when the central lab building exploded outward.

Her breath whooshed from her lungs. Lightning bolts of pain shot from her tailbone down to her legs and straight to her teeth.

Tara watched in mute horror as the behemoth shark rocketed through the disintegrating building, as straight and true as an ICBM.

She wanted to scream. She wanted to cry. But for the moment, she couldn't even draw a breath.

The Megalodon's enormous mouth was open wide, devouring brick and steel, powering into the air.

How the hell did it know Ollie and the smuggler were up there?

As gravity dragged the massive Megalodon back into the ocean, the remains of the building splashed around it. The air was choked with turgid water and debris.

"Oh my God, Ollie," she gasped, her lungs burning.

"Look!" Lenny gasped, pointing to the tumbling refuse.

The shadow of a man tumbled toward them. His arms and legs whirled in a vain attempt to find purchase where there was none to be had.

The building under them gave a fatal and grinding shake. Tara heard the foundation start to give way.

Somehow, Lenny had made it to his feet, running toward the falling man with outstretched arms. How he expected to catch him with only the one hand and all the strength of a kitten was anyone's guess.

Tara saw a flash of the man's face and the raw terror in his eyes.

It wasn't Ollie.

"Lenny, it's the smuggler!"

Lenny stopped short, letting the man fall just a couple of feet in front of him. Even from a distance, Tara could hear the man's bones snap. His body bounced not just once, but twice before settling into an unnatural heap. The man's bloody face was turned to her. His eyes were wide open and vacant.

Running past him, she peered over the edge of the roof.

Tara looked into the floating field of carnage. There was no sign of Ollie. It felt as if a fist were closing over her heart. Poor Ollie. He only wanted to make people happy after being denied happiness most of his life.

The Megalodon's fin sliced back and forth through the water, seeming to revel in the destruction it had wrought.

Glancing back at her, Lenny said, "Good eye. I'd hate to have sacrificed myself for that guy."

He collapsed onto his bad side when the building canted hard to the left. Tara clawed the rough surface of the roof to stop herself from sliding over the edge.

It was no use. The damage was done. The building was breaking up fast, tilting into the ocean like a wounded ship.

Slipping across the slick roof, she managed to grab hold of an outer pocket on Lenny's shorts. At least they would go down together.

Tara couldn't help the hot tears from burning her eyes. She didn't want to die. Especially not like this. She knew the second they hit the water, the shark would smell them. They were both cut up pretty bad, and Lenny was a blackening mass of whatever vileness that fed the beast. Would it tear her in half like it had done to Lae, or would the end come quickly? Just thinking about those massive teeth carving through her, being digested in the belly of the prehistoric creature made her wish her heart would just give out and spare her one more second of panic.

With one last heave, the building foundered. Tara and Lenny sprawled into the ocean. She landed on her belly, the impact punching the held breath from her lungs. She considered just sucking in as much seawater as she could and ending it right there, but her innate survival instincts had her struggling for the surface.

She broke through, fighting for a merciful breath.

"Over here," she heard Lenny cry.

He'd found a buoyant slab of driftwood and draped his good arm over it. She knifed through the water to latch onto it.

They floated right into a lone ray of sun. It was a meager spotlight on the stage of their undoing. Floating across from an illuminated Lenny, Tara saw how gray his skin had become, with lines of black blossoming on his jawline. He couldn't have much more to go.

Worse still for her, he was a living dinner bell for the shark. She could push away now and get as far from him as she could, forced to watch him get eaten before she met the same fate, or she could stay by him and not die alone.

The sound of a motor broke her from mulling over a winless choice.

She looked around for the source. The rough water had them bobbing so much, it was almost impossible to see anything for more than a fleeting moment.

Lenny rested his head on the driftwood. His eyes were closed.

Whatever was making the noise was coming closer because she could feel the rumbling in her chest.

Riding the crest of a whitecap, she spotted a boat.

A boat!

"Lenny, wake up."

Lenny's eyelids fluttered but he remained unconscious.

"Stump, I need you to wake up!"

At hearing his old nickname, he finally came out of it. "Please, just let me sleep, T-Mac."

"You can sleep all you want later, buddy. Right now, we need to hitch a ride."

***

When Steven steered Ollie's boat, the *Sarah Kay*, to where the lab once stood, his heart and stomach sank into his shoes. Everything was gone. The shattered remains of the lab littered the surface of the interloping ocean.

And somewhere within the mess was his wife.

He couldn't see her anywhere.

But he did spy Tara and a strange man clinging onto a long slab of wood.

Far from a boating expert, he eased back on the *Sarah Kay's* throttle and steered next to them. He didn't want to get too close because he was worried he'd ride right over them or get them caught in the motor's propeller. He was no sailor, having driven a speedboat once when he was seventeen at camp. That brief foray hardly qualified him to pilot anything more complex than a canoe.

He pulled a life preserver from the hook and tossed it over to Tara. She looked completely wiped out. He wrapped the end of the rope several times around his wrist.

"Take Lenny first," Tara said, trying to loop the circular tube over the gray man's upper body.

That's Lenny? Steven bit back his repulsion. He looked a lot like Heidi had before he'd left to find a way out of the lab and off this cursed island. He didn't know he'd end up getting swept into the sea, fighting to stay afloat. The current ripped him farther and farther from the lab. The circling fins of smaller sharks turned in his direction. He decided being eaten piece by piece by a gang of small sharks was far more terrifying than a single, swift chomp by the Megalodon. Paddling and kicking like a man possessed, he found himself deposited to where the dock and beach had once been.

The dock was gone, but Ollie's boat was still there, listing to the right and taking on water because it was still tethered to the submerged dock.

The smaller sharks were getting closer.

Steven dove under several times, having to undo the tether by feel in the dark, murky water. Just when he thought his lungs couldn't take any more, his arms weakening to the point of shaking uncontrollably, the rope pulled up and over the post.

The *Sarah Kay* immediately righted itself and Steven struggled to climb aboard. He flipped the bird defiantly at the disappointed sharks.

Ollie had left the key in the ignition. It was the only thing he could thank Ollie for. Exhausted, the scar on his head throbbing, he was tempted to let the darkness overtake him.

He fought it, knowing he had to get back to Heidi. If he could somehow get her to a medical facility on a nearby island, they might be able to save her.

Thankfully, the tempest had finally passed. It took some trial and error to get control of the boat.

He thought he'd be returning a hero.

He was wrong.

"Where's Heidi?"

"Get Lenny on board," Tara said, avoiding his gaze.

Steven had a hard time drawing his next breath, much less pulling Lenny's dead weight. Lenny looked like a diseased avocado. The last thing he wanted to do was come in contact with his infected skin.

"Come on, take him!" Tara shouted, looking over her shoulder repeatedly.

He leaned over the boat, hesitating. Lenny's eyes rolled into his head, revealing eyes that no longer looked human. How did eyes get that color?

"Steven!" Tara snapped.

"Let me help you," he said, reaching out to her.

"Lenny first," she insisted. "And hurry, goddammit!"

"But . . . he's infected. Is he even alive?"

"If you're worried about catching it, do I need to remind you that you were holding Heidi the entire time she was sick? Just grab him by his shirt and pants if you can."

Hearing Heidi's name made him forget his worries about the poison running through Lenny. Using both hands, he hauled Lenny aboard. His old friend's skin and muscles felt like porridge. He thought he felt bones snap under his grip.

Lenny moaned, flopping onto the deck. Thick, black fluid leaked from the corner of his mouth.

Tara managed to get herself onboard.

"Where's Heidi?" he asked again.

She shook her head. "She didn't make it. I'm so sorry, Steven. But she went out trying to save us."

It felt as if the world had been yanked out from under him.

She'd died trying to save them.

He wasn't sure what that entailed. He *was* sure he was in no state to comprehend whatever Tara would tell him.

Oh God, Heidi. You can't leave me.

He didn't realize Tara had grabbed his arms and was shaking him, shouting into his face.

"What?"

"We have to get the fuck out of here."

"I need to find Heidi. Where's her body?"

"I don't know. She was in the lab when it . . . when it blew up."

"Blew up? How did it blow up?"

A cold wind blew the wet strands of her hair from Tara's pale face. "It was the water . . . and the shark. Look, you have to get us as far away from here as you can, right now."

"Not without Heidi. I can't leave her out here."

Tara stormed past him and went to the pilot's seat. "Just tell me what the hell I need to do."

Steven couldn't feel his legs. He stared into the distance, images of Heidi playing out on the gray horizon as if it were a drive-in movie screen.

"Steven!"

"Need to take Heidi home," he mumbled.

A sudden sting in his cheek shook him from his fugue. When he didn't react, Tara slapped him again.

"Drive . . . the fucking . . . boat," she ordered. Her lips were curled into a snarl. The look on her face would have scared him any other time.

She roughly grabbed his face and twisted his head.

"See that? If you don't haul ass, it's going to find us."

He watched the impossibly large dorsal fin patrol the water. It was a hundred or so yards away now, but it had turned in their direction. The sight of the shark brought him crashing back to reality.

Tara was right. They had to get out of there, fast.

His cowardice, his inability to let the inevitable happen and be with Heidi once again, sickened him. He opened up the throttle and turned the wheel. Tara knelt by Lenny, propping his head up under the life preserver.

He fought against the ocean, trying to get the *Sarah Kay* going in the right direction, which was any direction opposite that shark. The back of the boat slid sideways as if it were a car on thin ice. He didn't know if he was supposed to steer into the curve or not.

Daring to look back, he caught the shark leaping from the ocean. Its mouth was open wide enough to swallow the Staten Island Ferry. It slammed into the water, sending a ripple of waves that nearly flipped the *Sarah Kay*.

"It's coming!" Tara screamed, a bit unnecessarily as far as Steven was concerned. Of course it was coming for them. The damn shark was like some kind of avenging demon, sent to destroy them for daring to live a life people only dreamed about.

"I'm trying," Steven shot back, wrestling with the wheel. At one point, it jerked so hard, it almost pulled his elbow from its socket.

"Wait! Wait!" Tara shouted, crossing the boat to tug on his arm. The boat bobbed on the high waves. They both almost hit the deck.

"There's someone out there," she said.

"So what?" He was finally starting to make some headway. And now she wanted him to stop?

"It might be Ollie."

He turned to her, unable to mask his ambivalence. "Not my problem. I'm getting us out of here."

With a shrug of his shoulders, he nudged Tara off him and she went sprawling, sliding next to an unconscious Lenny.

Fuck Ollie.

As far as he was concerned, Ollie had killed Heidi.

He'd earned whatever he had coming to him.

CHAPTER TWENTY-NINE

Captain Powell watched the monitor as the Megalodon thrashed about in the water. It definitely wasn't going far from home. That wasn't going to make things any easier.

Leuis, his XO, said beside him, "How in the holy hell are we supposed to capture that thing? It'll snap *Maximus* in two."

The Megalodon seemed bigger than he'd thought. At least it appeared bigger in motion. And it moved so damn fast. Jesus, no wonder they had tried to weaponize the thing. But how the hell did they think they could ever bend it to their will? The Megalodon was a force of nature, an extinct beast that no longer had a place in this world.

Powell was none too pleased with the orders he'd been given.

He wasn't a cowboy and the *Maximus* wasn't a horse. Somehow, they were supposed to get the shark's attention and corral it into the special holding pen under the island. He couldn't imagine a single scenario where the submarine wasn't smashed to bits.

"They said it should be weakening," Powell said, his face glowing green from the monitors.

"It sure as shit doesn't look that way to me," Leuis said, grinding his dentures. Always an intense man, he'd ground away his real teeth years ago.

Leuis was right. The actions of the shark were downright manic. It was circling the island, or what remained of it, jumping like a dolphin and then diving deep, barreling to the surface seconds later. If Powell was a shark psychologist, he'd say the creature had completely lost its mind.

Powell said, "The lunatics that designed it also put in a failsafe. It can't go for long without a special chemical that's fed to it. The lab is destroyed. Whatever remnants it had managed to get ahold of are gone. There's no more supply. It will burn itself out. Then we go in and get it back in its cage . . . after we repair it."

"And what if it decides it wants to take a stroll while it's still full of piss and vinegar?"

Powell drew in a sharp breath. "We're to discourage it from venturing any further from its current location."

"But we can't kill it?"

"No. If this bastard dies under our watch, we're cooked. And I'm not just talking career-wise. The words 'court-marshal' were mentioned more than once."

Leuis punched his fist against the bulkhead. "I could strangle the moron that sold that cursed island."

Powell spoke softly so no one else could overhear him. "That ship has sailed. No sense bemoaning it any further. It's our job to get it back in mothballs so someone can find a way to fix it. All without letting the administration find out. Simple."

Both men stared at the monitor, watching the shark circle round and round.

"Some things can't be fixed," Leuis said.

Captain Powell couldn't agree more.

***

Nacho was having a hard time staying awake. There was a constant buzzing in his head. His body was numb. Salty water burned his throat, filling his lungs.

At least his scar had stopped itching. Or had that gone numb, too?

His vision was blurry, but he could see that he still had a good hold on the man's leg. This little man who had somehow bested them all.

Well, no matter.

Nacho was dying. But when he did, he knew rigor mortis would make it impossible for the man to release his grip on him. Soon enough, Nacho's dead weight would be an anchor, dragging the son of a bitch into the sea.

The smuggler smiled for the first time that day.

Killing always made him happiest.

At least he'd go out doing what he loved.

***

Tara pounded on Steven's back to no avail. He was twice her size and determined to get as far away from the shark as possible.

Which would have been exactly what she would do if not for the possibility that Ollie was out there.

Of course, it could also be the smuggler. She hadn't checked to see if the fall had killed him. Or it could be another one that had managed to survive the tank blast.

No, it had to be Ollie.

"Steven, just listen to me," she said, taking a different tack. "If you turn around now, it'll take less than a minute to circle back and grab Ollie."

He looked down at her with fire in his eyes. "A minute is fifty nine seconds longer than that damned shark needs to devour us. There's no way I'm going back there."

"Not even to save our friend's life?"

He turned away from her. "Especially not."

She couldn't just leave Ollie out there, paddling for his life, waiting for the shark to chew him up.

Scanning the deck of the *Sarah Kay*, she found a retro aluminum cooler. She was sure Ollie had bought it thinking of all the ice cold beer he'd bring aboard as they went out to enjoy the beautiful ocean.

Tara grabbed the sides of the cooler, grateful it was empty and not full of melted ice water and bottles of warm beer.

She didn't want to hit Steven, but he wasn't giving her an option.

Heaving it with all her might, she brought the edge of the cooler down on the back of Steven's head. He slumped over the wheel, jerking the boat hard to the left. His body slid off the wheel onto the deck.

Tara watched in horror as the wheel spun. It looked as if an invisible man was piloting the boat to certain ruin.

She grabbed the wheel, crying out in pain as she struggled to get it under control. Once that was done, she checked on Steven. There was a nasty cut on his head but he was breathing steadily.

Turning the boat around, she operated the throttle as Steven had, not going too fast for fear of losing control. Lenny's body slid back and forth across the deck as she navigated the swells.

The shark, for the moment, was nowhere to be seen. That gave her very little comfort. She bit down hard on her back teeth, expecting it to slam the underside of the boat any second.

She searched for the human shape she'd seen flailing on the surface.

For all she knew, she was too late. If that had been Ollie, the bad swimmer that he was, he was probably making his descent to the bottom of the sea right now. And maybe that was a blessing. Drowning was far more preferable to being eaten by a prehistoric shark.

She was about to give up when she saw a hand claw through the rough water.

She sped as fast as she dared toward it.

Tara cut the engine back as soon as she got within ten yards of the hand. It was the only thing above water.

Damn you, Steven, she cursed, knowing his hesitation had cost Ollie his life. No matter. If all she could do was retrieve Ollie's body, that would have to be enough. Thinking that, she felt a sudden wave of pity toward Steven who wouldn't be able to do the same for Heidi.

Unable to navigate the boat comfortably, she hoped the tide would push her closer toward Ollie.

What she didn't expect was the rush of water from below as the ocean exploded, tipping the boat on its side.

CHAPTER THIRTY

Ollie felt something sharp and heavy slam into his legs.

The smuggler that he'd been struggling with on the roof held onto his leg and wouldn't let go, dragging Ollie down with him.

Suddenly he was rocketing toward the surface, breaking through the water and sailing into the sky. Tumbling ass over heels, he finally slipped free from the smuggler's dead grasp.

Ollie looked down before spinning skyward once more. What he saw made him wish he'd never survived the confrontation with the smuggler or subsequent demolition of the lab building.

The Megalodon poked its conical head from the ocean, rows of teeth pulling back, gums quavering as it waited for its next morsel. Before he turned completely around, he saw the smuggler slip into the shark's mouth, hitting its tongue before disappearing down its gullet.

That's going to be me, Ollie thought with sickening clarity.

There was nothing he could do about it. He'd run out of places to hide. It was just him, the ocean, and the Megalodon.

Falling toward the Pacific, he just hoped Tara and Lenny had somehow managed to find a way out.

It was funny. He wasn't afraid. When death was inevitable, there was no longer anything left to fear. The doubt of how the end would come was gone.

After everything that had happened, he welcomed it.

Arms and legs flailing, he turned around once again so he was facing the ocean.

The shark was gone . . . at least for the moment.

It would be back. And Ollie's body would be there, waiting for it.

He hit the water knees first. His shins felt as if they'd been smashed with a two-by-four. Ollie went under.

Just take a deep breath and end it, he thought, tumbling in the brine.

He couldn't make himself do it. Instead, he floated to the surface, gasping for air.

"Ollie!"

No. That was impossible.

"Ollie! Over here!"

He craned his neck to the sound of the woman's voice. When he saw Tara, tears sprung from his eyes.

"Tara," he croaked, feebly reaching out for her.

She was hanging onto the underside of a boat, extending her arm to him. She was too far away. He'd have to swim at least twenty-five yards to her, and he just didn't have the strength or ability. The simple act of keeping afloat was taxing his limited skills. The open wounds in his shoulder, nipple, and thigh burned from the salt water.

"I'm so sorry," he said.

"You don't have anything to be sorry for," she replied. She looked equally spent. They bobbed on the water, so close yet too far.

"Is Lenny . . ."

"I don't know," she said. "I lost him and Steven when we capsized."

"Steven's still alive?"

"He was," she said. "He got your boat and came back for us."

They gazed into each other's tired eyes. He could tell there was more she wanted to say, but she was keeping it to herself.

So this was it. They'd made it back to one another and just had to wait for the shark to finish them off. Ollie wished to hell there was some way to save Tara, but he knew that ship had sailed, so to speak.

"Look," Tara said. He paddled his body around to see where she was staring. It was so hard staying afloat. Every muscle felt like it was on fire.

The shark's fin cruised not far behind him.

It was coming for them.

"Tara, I just want you to know something," he said.

"I know," she said.

"I have to say it at least once before I die." His mouth dipped under water and he spit out a long stream of salty water. "I love you"

She gave him a weak smile. "I've known that for a long time."

"You have?"

"Subtlety isn't one of your strong points."

He laughed, despite their dire circumstances.

"I should have told you sooner," he said.

"I think you timed it just right. It's a beautiful thing to hear before . . . before . . ."

Her eyes grew as wide as dinner plates.

Ollie looked back.

The shark was coming right for them, fast as a bullet train.

He was finally at peace. It took winning an enormous lottery, rebuilding an island, uprooting the lives of his college friends, and watching it all fall to pieces to finally find comfort. Nothing made sense to Ollie in this world. Soon enough, that would no longer be a concern.

Ollie closed his eyes, waiting for the shark's jaws to clamp around him. The ocean surged, pushing him toward Tara. The overturned boat rose and dipped, Tara clinging to it desperately.

"Where did it go?" Tara said.

Ollie peeked over his shoulder. The dorsal fin was gone. The water calmed.

"I don't know," he said.

He'd bet everything he'd won that the damn demon shark was just under them, plotting the most hideous way to take their lives.

Tara managed to snag his shirt and pull him against her. He eagerly gripped the boat, the blessed relief from trying to tread water this side of euphoric, no matter how fleeting it would be.

"Hey!"

Ollie heard Steven but couldn't find him.

"Steven!" Ollie cried back.

"Where are you guys?"

"By the boat," Tara said.

"I can't see him anywhere," Ollie said.

"Me neither. He must be on the other side."

Ollie and Tara made their way around the upturned boat, sliding their hands across the hull. Rounding the bow, Ollie spotted Steven. He had one arm draped over Lenny, though the man's floating body no longer looked anything like him.

Steven managed to swim to the boat. Lenny floated on his back, oblivious to the carnage.

"Is he still alive?" Ollie asked.

Tara checked for a pulse. With the way his body was rising and falling in the water, it was impossible to tell if he was breathing by looking at his chest.

"I am," Lenny sputtered. Tara jerked her hand away. Like Ollie, she had assumed Lenny was gone.

"Just . . . just stay relaxed," Ollie said. He knew the moment Lenny stiffened, he was going to start to sink.

Lenny weakly lifted a blackened arm. "Jesus, look at me. I must look like a floating turd."

"How does it feel?" Tara asked.

"It doesn't burn so much anymore. I think my nerves got fried. Everything inside me feels, I don't know how to say it, it all feels off. Like there's stuff sloshing around my abdomen."

Steven said, "Ollie, have you seen Heidi?"

Ollie shook his head. He saw the grief in Steven's eyes and couldn't help feeling ashamed.

"Where's our friend, the shark?" Lenny said. He'd closed his eyes and had a serene smile on his charcoal lips.

"I don't know," Ollie said. "It disappeared. It could be anywhere."

The absence of the shark was starting to wear on Ollie's remaining resolve. It was one thing to grimly accept your fate. It was another to think it was coming and be forced to wait, not knowing when to expect it.

"How far are we from shore?" Lenny asked.

"I don't think there is a shore anymore," Ollie said. All he could see was water and floating debris.

"You need to find someplace safe and leave me here."

"We're not doing that," Tara said.

Lenny opened one eye, twisted his head and gazed at the water.

"You're going to have to. It looks like I've started to leak."

CHAPTER THIRTY-ONE

Lenny saw the undulating tendrils of what looked like an oil slick around him. Black ichor oozed from every pore, polluting the water. Ollie, Tara and Steven had smartly moved away from him, but only after his calm insistence.

"They turned me into a squid," he said, chuckling until it degenerated into a gurgling cough.

Oddly enough, he no longer felt any pain.

One small mercy.

Glancing out from the corner of his eye, his saw his friends clinging to the boat, too close for comfort.

"You guys need to haul some ass," Lenny said. "There may be some dry land left. Find it."

"We can't just leave you here to die," Tara protested.

"I'm already dead. Now I know how Heidi felt. At least let me die in peace thinking you knuckleheads found a way out of this."

No one spoke. Lenny closed his eyes again. Each breath was a struggle.

He was happy to hear the sound of their paddling away.

There had to be some high ground left, somewhere. Even if the island had been swamped by the storm, surely the ocean had started to retreat now that it had passed.

Lenny felt a pressure in his bowels, then a steady release. The stench of the discharge swirling around him made him wish his sense of smell would hurry up and die, too.

***

The creature sank into colder and colder layers of water. It was no longer able to maintain its frenzy. Its cells were switching off, returning to the dark, dormant place where it had lain for decades.

Not that it had any concept of time.

There was only the moment. And each moment was controlled by the simple instinct to feed.

But there was no longer enough of the special meat to sustain it.

The Megalodon had no thoughts as it plunged into the Pacific. Its hunger ceased to be a driving force.

Its ears and nose detected something strange in the distance, something large but not food. It was of no concern to the shark.

As the neurons in its prehistoric brain went to sleep, the electrical pulses in its synaptic pathways glowed less and less. Soon, only the bare minimum of brain function would remain—just enough to maintain stasis for as long as was needed.

Its vision had just begun to fade when the shark detected something else.

Its brain went into instant high alert.

Food was near.

The Megalodon shook off its impending slumber. Adrenaline shot through its system.

It soared toward the surface, following the chemical trail to the meat it craved.

***

Ollie kept looking back toward Lenny. His friend floated, hands clasped together and resting on his chest in a classic death repose. It looked as if his skin was actually starting to fall from his skull like melting candle wax. He couldn't begin to imagine what kind of chemical reaction was occurring inside Lenny. Harder to fathom was the diseased mind that would dream up such a thing.

Tara urged him on. Steven had pulled ahead of them. Ollie thought he heard Steven crying as he swam, once choking out Heidi's name.

What was the point? Everything was gone. All they were doing was delaying the inevitable.

Though if he kept this up, his body was going to give out sooner rather than later. He should be so lucky to drown.

But as long as Tara held out hope, so would he.

He wondered if she was thinking the same thing.

"I think I see something," Tara said.

All Ollie could see were breaks in the clouds, bars of sunlight poking through and illuminating the ocean.

"Over there," Tara said. She'd slowed down so he could catch up to her. She pointed to the top of a palm tree several hundred yards away. It was hard to tell from this distance, but he'd guess a good ten feet of the tree was visible above the water.

The skinny tree wasn't enough to renew his vigor and infuse him with optimism. It seemed so far away. There was no way he'd be able to make it. And even if he did, how long could three people manage to last clinging to the weakened branches of a tree in the middle of the ocean?

Again, his mind drifted to the movies. He thought of the couple stranded in the ocean in the shark movie *Open Water*. It was supposed to be based on a true story, the couple succumbing to their injuries and the dining desires of a shark as they paddled for days in the ocean. He remembered thinking it was a combination of the worse deaths possible—drowning and being eaten alive.

Would anyone make a movie about this?

Probably not. Who would believe it?

"Oh, thank God," he said with false enthusiasm. "It's about time we caught a break."

Tara smiled. "We were overdue."

"You think you can make it?" he asked.

"With my eyes closed."

"Best to keep them open. You don't want to swim in the wrong direction."

Steven saw it as well because he paused in his sidestroke to call back to them, "You guys see that? Come on!"

He attacked the water like an Olympian at tryouts.

Ollie toiled just to swim the next several yards. Tara sensed his flagging strength and stayed close to him.

"You go on ahead," Ollie said. "Don't worry, slow and steady wins the race."

"Then we'll go slow and steady together."

Ollie felt the water surge underneath him.

"Shit!" he exclaimed.

That could mean only one thing. The Megalodon was returning. It was so massive and so fast, even the ocean fled from it.

They stopped swimming and clung to one another.

Instead of the sensation of being run over by a train, they heard a tremendous explosion of water behind them.

Ollie turned to witness the moment the shark shattered the surface, swallowing Lenny whole.

The Megalodon flopped back into the water seconds after securing its prey.

***

"Skipper, it looks like the target has stopped."

Captain Powell looked at the monitor. Indeed, the Megalodon had gone still and was slowly sinking back to the ocean floor. He'd asked Leuis to prepare a team of divers. Once the shark had run out of gas, they would have to somehow lock the thing back up. If its cage was too badly damaged, he would make the call and they'd have to babysit it until a replacement was sent from the naval base in Australia.

He didn't relish the thought of spending any more time than was necessary around that abomination. If it came awake again, his instinct would be to unleash every torpedo the *Maximus* had at it.

But you can't do that. I'm not going to throw thirty-four years in the crapper over this.

Unless it's a matter of the lives of my crew over the science experiment cooked up by some eggheads before I was even born.

Captain Powell wiped the sweat from the back of his neck with a neatly folded handkerchief.

"Make a slow and steady approach. Let's wrap this up as soon as possible."

***

Seconds after devouring Lenny, the Megalodon went berserk. It writhed in the water, leaping and diving for no apparent reason.

The only silver lining was that in its mad water dance, it hadn't taken notice of the three humans desperately swimming for the lone palm tree.

Something about the manic intensity of the shark brought renewed strength to Ollie's spent muscles. He was even getting the hang of this whole swimming thing, following Tara's lead and copying her motions.

Great, you'll be a world class swimmer just in time to never have a chance to go in the water again.

Steven had put some serious distance between them and was almost at the tree.

Ollie knew Tara wasn't giving it her all so she didn't leave him in the dust.

"Almost there," she said.

Ollie's lungs labored too much to reply. He kept swallowing small mouthfuls of water. His tongue was swollen from all the salt.

His heart beat a little bit faster, if that was possible, when he saw that there was a patch of land just behind the palm tree.

Steven leapt out of the water and let out a primal scream. Ollie couldn't tell whether it was relief, victory, anger, or insanity. He suspected it was a combination of all of them.

He and Tara struggled to join him, the sight of land giving them strength. The patch of island above water was about ten feet by ten feet. The palm tree had been downhill of the dune, which was why only the top half was visible.

Limbs shaking uncontrollably, Ollie collapsed on his side. Tara and Steven dropped as well. All of them were breathing heavily, like a trio of dirty prank callers.

Ollie noticed with a tinge of relief that somewhere along the way, the butterfly knife had fallen out of his leg. Better yet, it didn't nick any major arteries, so he wasn't bleeding to death. Was it really better? Ollie was too tired to think.

Tara's face was just inches from Ollie's. Her eyes were so glassy, distant. He couldn't catch his breath to talk.

"Anyone kn-know what the fuck we do now?" Steven said, lying on his back, staring at the parting clouds.

Ollie tried to answer but could only flap his arm a bit before it fell into the sand.

He did manage to twist his body enough to look over where the shark still flipped about.

"I think it's lost its mind," Tara croaked.

"It's like whatever was inside Lenny was a kind of shark steroid," Steven said. Ollie was shocked by how right his friend probably was. Assuming it had gotten hold of Heidi in the lab, it went into full-on crazy mode. Then it disappeared moments before Ollie thought it was going to eat him and Tara. Everything had gone very, very still.

It wasn't a coincidence that it seemed to get a burst of adrenaline right after swallowing Lenny.

Ollie's gut twisted in a knot. He pictured the faces of Lenny, Heidi, Lae, and Marco staring back at him, angry as hell, bent on haunting him until he died and forever after.

"You think anyone will come out to check on us?" Tara asked. In a strange way, she looked extremely peaceful lying there in the wet sand, resting the side of her head on her arm.

"Eventually," Ollie managed to reply. "Lae's husband will head out the second it's possible. I just hope the storm missed his island. If it laid waste to the entire area, well . . ."

There was no reason to finish the thought.

Tara raised her hand with visible difficulty and laid it on the side of his neck. "None of this is your fault."

He wished he could believe her.

"It is if you ask me," Steven said.

That was more like it.

"You think Ollie set all of this up?" Tara shot back.

"I know Marco was responsible for some of it, and since he's not here, it looks like he got what was coming to him."

"Cut it out, Cooter," Tara said, adding insult.

"Fuck you."

"When did you become such a pussy?"

Ollie blurted, "Guys, stop it. Steven's right. If I didn't bring you all here, everyone would be alive."

Tara gave his neck a squeeze. "Don't you ever apologize for wanting to share your paradise with us."

"I just should have known better," Ollie said. "Since when did things ever go my way? That money came with a set of conditions I should have seen coming."

"No one, and I mean no one, could have seen this coming," Tara said. "Even Steven has to agree with me on that."

Steven didn't respond, but at least he wasn't fighting.

"So now I guess we just sit and wait," Tara said.

"And I haven't forgotten you hitting me in the head on the boat," Steven said to her.

"Fine," she said. "Happy to be on your shit list."

As much as he hated to do it, Ollie shifted away from Tara, her hand slipping from his neck. It took a monumental effort to get into a sitting position. With his arms resting on his knees, he watched the dorsal fin go round and round, still hovering over where the lab had been.

Even though he was sitting on firm ground, he didn't feel the least bit safe. That beast could swarm over them with a simple surge, its momentum carrying it over the tiny patch and back into the ocean before Ollie could scream, "Look out!"

"Just stay over there," he said.

The fin dipped under water, mammoth ripples spreading in every direction in its wake.

Ollie held his breath as he counted the seconds, waiting for it to return.

Ten Mississippi, eleven Mississippi, twelve Mississippi, thirteen Mississippi . . .

After two hundred and thirty of his scientifically inaccurate seconds, he finally ordered his brain to stop and collapsed onto his back. Maybe Lotano had returned to the sea goddess.

"I think it's gone," he said.

He looked over at Tara. She had fallen asleep. Even Steven had passed out. Ollie was exhausted. They had the right idea.

Closing his eyes, he wriggled until he could drape his arm over Tara.

If the shark wanted them so bad, there was nothing they could do about it. Ollie couldn't fight off a sand flea, much less an oceanic dinosaur.

He tried to find a happy place to retreat to, but could only relive every horrid moment of that day. Ollie struggled to shut his mind down.

What was left of their little world exploded before he could find peace.

CHAPTER THIRTY-TWO

Captain Powell couldn't believe what he was seeing.

"Goddammit! Pull back! Pull back!"

They had waited until the shark had finally gone still. Everyone on the bridge watched in rapt silence as the creature slowly sank.

The tempest had moved on the same time as the Megalodon had run out of gas. For the first time in this entire shit storm of an assignment, things were going their way.

Then something revived the damned beast and it was back in manic action.

Luckily, they were still submerged. The plan was to surface and deploy the divers to assess the damage to the special cage that had been installed under the island. Powell thanked God those men weren't in the water now. If they had been, he'd have had to make a difficult and unpopular decision between their safety and the safety of the rest of the crew, not to mention the billion-dollar *Maximus*.

Now it was all hands on deck as they veered away from the mad beast, hoping they didn't capture its attention.

"What the hell got it all started up again? I thought it was supposed to starve itself into dormancy."

Leuis consulted the debriefing they'd received.

"That's exactly what the science advisors said."

"Well, those eggheads either weren't born or were still messing their pants when that thing was hatched or however the hell they made it. Obviously something's changed." Powell took out a stick of gum and masticated it to shreds. He hadn't craved a cigarette more than he did at this moment.

"Maybe it changed after all these years," Leuis suggested. "It's not like they've kept a close eye on the thing, other than the occasional drive-by. Who knows what's been going on with it over the past fifty years? I can't see there being anything left on the island to feed it."

Powell pointed at the bank of glowing monitors, half of them tracking the gargantuan creature.

"Something is damn well feeding it," he said to his XO.

"But the lab and the island are wiped out. Any civilians that were on it are most assuredly gone, too."

"Maybe a little something was left behind in the lab and that thing somehow got ahold of it. Now there's no telling how long we'll have to wait before we can try again."

The captain paced in the cramped space, fists balled in his pockets.

"Sir, we have a problem."

Powell looked at the sonar.

It was coming right for them.

And it was coming fast.

The *Maximus* had been designed for speed and stealth, but it was still no match for the Megalodon. The shark could also out-maneuver them with ease.

So, there was no retreat, no evasive action they could take without getting rammed by the science experiment gone wrong.

A pained grin briefly touched Powell's lips.

The decision had been taken out of his hands. Everything that happened inside and outside the sub was recorded. Admiral Keyes would see there was nothing they could do to salvage the situation.

Right now, all that mattered were the lives of his crew and preserving the *Maximus*.

"Prepare to blow that thing out of the water," he ordered.

The alarms were set off so everyone aboard knew what to expect. Leuis called down to the torpedo room to make sure they were locked and loaded.

Powell ordered the sub to face the shark head on. He wanted to make as sure a shot as possible. There was no room for mistakes. If they missed, they were done for.

"Ready when you are," Leuis said.

"Hold steady," Powell replied curtly.

Just a little bit closer.

The shark cut through the water as if it were air. The *Maximus* stayed tried and true on a collision course with the beast.

"Keep coming, you mindless freak," he muttered, hoping no one could hear him.

"Sir," his navigator said, an uneasy edge to his voice. The automatic alarm tripped on, signaling a collision was imminent.

Powell calmly yet forcefully barked, "Fire."

The submarine shuddered as twin torpedoes shot forward.

They detonated shortly after launching.

Powell allowed himself to exhale.

"Direct hit, Skipper," Leuis reported.

The imminent collision alarm continued to bleat.

"Shut that damn thing off," Powell said.

"Incoming target," his navigator said.

"That's not possible."

"Five seconds to impact!"

It was never supposed to come to this. That goddamn Megalodon was supposed to be in hibernation and the *Maximus* was supposed to be parked safely off Australia.

The misguided intentions of the few were about to cost the lives of many.

"Liberal fuck ups," he muttered, seething. His body felt lighter than air, as if a part of him had already departed in anticipation of the oncoming calamity.

Leuis said something, but Powell couldn't hear him. His mind was on a million things right now. He thought of the sweet sixteen party they were going to throw for his daughter when he came home in a month. He'd been looking forward to seeing Abby's expression when he handed her the keys to the slightly used yellow Chevy Malibu.

"Abby."

The impact was jarring. Captain Powell was thrown off his feet, his skull crunching on metal.

The Maximus split in half. The only mercy was the fact that the death of all those aboard came swiftly. No one felt the Megalodon chew them to sinewy shreds as their bodies were sucked out of the damaged sub.

***

The creature felt pain for the first time in its existence. It had no word for the strange sensation, but it knew it didn't like it.

In fact, it made it angry.

Its anger fueled its attack on the long beast that had wounded it. Small, tasty morsels spilled from its guts. The Megalodon made quick work of them, filling its belly as it wound round and round the sinking beast.

When all was done and there was no more food to be found—especially not the food it truly craved—the Megalodon still smelled fresh blood in the water. It swam in swirls of it.

But something wasn't quite right about this blood. The scent didn't ignite its hunger.

There was no way for its prehistoric brain to know that it was awash in its own blood. Shrapnel from the exploding torpedoes had ripped away chunks of flesh and muscle from the creature.

Not that they had done enough to stop it.

The pain only seemed to make it stronger.

It needed something on which to take out its aggression.

The programming done to it prevented it from venturing too far. The lab had been obliterated and there would be no more of its special food, but there was no way for it to ever know that.

So it stalked the ocean, searching for food and prey, the searing pain in its flank driving it mad.

CHAPTER THIRTY-THREE

What was left of the island vibrated. The visible half of the palm tree swayed.

Ollie watched in horror as a gigantic plume of water exploded several hundred yards from their meager shelter.

"Now what the fuck was that?" Steven moaned, his voice cracking.

"You think those smugglers planted a bomb?" Tara asked, now up and sitting next to Ollie.

He watched the water shoot up and cascade back down. It fell in a tremendous shower, the pressure of which he was sure would have crushed them had they been anywhere near it.

"That's too far out," Ollie said. "The island didn't stretch that far."

"Then what could it be?"

"The shark?"

"Not without it breaching the surface," she said.

"Maybe the storm activated one of those underwater volcanoes or fault lines," Steven said. "This whole area could be ready to blow. Christ, what are we going to do?"

He jumped to his feet, pacing and running his hands over his scalp frantically.

"Just hold on a second," Ollie said, trying to keep his tone as measured as possible. "I don't feel anything else."

The island and the ocean had gone still. The great geyser of water had returned to its rightful place.

The trio remained stock-still for minutes that felt like days. When nothing further happened, Ollie finally allowed his frayed nerves and muscles to relax.

"Whatever it was, it's gone," he said.

"Maybe that shark tripped a mine that was leftover from the war or something," Steven suggested. His teeth were chattering so loud, Ollie worried they'd break. There was nothing he could give Steven to bite down on or warm him up. They were all soaked to the bone, chilled from shock and exhaustion.

Ollie didn't think there were any old mines around the island. Steven watched way too much History Channel for his own good.

Tara tugged on his arm, pointing.

"Look at all that," she said.

It was hard to make out any details, but it looked like all sorts of debris was making its way to the ocean's surface. Hundreds, if not thousands of bits of flotsam had appeared from nowhere.

Standing up to get a better look, Ollie strained his eyes. "What is all that stuff?"

It didn't look like anything natural from the sea.

He remembered seeing video on the news of a commercial plane in Thailand that had crashed into the ocean several years ago. A chopper had been deployed right after the deadly accident, filming the desperate attempt to search for survivors. He'd been shocked by how many pieces the massive plane had shattered into.

This looked exactly like that, except there hadn't been any planes for hundreds of miles.

"Something exploded," Tara said. "And I don't think it was the shark."

"I bet it was a submarine," Steven said. "It was a submarine that had been sent to save us and n-n-now even that's gone. Fuck!"

Ollie was too exhausted to try to settle the big man down. Odds were, if he so much as touched Steven, he'd catch holy hell for it. Ollie knew he wasn't high on his list of favorite people, and he couldn't blame him.

That didn't stop Tara from saying, "Calm the hell down, Steven. Why would a submarine be sent to this island? That doesn't make any sense. We haven't been able to send out a distress call. No one knows what happened out here."

Steven jabbed his finger in the direction of the floating wreckage. "Somebody knows. Somebody kn-knows for sure. And n-now they're dead, too. Everybody dies out here. Just like we're going to die."

Tara looked to Ollie. What could he say? At the moment, he thought Steven was right. The only difference was, he refused to get hysterical about it.

He checked the tidemark on the sand. It hadn't receded so much as an inch, but it also hadn't crept further up their tiny patch of temporary salvation.

Ollie wondered what all of the bungalows looked like. Were they intact, like towns that were flooded when dams were built? Or had all of the work been reduced to splinters? And was there a possibility that the tide had washed it all out there and what they were seeing was the bobbing remains of his dream?

It didn't matter.

All that was left to them was sitting out here and dying of thirst.

Unless, of course, Lae's husband Lucky would make a dash for the island. Ollie's heart quickened. In the midst of struggling to simply survive, he'd forgotten about Lucky. He was sure the man would be on a boat headed their way the second it was possible.

He saw Tara shivering and put an arm over her. She rested her head against him.

"What I wouldn't give for a warm blanket and a bottle of whiskey," she said.

"I'd settle for just the whiskey," Ollie said. "Wild Turkey Reserve. We deserve the good stuff."

Steven continued to pace behind them, muttering to himself.

"Remember when we found a bottle of Turkey Reserve in New Hampshire on that skiing trip on Christmas break?" Tara said.

"That's where I fell in love with it. We were so smashed that whole time, it's a miracle we didn't end up in traction."

"I guess we used up all of our miracles on that trip."

He pulled her closer, smelling the brine in her hair. "The fact that we're still here talking about it is a miracle."

"Oh yeah, then what's that?" Steven blurted.

The shark's dorsal fin crept into view, cleaving through the wreckage.

Ollie felt all of his muscles go limp.

Shit.

There was no way Lucky could make it past the shark. Now he prayed the man *wasn't* speeding toward the island. If the shark got him, yes, a search party would be sent to find him.

The shark would be sure to devour them, too. All Ollie, Tara and Steven could do was cling to the remains of his island and watch the cavalry get cut down, one by one, while dehydration worked on stopping their hearts.

Ollie abruptly stood and stormed into the water, stopping when it was up to his hips.

"Ollie, get out of the water," Tara said.

"Don't tempt that thing," Steven added.

He leveled his gaze at the visible triangle of the shark. If looks could kill...

But they couldn't. Not even wound.

"It can't come here," Ollie said. "It's too shallow."

"But maybe it can get under us, just like at the lab," Steven said. "Get out of the goddamn water."

He headed toward Ollie, stopping the moment his feet touched the water.

Ollie would give anything for a chance to take that abomination out. If he could be granted one wish, he'd ask for a bazooka or grenade launcher. Anything that he could hold in his hands, giving him the satisfaction of taking down the Megalodon.

Or better yet, he'd wish to be made large enough to grab hold of its jaws and pry them apart with his bare hands. Just thinking about the sound it would make, watching the life bleed from its cold black eyes, gave Ollie a thrill. His soul seethed with hatred for the wretched shark and all the people who thought to bring it to life, leaving it out here to destroy everything and everyone he held dear.

Instead, all he could do was stand in its territory and pound his fists impotently into the water. He'd never felt so small in his life.

He gave a start when Tara grabbed his hand.

"Come on. There's nothing we can do," she said, leading him back to semi-dry land.

Ollie sighed. She was right. What could he do against a dinosaur shark?

He looked down and saw blood in the water around Tara.

"Hey, are you okay?" he said.

She followed his gaze and nudged him away from her.

"Great. Now I have my period. Why not?"

She laughed, crying at the same time. Ollie wanted to console her, but a quick look told him he would embarrass her if he got too close.

"Ollie. Ollie. Ollie! Ollie!" Steven blabbered.

Ollie's spine went rigid.

The shark was heading right for them, coming on faster now.

He grabbed Tara by the waist and carried her to the meager shore. She protested at first, until she spotted the approaching fin.

"You said it can't get us, right?" Steven said.

Ollie couldn't take his eyes off the fin.

How could something that big move so fast?

"We're safe here. Right, Ollie? Right?"

Ollie made sure Tara was behind him, a futile gesture at best, and braced for impact.

CHAPTER THIRTY-FOUR

Tara watched in horror as the Megalodon shot out of the ocean. Its gargantuan body blocked out the reappearing sun as it sailed toward them.

Her only thought was *this isn't possible!*

How could it know they were here?

Its lair was the ocean. It should be as unaware of what happened on land as they were of what went on in the murky depths of the sea.

As it sailed toward them like a fighter jet, she knew the answer.

It was coming for her.

If she hadn't gone in the water for Ollie, it would have continued to patrol the water, blissfully unaware of their existence.

Now she knew why people referred to it as *the curse.* There was nothing a voodoo priest could have done worse to seal their fate than this simple act of human nature.

Ollie shoved her so hard, she lost her footing and landed on her back.

The entire Megalodon was now out of the water.

This close, it was the largest thing she or any living person would ever see.

Not that she'd be among the living for long.

"Get down, Steven!" Ollie shouted as he dove on top of Tara.

The shark's momentum had been too great. There was a tremendous crack. It sailed over the small parcel left of Grand Isla Tiburon, landing with a tremendous splash back into the ocean behind them. She squirmed under Ollie, trying to catch a glimpse of it. She spotted its sleek, silvery body as it slipped back into the sea.

Tara and Ollie separated, rising to their hands and knees.

The palm tree had been obliterated by the passing beast.

Steven was somehow still on his feet.

"You okay, Steven?" Tara asked.

His eyes swiveled toward her, but his head remained in a fixed position, pointing out to where the shark had come from.

"Steven?"

Ollie helped her to her feet.

Steven's arms dropped limply at his sides.

"I think he's lost it," Ollie said.

Slowly, they approached him.

Tara was the first to see the blood leaking down his neck. She gasped when she edged around him.

The entire top of his skull was gone.

Blood and brain matter pulped from the open wound, trickling down his neck.

"Ollie," she cried, hoping he'd help her lay Steven down.

It was too late.

Steven's legs went out from under him. The second his head hit the sand, his brain poured from his open skull.

Even Ollie shrieked at the grisly sight.

"Holy crapping Christ!"

Steven's limbs twitched as his eyes rolled to the top of his head, his mouth going slack.

Tara wanted to help him, but what could she possibly do? Ollie's hands gripped her upper arms, keeping her from rushing to Steven's side.

In a few seconds, the twitching stopped. Steven's chest rose once, then deflated forever.

"How?" Ollie said.

"The shark's skin must have grazed him," Tara said. "It's the only thing I can think of. Their skin looks smooth, but it's actually like a cheese grater if you run your hand along it the wrong way. Oh, Steven."

For the first time since everything had gone haywire, Tara cried. It wasn't necessarily for Steven, but for everyone. She collapsed into Ollie, who managed to guide them as far as they could get from his body, which wasn't far at all.

"It's going to come back," she said between heaving sobs. "And it'll do the same thing to us."

"I won't let it."

She pulled away from him. "How? How can you say that?"

Ollie's jaw tightened, eyes narrowing.

"Because I won't."

Tara didn't try to refute him. What was the point? The poor guy's inner rage had always gotten the best of him. Maybe this time, that rage would save him from losing what little senses he had left, as she felt her own slipping away.

Perhaps his rage would assure him that he would die fighting, never lingering on fear or regret.

She wished she had that same fire.

Ollie tromped into the water where the palm tree had stood. Jagged shards were all that was left. Grabbing one of the thickest shards with both hands, he began to tug at it, grunting heavily.

"What are you doing?"

He paused for a second, his face red bordering on purple. "I don't really fucking know. I just know that I need some kind of weapon."

Ollie continued trying to break the wood shard free. Tara scanned the ocean, searching for the shark. It had gone under, which made her even more nervous. It could be anywhere right now.

"Yeaggghhh!"

Ollie's scream gave her a scare. She whipped around to see what had happened. He stood in the water smiling, holding a makeshift spear in one hand.

"Now, first things first," he said, striding back onto the remains of the island. He jammed the blunt end of the spear in the sand and started digging. "Feel free to give me a hand."

"With what?"

"Making you a shelter."

"A shelter?"

"Please, just dig."

She saw there was no arguing with him, so she dropped to her knees and scooped out sand with her hands. Together, they managed to make a good-sized hole, big enough for her to lie in.

"Now what?"

He pointed the sharp end of the shard over her shoulder. The shark's fin had returned.

"Now you get in that hole so it can't get you," he said.

She tugged at his arm. "You're getting in, too."

"It's not big enough."

"We can squeeze in. Stop being ridiculous."

He cupped her face in his hand. "Tara. Please, get in the hole. It's coming. We don't have much time."

When she didn't move, he pushed her into the hole. She landed on her tailbone. A sliver of pain rocketed up her spine.

She heard the shark burst from the ocean.

Ollie, standing by the edge of the hole, hoisted the shard over his head with both hands. The shadow of the shark came into view before the actual Megalodon.

"Ollie!"

In a flash, the shark sailed over the hole and Ollie and the shark were gone.

Tara scrabbled up the crumbling sand, her chest heaving so hard, she thought her heart would burst.

CHAPTER THIRTY-FIVE

Tara made her way out of the hole, shouted Ollie's name over and over again. Tears streamed down her face.

Ollie lay at the water's edge, writhing in pain.

He was pretty sure both of his shoulders were dislocated. The pain was mind numbing. His hands tingled.

The pain was all the proof he needed that he was alive.

Tara dropped into the water next to him.

"I thought you were…"

"Knock on wood," he said, looking around. "Oh. Looks like I lost it."

When she tried to help him up, he howled in agony.

"Where does it hurt?"

"I think my shoulders are out."

She inspected both shoulders, her brows knit in concern. "I can see the bones are where they shouldn't be, even without an X-ray."

"Whatever you do, don't try to put them in," he said. "This isn't a *Lethal Weapon* movie. If you do, I'll pass out."

"But it'll stop the pain."

"I'll live with it. Besides, have you ever put a shoulder back in place?"

"There wasn't much call for it at the vet's."

"Exactly."

With her gentle assistance, he was able to stand. He kept looking back at the ocean, expecting that vile fin to pop up.

She half-carried him to the hole, helping him slip inside. She worked hard and fast to expand it so they could both fit inside. He wished he could help her. At the moment, he couldn't even wipe his ass if he tried. The pain was morphing into a dull hum, both arms deadening. He hoped it was just his nerves shorting out rather than a sign of a blood clot or something worse.

"What the hell did you do?" Tara asked once they were settled in. The sun had fully broken from the clouds, drying their drenched clothes and flesh.

"I think I stabbed it," Ollie said, recalling the massive blow as he jabbed the shard into the shark as it careened into him. He felt something give way, and then the shard was ripped from his hands, nearly taking his arms with it.

Of course, the shark didn't make a sound. There was no way to tell if Ollie had done anything more than scratch it.

But he was pretty sure that by some sort of divine intervention, he had managed to spear the damned creature's eye.

There were remnants of some strange, viscous jelly on his hands.

"Does that look like eye juice to you?" he asked her.

He closed his fingers together, then pulled them apart, the sticky fluid forming little glue-like strands between them.

Tara's lip curled. "I don't know, but it smells awful."

Ollie lay his head back. "Smells like victory to me." He wanted to tell her the line was from *Apocalypse Now*, but he was too tired to keep his eyes open. His battered body was turning the lights out to save itself from another moment of pain.

It can't get us in here, he thought, the darkness creeping toward him.

This hole will be a grave before we know it. I don't care anymore. At least we'll die together.

***

The creature's vision wavered.

It was confused.

There was new pain now, arcing through its head.

Its sight, never being one of its strengths, was now severely compromised.

It wanted to kill, to eat the pain away.

But something else was wrong.

Swimming became more difficult.

An unbearable weariness swept through its gigantic body. Growing weaker by the moment, it searched for the food it needed to sustain itself.

There was none to be had.

Even its anger couldn't overcome the pull of hibernation.

The Megalodon began to sink, no longer able to propel itself through the water.

Bit by bit, its brain began to shut down.

The long, dark place was waiting for it.

Waiting.

Wait.

Wa...

***

Tara's loud whooping woke Ollie from his slumber.

Was it sleep when you passed into unconsciousness?

Tara.

Where was she?

Ollie tried to move, but bolts of pain kept him cemented to the sandy floor.

"Tara?" he croaked.

Her head popped over the hole.

"There's a boat!" she cried, the smile taking up half her face.

"Is it close?"

"Yes. They saw me wave them down."

He dared to ask, "You see the shark?"

"No. I haven't seen it for hours."

"How long have I been out?"

"A long time. You slept all day and night."

The sun slanted into the hole. "I slept a whole day?"

"Pretty close."

A whole day without the shark being spotted.

Was it possible?

Tara slipped out of view. He heard her shout, "Over here! Over here!"

The sound of a boat's engine lulled him back to sleep.

CHAPTER THIRTY-SIX

"You awake?"

He rubbed his eyes, sitting up in the bed.

"I am now."

Tara slipped into the room. She wore a fluffy white robe, courtesy of the hotel.

"Breakfast is here. I had them set it up on the balcony. It's a beautiful day."

"I'll be right there."

She closed the door behind her and he got up to piss. The body slings he'd had to wear on both arms had come off yesterday. His arms were a pair of sticks, his muscles atrophying after eight weeks in the slings. He had a lot of physical therapy ahead of him.

But it felt great to hold his own dick.

"Guess this is all part of learning to appreciate the little things," he said, his voice echoing in the swanky bathroom.

After slowly and carefully putting on his own robe, Ollie walked to the suite's main living area. A stack of Tara's paperbacks were on one end of the couch, next to her gym bag. Her sneakers were on the floor, nestled under the glass top table, where Ollie couldn't trip over them.

The sliding door to the balcony was wide open, letting in a crisp mountain breeze. It was an unseasonably warm day, but there was still a slight chill in the air. It felt amazing. Tara sat at the table, spreading marmalade on wheat toast.

"Look at you dressing yourself," Tara said, smiling. "How does it feel?"

"Like I'm no longer a helpless baby." He sat opposite her, shakily reaching for a small glass of orange juice.

"I told the nurse her services were no longer needed."

"Thank you."

The last thing Ollie wanted was for Tara to be tasked with being his nurse/helper while he recovered. She'd offered at least a hundred times, but there was no way he was going to let her feed and dress him, give him showers and least of all, wipe his butt. It was difficult enough putting himself in the hands of a nurse who had been a total stranger.

"You want the paper?" she asked.

"I'm good. No news is good news."

"That it is. So, you want to do anything special today?"

He looked out at the trees and mountains, the sun peeking over the ridge. It was breathtaking. And best of all, there was nary a sign of water. The high-priced resort was blessedly landlocked.

"We could go to the movies," he said.

Tara rolled her eyes. "You did that when you were laid up. Let's do something different."

"Like what?"

"We could go to the driving range and crush some balls."

"At this stage, the only balls I'll crush are my own if I bang them into something."

Tara giggled. "Okay, I'll crush some balls and you give them love taps."

Ollie was never one for golf, but she'd been so wonderful, so patient, he couldn't say no. Besides, driving ranges weren't really golf. It was like a shooting range for old people.

"After that, I have a call with the contractor around two."

"I guess you don't need me to take notes anymore," Tara said.

"No, but I want you there. One of the houses they're building is yours. I know he loves to hear your two cents."

"Har-dee-har-har."

She munched on her toast.

Once they made it back stateside, Ollie had gotten right to work looking for someplace for him and Tara to live. They couldn't stay in this hotel forever. Well, they could. He had more than enough money left. But they needed to have their own place.

Tara's would be right next to his, in a wooded area in Colorado.

Staying in the hotel had actually been part of the healing process, both physically and mentally. Tara's night terrors had decreased, but at least Ollie was always nearby to comfort her when they hit. But the time would come when they needed to move on.

They had a hell of a fish story to tell, but they'd been sworn to secrecy by the US military. Ollie got the feeling that if word ever got out what happened on the island, he and Tara would disappear. It would have been the stuff of legend, his killing the Megalodon with nothing but a shard of wood.

After Lucky had rescued them, a Navy frigate had come to the island. Ollie and Tara had become reluctant sensations, the nearby islands abuzz over the lone survivors of the storm. Ollie and Tara had been smart not to tell Lucky or anyone else about the shark or the smugglers.

Poor Lucky had been devastated. Ollie promised to make sure that he and his entire family would be taken care of, but it couldn't replace lovely Lae.

He and Tara had been called to a debriefing with an admiral. The man's presence was enough to convey the importance of what had gone down. He never outright claimed proprietorship over the Megalodon, but he didn't have to. Ollie and Tara were interviewed—or grilled was more like it—for five days. Every scrap of information was extracted from them. When he told the admiral that he had slayed the beast, the stern man flashed a hint of a smile, as if to say, *Sure, son, you go on believing that.*

Ollie had the feeling that the drug lord, Donovan Bailey, was going to be paid a visit. Even though he hadn't been witness to what happened, the Navy wasn't going to take any chances. If they dumped him in the ocean, it would be one good thing to come out of this.

For now, Ollie and Tara were safe. They would remain so as long as they never spoke a word of what had happened to them. The threats they had received in that regard weren't the least bit veiled or vague.

His dreams of he and Tara falling in love after surviving their ordeal had to be . . . readjusted after she confessed to him that she had come out as a lesbian the year after they'd graduated college.

"I have guys like Lenny and Steven to thank for helping me come to my senses," she joked at the time, the mention of their names bringing tears to both their eyes.

So they might never become lovers, but they would always be the best of friends. And Ollie was okay with that.

He picked up a knife and fork for the first time in months and got to work on his eggs and sausage.

Simple pleasures.

Just keep it simple.

***

Admiral Keyes stationed himself on the bridge, scanning the horizon with binoculars.

"Looks like there's nothing left."

"The storm did a damn good job leveling the island," Captain Campisi replied.

"No matter. It's what's below that matters most."

Operation Revive was going to be a massive undertaking. Submarines had located the asset. The admiral wanted to be on hand to make sure the transport to the new underwater facility went off without a hitch. A lot of money had been spent to get it right this time. Billions of black budget funds went into making sure the Megalodon was secure.

The power of the creature was undeniable. If it could do to the Russian and Chinese fleets what it had done to the *Maximus*, the United States would control the water, and the world.

They just needed to fine-tune the beast. How that was to be done, the admiral would leave to the scientists. Plans were already underway for making a second Megalodon, and a third and so on until they had an asset in every major body of water.

There might come a day when ships like the one he was on were obsolete.

Robots on land, drones in the air, and fucking sharks in the water, he mused.

The world was on the brink of wholesale change. He knew he wouldn't be alive to see it all come to fruition. And in a way, he was glad of that. What would be his place in such a world?

Captain Campisi consulted his tablet and leaned into the admiral.

"We just got word that the civilians who survived the island massacre have moved out of the hotel."

"We'll have to keep our eye on them."

Admiral Keyes had personally interrogated Ollie Arias and Tara McShane after they'd been rescued from the island. He'd made it abundantly clear that they were to never speak of what happened. His original intention was to make them disappear. But after spending time with them and hearing what they'd been through, he'd decided to let them pick up the pieces and live their lives.

He was sworn to protect US citizens, not kill them.

So far, they'd kept quiet.

He hoped it would stay that way.

"We have the asset locked and ready to roll," the voice said over the speaker system.

Admiral Keyes puffed out his chest.

"Gentlemen, proceed."

ACKNOWLEDGEMENTS

I hope you had fun with my unusual take on a Meg tale . . . or tail. This was supposed to be a neat little novella, but it took on a life of its own and blossomed into a full, insane novel. My main goal was to plop a group of old friends on an island with a dormant Megalodon lurking beneath them. I quickly realized that to fully flesh out each character, the book would need more space for them to breathe— kind of like a fine wine. Or in Lenny's case, a domestic beer at the ballpark.

Unlike Grand Isla Tiburon, no man—or writer—is an island.

I can't thank my team of beta readers for tackling this beast of a manuscript and taming it. Carolyn Wolstencroft, Erin Al-Mehairi, Tim Feely and Tim Meyer are my Mount Rushmore of support. Gary and the entire team at Severed Press kick some serious ass. Thank you for allowing me the chance to spread my madness to readers all across the globe. I'm eternally in your debt.

CHECK OUT OTHER GREAT
DEEP SEA THRILLERS

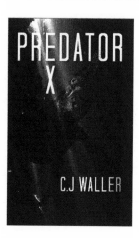

PREDATOR X
by C.J Waller

When deep level oil fracking uncovers a vast subterranean sea, a crack team of cavers and scientists are sent down to investigate. Upon their arrival, they disappear without a trace. A second team, including sedimentologist Dr Megan Stoker, are ordered to seek out Alpha Team and report back their findings. But Alpha team are nowhere to be found – instead, they are faced with something unexpected in the depths. Something ancient. Something huge. Something dangerous. Predator X

DEAD BAIT
by Tim Curran

A husband hell-bent on revenge hunts a Wereshark...A Russian mail order bride with a fishy secret...Crabs with a collective consciousness...A vampire who transforms into a Candiru...Zombie piranha...Bait that will have you crawling out of your skin and more. Drawing on horror, humor with a helping of dark fantasy and a touch of deviance, these 19 contemporary stories pay homage to the monsters that lurk in the murky waters of our imaginations. If you thought it was safe to go back in the water...Think Again!

CHECK OUT OTHER GREAT
DEEP SEA THRILLERS

MEGA
by Jake Bible

There is something in the deep. Something large. Something hungry. Something prehistoric.
And Team Grendel must find it, fight it, and kill it.
Kinsey Thorne, the first female US Navy SEAL candidate has hit rock bottom. Having washed out of the Navy, she turned to every drink and drug she could get her hands on. Until her father and cousins, all ex-Navy SEALS themselves, offer her a way back into the life: as part of a private, elite combat Team being put together to find and hunt down an impossible monster in the Indian Ocean. Kinsey has a second chance, but can she live through it?

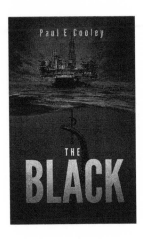

THE BLACK
by Paul E Cooley

Under 30,000 feet of water, the exploration rig Leaguer has discovered an oil field larger than Saudi Arabia, with oil so sweet and pure, nations would go to war for the rights to it. But as the team starts drilling exploration well after exploration well in their race to claim the sweet crude, a deep rumbling beneath the ocean floor shakes them all to their core. Something has been living in the oil and it's about to give birth to the greatest threat humanity has ever seen.

"The Black" is a techno/horror-thriller that puts the horror and action of movies such as Leviathan and The Thing right into readers' hands. Ocean exploration will never be the same."

SEVEREDPRESS

CHECK OUT OTHER GREAT
DEEP SEA THRILLERS

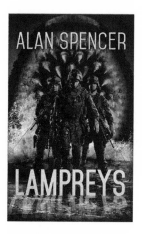

LAMPREYS
by Alan Spencer

A secret government tactical team is sent to perform a clean sweep of a private research installation. Horrible atrocities lurk within the abandoned corridors. Mutated sea creatures with insane killing abilities are waiting to suck the blood and meat from their prey.

Unemployed college professor Conrad Garfield is forced to assist and is soon separated from the team. Alone and afraid, Conrad must use his wits to battle mutated lampreys, infected scientists and go head-to-head with the biggest monstrosity of all.

Can Conrad survive, or will the deadly monsters suck the very life from his body?

DEEP DEVOTION
by M.C. Norris

Rising from the depths, a mind-bending monster unleashes a wave of terror across the American heartland. Kate Browning, a Kansas City EMT confronts her paralyzing fear of water when she traces the source of a deadly parasitic affliction to the Gulf of Mexico. Cooperating with a marine biologist, she travels to Florida in an effort to save the life of one very special patient, but the source of the epidemic happens to be the nest of a terrifying monster, one that last rose from the depths to annihilate the lost continent of Atlantis.

Leviathan, destroyer, devoted lifemate and parent, the abomination is not going to take the extermination of its brood well.

Made in the USA
Middletown, DE
13 July 2023

34994522R00144